Love of the Dragon

Book 5
Aloha Shifters: Jewels of the Heart

by Anna Lowe

Contents

Other books in this series

Aloha Shifters - Jewels of the Heart

Lure of the Dragon (Book 1)

Lure of the Wolf (Book 2)

Lure of the Bear (Book 3)

Lure of the Tiger (Book 4)

Love of the Dragon (Book 5)

Lure of the Fox (Book 6)

visit www.annalowebooks.com

Free Books

Get your free e-books now!

Sign up for my newsletter at *annalowebooks.com* to get three free books!

- *Desert Wolf*: Friend or Foe (Book 1.1 in the Twin Moon Ranch series)

- *Off the Charts* (the prequel to the Serendipity Adventure series)

- *Perfection* (the prequel to the Blue Moon Saloon series)

Chapter One

"Going once. Going twice... Gone."

The auctioneer slammed his gavel, and a murmur rippled through the crowd.

Silas went very still. The next item for sale was the one that had brought him all the way from Maui to this swanky event in New York. The one he *needed*. Badly.

"We're up next," Kai said in a low, growly voice to Silas's left.

Silas didn't look at his cousin. Instead, he glanced across the auction hall, ignoring the crystal chandeliers and gold accents that hinted at wealth and treasures to be obtained. No matter how hard he tried to keep his eyes trained straight ahead, they kept roving over to the gray-haired man in the third row. A man who fit in perfectly with the crowd — tailored suit, diamond cuff links, silk tie. One of the well-to-do in New York's high society. But that man was different in one critical way.

Drax — the mightiest dragon lord of them all. Silas's bitter enemy.

Drax folded his hands on his lap and cast a bored glance at Silas.

I am king here, his smug, disdainful look said. *I have it all, and I will keep it all.*

And Drax really meant *all*. Properties around the world. A dragon hoard beyond compare. The riches Drax had seized from Silas's family a generation before. And above all, the woman Drax had wooed away from Silas less than a decade ago.

Moira.

1

Just thinking of her together with Drax made a thousand emotions roil.

Then something red and silky flashed, and those emotions turned into a whirling storm.

Moira, his inner dragon muttered through clenched teeth.

The people in the third row stirred as Moira made her grand entrance. She nodded as she swept by them the way a queen might nod to peasants. Halfway along the row, she paused and lifted her right heel to inspect some invisible imperfection.

Silas grimaced. That was all part of Moira's show. The woman craved attention. She was addicted to it, just as she was addicted to wealth and power.

She sashayed to the empty seat beside Drax and sat with her hands folded neatly, casually. On the outside, a perfect lady. On the inside, a ruthless abuser of hearts, fortunes, and souls.

She was younger than Drax — much younger — but the hand she placed high on Drax's thigh advertised to the world how intimate they were.

Silas's hands clenched into fists as he ordered himself to remain cool. So Moira had broken his heart when she'd left him for Drax, eight years ago. That was all water under the bridge, right?

His dragon snorted. *Right. That's why your pulse is through the roof.*

Okay, so maybe he had loved Moira, once upon a time. That was all over now.

It's not over because it never started, his dragon insisted. *We never truly loved her. We just thought we did.*

Silas made a face. Love was all in the head anyway.

Love is in the heart, and hers is made of stone. His dragon lashed its tail.

Silas looked around. What would the people in attendance do if they discovered dragon shifters in their midst? He almost wondered if the guests would care, given how intently they focused on the next item for sale.

An attendant with white gloves stepped forward with a black velvet box, and the auctioneer tapped his gavel. Everyone leaned forward, including Silas and his companions. Even Drax, he sensed, leaned forward and held his breath.

Is that it? Is it a Spirit Stone? Tessa, Kai's mate, whispered into Silas's mind.

He pursed his lips. From this distance, it was impossible to tell.

The auctioneer cleared his voice and spoke. "Lot number 457. An exquisite thirty-six-carat diamond from an anonymous collection."

At *anonymous*, a low snort went out from the back of the crowd. Silas craned his neck and caught a glimpse of a woman whose arms were crossed tightly over her chest. Her chestnut hair reflected the light of the chandeliers, and for some reason, his heart skipped a beat or two. But the room was so packed, she was blocked from view a moment later.

"Lady Montgomery DeWitt was known to have worn this diamond before it was lost to the public eye, and before her..."

The auctioneer droned on with a long list of eighteenth- and nineteenth-century socialites who had once owned the diamond. None of those facts was new to Silas. He'd been feverishly researching the Windstone ever since the first of the Spirit Stones appeared on Maui less than a year ago. The Windstone was far older than that recent history implied. Far more important than any other jewel — if that diamond truly was The One.

He closed his eyes, trying to pick up on the subtle radiation of power all the Spirit Stones exuded. But when a Spirit Stone slumbered, there was no way to tell it from just another jewel.

Just another jewel? his cousin, Kai, huffed, reading Silas's mind as all closely bonded shifters could.

"Are you picking up on anything?" Tessa whispered.

Kai shook his head. "I can't tell yet."

Silas's eyes slid to Drax. The man sat ramrod stiff, and his eyes had the slightest hint of dragon glow.

That has to be a Spirit Stone, Silas's dragon whispered. *It has to be.*

He took a deep breath. Even without more evidence, he knew this was it. Slowly, inexorably, everything was coming to a head. He and Drax had been steering toward all-out conflict for years. First over Moira, and then over the Spirit Stones. Their indirect power struggle had become increasingly intense, as if destiny wanted to unleash a new shifter war upon the world.

Was it coincidence that the Windstone had surfaced now? Hardly. Like the other Spirit Stones, it was part of a collection of precious stones with magical powers. But the dragon that had watched over the Spirit Stones had died generations ago, and the jewels had been scattered and lost.

Until now. One by one, the Spirit Stones had resurfaced. And one by one, they'd ratcheted Silas's conflict with Drax to ever-higher levels. Drax had refused to acknowledge Silas for years, but not any more. Not with Silas gaining his own power, experience, and supporters.

Silas ignored the look of open appraisal Drax threw his way.

Look all you want, his inner dragon growled. *I have nothing to fear from you.*

Except he did, and he knew it. He had strengthened his position over time, but he'd become more vulnerable too. The very men and women who gave him strength — the shifters of Koa Point — were also his Achilles' heel. Some of the couples were close to starting families, and Drax wouldn't hold back from exploiting any advantage he could.

Drax smirked, and Silas nearly bared his teeth to show his fangs.

We need that diamond, Kai grunted.

"Bidding opens at $500,000," the auctioneer announced.

Kai caught his gaze, but Silas shook his head. There was no need to bid early on. He would draw too much attention as it was when bidding reached the serious stages.

Silas gripped the edge of his seat, frowning. The problem wasn't bidding, but whether he could match other bids. Drax had far more money, resources, and power scattered in dark, shadowy corners of the globe than Silas could ever amass. All Silas and his clan really had was a generous benefactor and the other four Spirit Stones: the Firestone, the Lifestone, the Earthstone, and the Waterstone.

Surely, the power of those four outweighs that of a single Windstone, his dragon said.

Silas wanted to believe it, but with Spirit Stones, you never knew. And according to legend, the five Spirit Stones would create a single, combined power if they were reunited. They could be used to aggregate incredible wealth and power — something Silas had no doubt Drax would do, given half a chance. But other shifters understood that such power was better left untouched. Silas and his friends would protect the Spirit Stones, and the Stones would protect them in turn, allowing them to live in peace and prosperity.

Silas sighed. Prosperity came and went; he wasn't concerned about that. But peace — true peace, mental and physical... God, that would be nice. Not just for him, but for all the shifters of Koa Point — and for generations to come. Nina and Boone were already expecting — twins, as the proud papa wolf had predicted. And it was only a question of time before Kai and Tessa started their own family too.

So much was at stake. So much depended on the Windstone.

Silas watched closely as the auctioneer's assistant tilted the case for the crowd to see. Rays of light caught in the diamond's facets and shot across the ceiling. The moment that light flashed across Drax's greedy face, Silas knew. That was the Windstone.

Moira licked her lips and whispered into Drax's ear. Something like, *That's the one,* no doubt. *It's beautiful. It's powerful. And I want it. Now.*

Silas took a deep breath. At least there was that — the only emotion Moira stirred in him these days was anger. Still, his heart hammered away. So much depended on what happened next.

"$500,000," the auctioneer said, pointing to a bidder in the fifth row.

Another hand shot up, and the auctioneer swung around. "$600,000."

Kai nudged Silas, but he kept his hands folded firmly in his lap. *Too soon.*

When the bidding hit one million, Drax casually raised one manicured finger.

The auctioneer pointed. "One million dollars to Mr. Drax."

A murmur of recognition went through the crowd, and Kai made a face. *What kind of shifter draws attention to himself by living big in high society?*

The kind who thinks he can get away with anything, Silas replied in his driest tone.

Drax's smirk grew as bidder after bidder dropped away.

"One-point-five million dollars... One-point-six..." The auctioneer pointed at each successive bid. "One-point-nine. Ms. Lee?" He raised his eyebrows at an Asian woman with a phone pressed to one ear. She held her hand out in a flat, *stand-by* position.

"Who is that?" Tessa whispered.

"A rep for an absentee buyer," Kai murmured as the woman spoke into her phone.

"Anyone you know?" Tessa asked.

Silas shook his head. "It could be anyone."

Ms. Lee turned her thumb down. No go.

"I have one-point-nine million dollars with Mr. Drax's bid." The auctioneer scanned the crowd. "Going once..."

Kai looked at Silas as the tension in the room rose.

"Going twice..."

"Silas..." Kai started, but Silas already had his hand up.

"Two million dollars," the auctioneer cried.

Every head swiveled toward Silas, and he took a deep breath. Like any self-respecting dragon, he hated the limelight. He'd grown accustomed to a certain level of scrutiny on Maui, but he still hated the prying, appraising looks. If only people knew how little wealth he had left, given that Drax had stolen most of his inheritance decades ago.

A long minute later, everyone looked at Drax, who nodded. Moira's lips curled in one of her carefully calculated, *I'm so rich, everything bores me — but why not indulge myself?* smiles.

"Two-point-one," the auctioneer said.

Two-point-two million dollars came from an oil magnate Silas recognized from the newspapers. Fine. Let Drax and that man duke it out for a while.

Fine — except for one thing, his dragon reminded him.

The higher the bidding went, the less likely he was to be able to keep up. Drax and the oil magnate might have unlimited resources, but he didn't.

How much did Uncle Filimore leave you? Kai asked.

A blur of sentimental images swept through his mind. His great-uncle waving him toward a chair in the library of the family estate in southern France, where Silas had spent summers as a child. Or his uncle kneeling to hug him goodbye the first time Silas had left for boarding school after his parents died.

A pang of regret sliced into his side. Filimore had become a father to him, and Silas hadn't visited nearly enough in recent years. His uncle's recent death from mysterious causes had left a gaping hole in Silas's heart — and in the dragon world. As the last of the ancient dragons, Filimore had maintained a certain degree of law and order among their volatile species. Since then, the dragon world had been holding its breath for a new leader to emerge — or for chaos to break out.

Silas blinked a few times, fighting away a burning sensation. His eyes were starting to glow. He couldn't allow that in public, no matter how much he despised the idea of Drax ascending to power.

Silas? Tessa called softly, pulling him back to Kai's question. How much had Filimore left to him?

He gritted his teeth. *Three million.*

The other two winced.

That's it? Kai protested.

Filimore's fortune was vast — even greater than Drax's. But he had only bequeathed three million in cash to Silas. The rest was being held back as lawyers pored over the will. And truthfully, Silas wasn't interested in the luxury properties, ten-digit accounts, or glittering treasure said to be hidden in various corners of the globe. All he really wanted was peace for the shifter world. Everything he treasured — his home and the future of his clan — hung in the balance.

The diamond glittered from the podium.

"Two-point-five million dollars," the auctioneer cried, pointing at Drax.

Silas hid a scowl. Drax was bidding with money he'd stolen when Silas's parents died, years before. In fact, Silas suspected Drax of orchestrating his father's death, even if Drax hadn't directly participated in that fight.

Drax grinned as if to rub in the point. *Two-point-five million dollars. What do you say to that?*

Silas kept his lips sealed as a hundred pairs of curious eyes peered at him. Drax's haughty black eyes pierced his, while Moira's deep grays mocked everyone. But the gaze that captured Silas's attention came from the back of the room — so intense, he had to fight the urge to turn around.

Must find out who that is, his dragon cried, more agitated than ever.

Silas told himself it didn't matter, but the itch remained.

It's important, his dragon insisted.

He kept his eyes firmly ahead. Nothing was more important than the Spirit Stone. He raised his hand.

"Two-point-six million dollars," the auctioneer crowed.

Silas sucked in a slow breath. Bidding against a billionaire might be a losing battle, but he would push Drax as high as he could go. And meanwhile, he'd think of a Plan B.

But he couldn't think, somehow. Not with that magnetic force drawing him toward the back of the room. He turned his head slowly, wondering who or what it was.

There were a dozen rows of chairs behind Silas, all filled, and beyond that, a packed standing-room-only section at least five deep. For all the faces in that crowd — the business types watching proceedings with eagle eyes, the painted beauties seeking to make eye contact, the curious reporters — his eyes landed right on the woman with the chestnut hair.

Her arms were still crossed, her face furious. She tapped her foot while her eyes threw daggers at a man in a brown suit slowly making his way to the podium. Why did she seem so important? She was a stranger to him.

We've never met, but she's not a stranger, his dragon said in a choked voice.

Her eyes darted over the crowd and stopped right on him. Silas's breath caught in his throat, and his blood rushed.

"Two-point-seven million dollars," the auctioneer announced.

Drax was bidding. Kai was nudging his elbow, and Tessa was whispering something. But all Silas could see, hear, or sense was the stranger at the back of the room. Everything became muted and fuzzy except her, and time slowed until he could feel each thump of his heart, each heavy rush of blood through his veins. They stared at each other through what seemed like a long tunnel of light in an otherwise dark and dreary world. When she tilted her head, her hair swung in a slow wave, mesmerizing him. He nearly reached out a hand as if she were right behind him and not several yards away.

"Silas," Kai hissed, elbowing him hard.

"Going twice—" the auctioneer said.

Silas blinked as Kai pushed his hand up to bid. Whoa. What had just happened?

"Two-point-eight million dollars."

"Damn it, man. Keep your head in the game," Kai muttered.

A bead of sweat ran down Silas's brow. *It doesn't matter who she is,* he berated his dragon.

She does matter, his dragon insisted. *Can't you see?*

He kept his eyes firmly forward, trying to focus on the diamond. But with the tunnel vision gone, he saw Drax and Moira too. Moira tossed her head, making the light glint off her hair in a forced effect that made him want to turn around and point to the woman at the back of the room.

That's beauty, he wanted to tell Moira. *Natural beauty, because it comes from the inside. From confidence, and from the instinct to fight for what's right.*

9

A second later, he shook his head, trying to clear those crazy thoughts. He didn't know that mystery woman or what drove her. Was he losing his mind?

Not losing, his dragon murmured. *Finding.*

He didn't have time to ask, *Finding what?* because a movement caught his attention. The man in the brown suit was still making his way forward — the one the mystery woman had been watching so intently. He edged past a long table of champagne flutes then leaned in to whisper to a security guard.

"What's that about?" Kai murmured, studying the same man.

Moira arched an eye at Silas as if wondering why he would pay attention to anyone but her.

I don't love you, he wanted to say. *I don't care any more.*

"Two-point-nine million dollars." The auctioneer pointed at Drax.

Shit, Kai said.

Shit was right. Three million was Silas's hard limit, and he still didn't have a Plan B — other than cornering Drax on the way out of the auction house and wrestling the Spirit Stone from him.

One of two linebacker types standing by the doors cracked his meaty knuckles and scowled as if reading Silas's mind. Those two were just the most obvious members of Drax's security force — a wolf and a boar shifter, if Silas's nose was right. Drax would have more bodyguards outside, of course.

I can take them, his dragon huffed.

Silas kept perfectly still. Yes, he could take on any one of them. Hell, he could take them on in pairs or in threes, but not a whole gang at the same time. He had his own backup in Kai and Tessa, but there had to be a better option than fighting.

Sooner or later, we have to fight Drax. We have to kill him, his dragon roared.

Silas knew that. He even looked forward to it, in a way. But if he were to succeed, he'd have to use his brain. New York was Drax's home turf — not the place or time for that fight.

When, then? his dragon demanded.

He wished he knew, but destiny never revealed her plans, and fate loved springing surprises on a man.

Moira's eyes glittered at his, suggesting something.

He furrowed his brow. What the hell was that about? He could feel Moira's mind tapping at his, demanding to be let in. The woman could worm her way into a man's soul if he didn't watch out — a lesson he'd learned the hard way.

He blocked her out and raised his hand.

"Three million dollars," the auctioneer noted.

Silas's stomach sank, because the woman at the back of the room was glaring at him. And somehow, that hurt. He didn't want her to hate him. He wanted...

He scratched his chin. What did he want?

Her, his dragon murmured. *Want her.*

He might as well have been sucker-punched in the stomach, he was so surprised. So caught off guard by his dragon showing an interest in anyone. Genuine interest, not a passing little burst of lust.

Lust too. His dragon grinned. *Want her every way. Want her to want me too.*

Fat chance of that if she had already pegged him as an enemy.

"Mr. Drax?" the auctioneer asked.

Tessa gripped Kai's hand. The whole crowd hushed as Drax made a show of deciding, torturing Silas by drawing out the process as long as possible. Finally, the gray-haired dragon raised a single finger with a look that said, *A single finger is all I need to crush you, boy.*

The auctioneer smiled broadly. "Three-point-one million dollars from Mr. Drax." He turned back to Silas. "You, sir?"

The assistant tipped the velvet box his way, letting the diamond toss out one last ray of light. A hopeful, almost plaintive light, as if the stone knew exactly what was at stake.

Don't let me go to that bastard. Don't let him win.

Kai nudged him. *Remember what Nina said.*

Nina, one of the wolf shifters of Koa Point, had recently inherited fifty million dollars. She'd given half to cancer research

11

and kept half — twenty-five million she'd offered to Silas to use for the greater good.

Silas's fingers itched, begging to jump up and place a higher bid. Instead, he gave a curt shake of his head. No matter how high he bid, Drax would bid higher. It was time for Plan B or C. Time to go through every letter of the alphabet and figure out what the hell to do.

"No?" the auctioneer asked. "No more? Three-point-two?"

Silas shook his head, refusing to let any emotion show.

"I have three-point-one million dollars from Mr. Drax. Going once..." the auctioneer started.

Drax flashed a triumphant grin, letting the points of his fangs show. *The Windstone is mine, and soon, I will find a way to rob you of the others.*

Moira's eyes flashed too. *Tsk, tsk. You lost your chance.*

There was something sneaky and disappointed in her gaze. Something Silas couldn't pin down.

"Going twice..."

Kai bristled. *Let that asshole have it. We have the other four stones, and those will keep us strong.*

They would. But five Spirit Stones would have made them nearly invincible, and Silas would have liked that buffer for the future. So far, Drax had left the shifters of Koa Point in relative peace. But who knew what he might attempt in his quest for supreme power?

The auctioneer raised his gavel, ready to close the sale. Silas could read the word forming on his lips. *Gone.* The diamond was gone.

But the man in the brown suit had been waved forward by the security guard, and he raced to the podium, halting the auctioneer before he could actually call the bidding to a close.

The crowd broke out in a hubbub as the frowning auctioneer leaned down, listening to the man's urgent whispers.

"What's going on?" Tessa asked.

Silas had no clue. Even Drax furrowed his brow as the two men at the front gestured and spoke in low tones. The man in the brown suit looked toward the back of the room — just once, and only briefly, but Silas whipped around.

The chestnut-haired beauty was there, staring at the front of the hall with her hands clasped as if praying for something.

Silas pursed his lips. What was that all about?

Quick, turn away, his dragon bellowed.

But he was too late. Drax had followed his gaze and spotted the woman. He frowned at her — a menacing frown that told the woman she'd better not mess with him, or else.

Her knees wobbled for a split second, but then she straightened and glared back.

No, Silas wanted to yell. *You don't know who you're crossing!* She was a mere human, and Drax was a ruthless dragon.

"Ladies and gentlemen, pardon the interruption," the flustered auctioneer said. "But we have discovered an irregularity. I regret to announce that Lot 457 has been removed from sale."

"Removed?" Drax jumped to his feet and shook a fist. "What do you mean, removed?"

The auctioneer shrank away. The attendant hurried off-stage with the velvet box. The man in the brown suit and a security man shot pained looks at the woman at the back of the room.

Silas spun around, catching her flash a brief smile before slipping toward the door.

"What the hell is going on?" Kai muttered.

Silas stood quickly and headed for the exit, wondering the same thing.

Chapter Two

Cassandra smoothed her hands over her dress to keep them from trembling as she looked around the auction room. Everyone was chattering and gesturing — some of them at her. The man in the brown suit and the auctioneer had whispered just loudly enough to be overheard by guests in the front, who were spreading the news.

" 'The authorities have belatedly identified the true owner of the diamond'? What the hell does that mean?" someone demanded.

"Can you do that?" a woman asked as the news spread. "Just stop a sale?"

You bet your ass, I can, Cassandra wanted to say.

But it had been a damn close call, and crap — the last thing she needed was to be identified. Most of the gawking guests were harmless enough, but two men pinned her with killer stares. One was the silver-haired gent in the front row who'd nearly bought the diamond.

His withering look said, *You don't know who you've just tangled with.*

Ah, but she did, and that's what made her tremble. That was Drax, a dragon shifter. The mortal enemy her aunt had warned her of.

She took a step back and placed a hand against the wall for support. She wouldn't turn and run — yet — no matter how tempted she was. But she needed the support badly. It was all she had.

You are the last of our line, her aunt Eloise had said in a hoarse, urgent voice, three weeks earlier. *You are our last hope. No evil can be allowed to command the powers contained in the Windstone, the most powerful Spirit Stone.*

And according to Eloise, dragons were the worst evil of all.

Cassandra tore her gaze away from Drax, only to have it land on the second man who was watching her closely. For a moment, her breath hitched, just as it had when she'd first laid eyes on him. She had hurried into the auction room late, intent solely on the diamond. But a second later, she'd only had eyes for the striking, younger man with dark, flashing eyes, sharply angled eyebrows, and wide shoulders. Who could blame her for having a second look?

Even now, she could barely keep her eyes off him, though she couldn't understand why. Something beyond good looks or the strength that emanated so clearly from under the finely cut suit made her heart race. Something that made her stand in breathless silence, forgetting why she'd come to this place.

Then she shivered, spotting the red glow in his eyes.

Another dragon? She looked around the room, hugging herself. How many other shifters were lurking out there?

Suddenly, everyone looked suspicious — and, shit. There she stood, all alone, a woman who hadn't known a thing about the supernatural world until three weeks ago.

You're not just any woman, Eloise had insisted. *You're part witch, like me. It's in your blood.*

Cassandra forced herself to breathe evenly and focus on one thing at a time. The good news was, she'd succeeded in keeping the Spirit Stone out of enemy hands.

She gulped and peered around. The bad news was, those dragons still wanted the gem. Worse, she'd given herself away. Maybe it was time for a quick exit, after all.

She spun on her heel and forced herself to walk casually out the door as her mind revved into overdrive. How could she protect the gem?

Hide it. Conceal it. If you have no other choice, destroy it. Anything to prevent them from abusing its powers, Eloise had said. *Generations ago, we witches created the Spirit Stones. We can destroy them too.*

The problem was, *we* referred to trained, full-blooded witches. Cassandra was only one-eighth witch, and even after a few rushed lessons, she couldn't conjure a single spell.

The empty corridor was an eerie contrast to the clamor of the auction room. With a sharp click of her heels, she headed to the women's room. The wimp's option, but hell, she needed to collect her nerves and formulate some kind of a plan. There was a diamond to claim, for starters. And shit, what would she do then? She was a novice, totally unprepared for the task that had been thrust upon her.

You, Eloise had said in that surprise meeting when she'd revealed the long-kept secret of Cassandra's heritage. *You are our last hope.*

At first, she hadn't taken Eloise seriously. But after witnessing a few spells — like a levitated chair and a candle that lit out of nowhere — Cassandra had progressed to sputtering in protest. Surely, if any member of her family were a witch, it would be her bitchy cousin, Rita. But Rita was from the all-human side of the family, Eloise explained, not the side with a tiny splash of witch's blood.

There's no one else. If you don't rescue the gem, no one will. You, Cassandra. Everything rests in your hands.

Why not you? she'd retorted.

Believe me, I'm doing my part, the old woman had said with a mischievous glint in her eye.

And now, Cassandra really was the last one, because Eloise had been murdered just days after that impromptu meeting.

Cassandra swallowed hard, looking at her haggard reflection in the mirror. Her eyes were wide and bugged-out, and who could blame her? She washed her hands and took a couple of deep, steadying breaths. She had to figure out how to get the gem — and herself — out of here. Fast.

Her mind was anything but fast, though, drawing blank after blank when it came to an escape plan, so she leaned over the sink and splashed her face. She was still blinking the water out of her eyes when the door to the ladies' room opened then closed with an ominous click. The space around her spiked

17

with tension as if a storm system had just squeezed into the room.

Cassandra snapped her head up just in time to see a woman in a red dress scowl at her in the mirror. She spun to face the newcomer, reminding herself she was a badass New York bartender. She could handle anyone.

But, shit. It was the woman who'd been sitting beside Drax, and her eyes glowed red. A dragon glow?

"So," Red Dress said, looking Cassandra over slowly, dismissively. "You're the one who halted the sale. Bad idea. Very bad idea."

And holy shit, the points of the woman's canines extended. She was a dragon, for sure.

Cassandra cursed Eloise under her breath. Couldn't her aunt have offered a few pointers in handling angry dragons before sending her off on what seemed more and more like a suicide mission?

"What are you going to do now?" Red Dress hissed. "Do you really think you can just walk out of here with my diamond?"

It might as well have been Cassandra's own subconscious posing the question. What the hell *was* she going to do?

The she-dragon was gorgeous in a too-thin, too-painted kind of way, with shiny black hair and scarlet lipstick the color of her dress. She was shorter than Cassandra by at least two inches, but the heels made up for that. Her appraising eyes were a haunting silver color, her lips turned down in a permanent scowl.

"I'll do whatever I please with *my* diamond," Cassandra retorted, telling herself she was dealing with a rowdy customer and not a shifter who could breathe fire.

The black-haired woman laughed. "Your diamond?" She stepped closer, dark as a cloud. "It will soon be mine." A moment later, she laughed again. It was eerie, the way she flipped from one mood to another. "Silly human, you don't know what you've gotten yourself into, do you?"

No, she didn't. A magic spell would have been awfully handy, but, crap. The few lessons Eloise had rushed her through had all ended the same way: in abject failure.

So, all Cassandra could do was resort to her I-don't-take-shit-from-anyone Brooklyn attitude.

"Maybe you're the one who doesn't know what she's gotten herself into," she spat.

Moira tossed her head back and cackled, making her silky mane wave and bounce. "Ha. You're bluffing. I want the Spirit Stone, and you will give it to me."

"Sure. And then you'll give it to him, right?"

Him was Drax, of course. Cassandra watched as the woman's eyes sparkled with mischief and some hidden plan.

Crap. Did the levels of intrigue in the paranormal world run even deeper than she'd imagined?

"No dragon will ever have the Windstone. Not if I can help it," Cassandra said, sounder braver than she felt.

Red Dress scowled and stepped closer. "But that's the problem, my friend. You can't prevent it."

Not your friend, she wanted to say, but the she-dragon started pacing around her in half circles, like a cat. She prowled back and forth, coming closer each time, spinning a web of fear with her looks and words.

"You can try, of course. And die." Red Dress shrugged. "Either way, the Spirit Stone will be mine."

Cassandra crossed her arms and let her chin jut, about to retort. But the bathroom door flew open, and a second woman burst in. A woman every inch as tall as Cassandra and every bit as beautiful as Moira, but the exact opposite at the same time. Her fiery red hair and flashing green eyes filled the room with energy and light, and something about her put Cassandra at ease. Which was nuts, because those green eyes glowed, giving her away as a dragon.

Cassandra's hopes plummeted. Now she had two she-dragons to deal with, and who knew how many others outside?

"Moira." The redhead glared, kicking her foot up against the door and crossing her arms. "Can't say it's a pleasure to meet you."

"And you must be the new kid on the block. Tessa, right?" Red Dress sniffed, looking over the newcomer from head to toe, unimpressed.

Well, Cassandra sure as hell was impressed. If she could stare down Moira the way this Tessa woman did, she'd be pretty proud of herself.

"That Spirit Stone isn't yours, Moira," Tessa said.

"It will be," Moira snarled.

"It will never be yours," Cassandra cut in.

"Exactly," the redhead said, stepping sideways to stand beside her.

Cassandra nearly did a double take. Tessa was on her side? It had to be some kind of trick, right? A good-cop, bad-cop combo the two she-dragons had worked out ahead of time, perhaps.

But Tessa shot her a kind look that bolstered her nerves and said, *Just play along. I'll explain as soon as I can.*

Cassandra stared. Dare she trust this stranger?

"What are you doing here, Moira?" Tessa demanded. "Planning to steal the diamond from its rightful owner?"

Cassandra gaped. Was Tessa acknowledging the diamond as hers? That sure didn't fit the description of greedy dragons Eloise had warned her about.

Tessa went on bitterly. "And then you and Drax will fly off into the sunset and make more trouble for everyone. Am I right?"

"Something like that," Moira murmured. Again, there was a hint of something mischievous, something not quite right. "And you, fire maiden, can't stop me. Not even Silas can stop me. No one can." Her voice held a hysterical note, as if just the thought of power wound this woman up.

Cassandra eyed the door, thinking about escape. The situation was rapidly spinning out of control.

"Listen to yourself," Tessa spat, her eyes glowing with rage. "I don't know what Silas ever saw in you. Or did you bewitch him?"

Cassandra gulped quietly. Tessa had seemed like a potential ally, but what if she discovered she was defending someone who was part witch?

Red Dress — er, Moira — just laughed. "I don't need to bewitch men. Silas still loves me. You'll see."

Cassandra wondered who the poor fool was.

Moira stepped toward the door, apparently ready to retreat — at least, for the time being. She smiled all too sweetly at Cassandra.

"Enjoy the diamond while you can. Hold it in both hands and dream of harnessing its power." Her voice grew wistful, and her gaze was far away. "Watch the light glint off its facets..." Then she snapped her chin up and shook herself as if from a dream. "Like I said. Enjoy the diamond while you can. It won't be yours for long."

And with that, Moira tossed her hair and strode out as sure and regal as a queen.

The minute the door slammed, Cassandra shrank back against the sink and exhaled.

"Whew," Tessa said. "Goodbye and good riddance. And wow — good job, you." She smiled broadly, and her green eyes danced. "Sorry — manners. I'm Tessa Byrne. Nice to meet you."

Cassandra stuck her hand out, working hard to remember the redhead was a dragon and thus someone to suspect. A pity, because she liked the woman already — unlike Moira. But if both were dragon shifters, she'd have to stay on her toes.

"Cassandra Nichols."

The woman's green eyes shone as brightly as the pendant around her neck, and Cassandra stared. Was that a Spirit Stone too?

"Listen, we need to get out of here," Tessa said.

We? Cassandra wanted to yelp.

"You need help," the redhead continued. "There's no telling what Drax will do to get his claws on the diamond."

Claws. Cassandra cringed. Only a few days after her aunt had warned Cassandra about dragons, she was dead, the victim of a gruesome attack.

21

We're still trying to identify the killer and weapon, the baffled police investigator had said.

Try dragons with huge claws, she'd thought the moment she'd seen the awful wounds.

The murder — like the news about her heritage — had thrown Cassandra's life into a tailspin. All of Eloise's effects had been locked up by the police — including the contents of her bank vault, which included the diamond. Her estranged son on the West Coast obviously hadn't known about it, because he'd arranged for all of Eloise's modest effects to be auctioned. Which meant the diamond had gone off to auction, as well — until Eloise's will was discovered and authenticated, naming Cassandra as heir to the gem.

"You're not with Drax?" Cassandra asked. She really had to get moving and talk to the auction director before Drax did. But she had to figure out how Tessa fit in, too.

Tessa made a face. "God, no. I'm with Silas. Well, I'm with Kai." She beamed, clearly in love.

Cassandra nearly sighed at the reminder of everything her life lacked. No boyfriend. No lover. No shoulder to lean on, and certainly, no hero to save her when she needed it most.

She straightened her shoulders and reminded herself she could damn well stand on her own two feet. So she'd better start now — especially if there were more dragons outside. Silas? Kai? Was one of them the striking man with dark eyes?

"Anyway, it's a long story," Tessa said. "Right now, we have to get you out of here. You're in danger."

No kidding. The question was, could she trust this woman? *Trust no one,* Eloise had said. *Especially not a dragon.*

"We can help," Tessa said, growing urgent again.

Cassandra bit her lip. Help would be great. She'd never felt so painfully alone in her life.

She turned to splash water over her face, buying time. Plan A — to remain anonymous and stay out of trouble — had gone down the drain. Not that she'd had any choice since Eloise's will had only been authenticated at the last possible minute. Cassandra was lucky to have stopped the sale in time.

But, damn. Her luck had screeched to a halt there. Now what?

"Moira will do anything to get the diamond," Tessa warned.

Forcing her hands not to shake, Cassandra dried her face, spying around for some way out. The door to the ladies' room swung open, and two women stepped in.

"Can you believe it?" one said to the other.

"Never seen anything like it," the second woman agreed. "A three-million-dollar auction halted at the last possible second?"

The hallway outside filled with the sound of a crowd, and a plan formed in Cassandra's mind. She sidestepped, putting the women between her and Tessa.

"The buyer looked really mad. Did you see how red in the face that man went?"

Cassandra frowned. As if she needed a reminder of Drax's wrath.

"Wait," Tessa said, leaning left and right, seeking eye contact.

Cassandra slipped out into the hallway.

"Wait!" Tessa called.

Cassandra was tempted — so, so tempted — to turn her problems over to someone else. But she had a mission to fulfill, damn it, and that meant not trusting anyone.

"Let us help," Tessa called in an urgent undertone.

Cassandra forced herself onward, slipping away through the crowd.

Chapter Three

Less than an hour later, Cassandra pushed out the doors of the auction house and hurried down the sidewalk. Never had she experienced anything like the past forty minutes — minutes that were excruciatingly slow but rushed at the same time.

The important thing was, she'd given everyone the slip and taken care of the diamond. Now, all she had to do was speed away from the dragons she'd evaded and figure out what to do next.

She hurried down a side alley, listening to her own muted footsteps. She was still reeling from it all — her quick exit from the women's room, followed by her visit to the auction director's office, where she'd channeled *indignant New Yorker*.

"Well, I'm glad I won't have to press charges against Westmore Brothers Auctioneers," she'd snipped. "Especially now that I have my property back. And I expect no further indiscretions as to my identity."

God, she sounded like a real bitch. But it had worked, right down to the snap of her fingers. The director had checked her ID and the court order then signed the diamond over to her.

"We take the privacy of our clients very seriously," he assured her.

Boy, she hoped so. Someone like Drax probably had the power to buy off the entire staff, but maybe if they feared for their jobs, they'd keep their mouths shut.

"Good," she'd sniffed. "I'm sure Westmore Brothers doesn't want any bad press."

She'd spotted Tessa with two men at the end of the private hall to the director's office. In fact, she could *sense* them there — especially the man with dark hair and dark eyes. His presence was that powerful, calling to her in a way she couldn't define. So much, she was tempted to give in and approach him — whoever he was. Tessa had mentioned a Kai and a Silas. But if Tessa was with Kai, that had to be the guy holding hands with the redhead. Which meant the dark-haired man was Silas.

Silas, she whispered his name in her mind.

Wait, Tessa had said. *You need help.*

Silas's eyes said the same thing, and she knew he was right. But the second she remembered who he was, she froze. No way could she trust a dragon.

Silas, Tessa, and Kai had been held back by security guards who probably had no clue who they were dealing with. Then a passing waiter walked by, carrying a tray of empty champagne glasses. His foot caught in a fold in the carpet, and he tripped. With an ear-splitting sound, glasses shattered into thousands of shards, each reflecting the light. Just the distraction she needed.

Swift and stealthy as a black cat, she rushed down the stairs and out into one of those crisp fall nights in New York. It was ten o'clock on a Tuesday evening, and traffic was flowing freely. Her throat was so dry, it hurt to swallow her fear and carry on. A tiny twinge of pride helped, though. She'd done it — she'd eluded them all.

Her shoes clicked down the sidewalk as she turned several corners then paused at a mailbox. Opening it with a screech, she winced and looked over her shoulder. No dragons in hot pursuit — yet.

Her hand trembled as she pulled a small package from her purse. The auction director had offered her a jewelry box to transport the diamond, but she'd taken bubble wrap and a plain, pre-paid envelope instead. The result was a package so ordinary, it could have held anything. Yet if she concentrated, she could feel the faint throb from within. The Spirit Stone.

"Shh," she whispered. "None of that."

Eloise had mentioned something about Spirit Stones slumbering, but damn — she needed it to do more than just snooze.

"Keep quiet," she ordered as if it were a person and not a jewel.

It was eerie, the way the Stone's energy reached out and clawed at her, begging.

I've waited for so long.

"Well, you have to wait a little longer," she hissed while she scribbled an address on the envelope from memory. The easiest address she could think of, one that was thousands of miles away. The dragons would never find the diamond there.

"I'll come for you soon," she promised, hoping it wouldn't turn out to be a lie.

A couple walked past, giving her strange looks.

Cassandra shot them her best mind-your-own-business glare and dropped the package into the mailbox. The flap creaked twice as she checked that it had really gone in. Then, with a last look over her shoulder, she hurried on. The subway was at the end of the next block, but she headed for an alley rather than taking the too-obvious route. A second later, she stepped into the dark slot between buildings and race-walked on, throwing furtive looks over her shoulder every few steps.

Trash rustled in the shadows. A taxi beeped in the cross street that seemed miles behind. The man lying in a doorway ahead — a drunk? Homeless? — didn't stir as she leaped over his outstretched legs. Two pigeons fluttered away, nearly giving her a heart attack.

"I love New York. I love New York," she whispered through clenched teeth.

She was two-thirds of the way down to a large cross street at the end of the alley when a voice rang out.

"Wait! Please, wait."

She halted in her tracks. Really, she ought to have bolted, but something about that voice reached deep into her soul.

"Please," the man called again, asking rather than demanding. Begging, almost.

She whirled and immediately held her breath. It was him — the man who had so captivated her at the auction.

He'll captivate you in a bad way if you don't watch out, an inner voice warned. *He's a dragon, remember?*

"Who are you? What do you want?" she demanded, jamming her hands on her hips.

"I'm Silas Llewellyn. And I just want a word," he said. "Just a word. Please."

She made a face. Why hadn't Eloise warned her about polite, drop-dead gorgeous dragon shifters? Drax and Moira were easy to hate. This man, however, kept drawing her in.

She walked on and turned into another alley. He was beside her in a flash, though his movements were slow and graceful. She clenched her right hand into a fist and mentally reviewed a list of male soft spots she could knee, punch, or elbow in self-defense. The fingers of her left hand flexed as if trying to conjure up a spell against dragons.

She snorted inwardly. Yeah, that would be handy, all right.

"Look," he said in a deep, sincere voice. "The diamond is yours. I respect that. But I'm not sure you understand what it really is." His voice grew urgent, even anxious.

She stopped to study him. The man was so perfectly proportioned, she hadn't realized how big he was until now. The fabric of his tailored suit swelled at his chest and shoulders and tapered at the waist.

Danger, her inner radar announced. A whole different kind of danger than she'd anticipated. The danger of letting her heart — or hormones — take over instead of her mind.

She started walking down the alley again, and he followed, taking one long stride to every two of hers. He was that tall, that quick — and quiet. *Sneak-up-on-you-in-an-alley* kind of quiet.

She hid a shiver, pretending it was the chilly night.

"Believe me, I know what the diamond is," she said. But all she really knew were the basics Eloise had shared in that last rushed visit.

A powerful stone created generations ago by our ancestors. A jewel with incredible powers.

Just about the only thing Eloise had been specific about was the *keep it out of the hands of greedy dragons* part.

"So you know the danger you're in now," Silas murmured.

She scurried along. Oh, she knew, all right. The hairs on the back of her neck told her, as did the goose bumps on her arms.

"Right. Danger. So how about you leave me alone?"

"It's not me you should fear. I would never hurt you."

Really, she ought to have focused on the word *fear*. But all that echoed in her mind was *never hurt you*. The words had come out low, gritty, and sincere, as if he were taking a vow.

She pulled up the lapel on her coat — as if that would protect her. "Well, I don't have it any more, so that's that."

He stared. "You... what?"

She shrugged. "I don't have it any more."

For a moment, she feared he might pick her up, shake her, and demand to know what she'd done with the Spirit Stone. But then his gaze softened, and he looked around the alley, running a hand through his hair. He turned back to her with an intense, protective look in his eyes.

"Good, but not so good. Drax will still be after you."

She studied him carefully. Did that mean he — Silas — would leave her alone? For some strange reason, the thought unsettled her more than it gave her a sense of relief.

She picked up her pace. "Exactly why I'm getting out of here. So if you'll excuse me... "

"Listen," he said, touching her arm.

Not tugging, not forcing. All his gesture conveyed was concern. The second they made contact, a zing went through her body. Make that, a wave of something primal, instinctive. The urge to slide closer to him and let that sensation intensify.

For a moment, her eyes fluttered, and she very nearly gave in. But when her inner alarms went off again, she yanked away and backed up.

"Leave me alone!"

She whirled into the darkness of the alley, ready to escape him for good. But half a step later, she halted in her tracks at the sight of an imposing silhouette.

"You," a gray-haired man hissed, stepping into the light at the end of the alley.

The outline of his body was broad and boxy, and his voice was harsh. "I should have known you would be here, Silas."

"Drax," Silas growled.

Cassandra whirled back and forth, fighting panic. She was trapped between two rival dragon shifters. What the hell could she do now?

"Give it to me," Drax snarled at Cassandra, his voice low and dangerous. He smelled of old cigars — or was that the scent of dragon smoke?

"The hell I will," she cried. And damn it, her voice trembled.

Silas stepped beside her, glaring at Drax. She looked back down the alley, ready to run. But for some reason, her body refused to leave Silas's side.

"Leave her alone, Drax," Silas snarled.

"Oh, I will, as soon as she gives me the diamond," Drax rumbled. "And if you do so quickly, miss, I might even release you alive. If you don't..."

His words hung in the air, evoking images of Eloise's lifeless body after the attack. The blood. The slash marks. The startled expression on her face.

But Cassandra had never been one to back down from a blustery man, and she wasn't about to start now.

"I don't have it any more," she said in a *So there, asshole* tone.

"What have you done with it?" Drax roared, stepping closer.

"It's someplace safe," she retorted. At least, it would be soon. "Someplace you will never track down." She shook her fist in the air. No bluff this time. The moment that mailbox was emptied, the Spirit Stone would be on its way to the other side of the world. How safe that really was, only time would tell. She might not live to find out for herself. But there was a certain high to knowing that she'd foiled Drax, at least for now.

"You don't seem to understand one fundamental point, miss," Drax said. "I take what I want. I get what I want. Now tell me what you have done with the Windstone."

A subway car hurtled by somewhere deep underground, sending air rushing through a vent. Dust flew, and a crumpled sheet of newspaper rustled through the alley. Drax stepped forward, raising his arms. His eyes glowed an evil, flickering red.

"You will give it to me," he said, stretching to his full height.

Cassandra gaped as Drax stretched ever higher, until he wasn't just a formidable six feet but closer to eight...nine...ten...

She leaned back in horror as the clothes ripped from Drax's body, revealing a set of interlocked gray scales. When his arms rose farther, his jacket swept back like a cape.

"Jesus," she muttered. That wasn't Drax's dinner jacket. His arms were turning into wings. Broad, leathery wings and talons that ended in long, pointy claws.

"I will never give it to you," she yelled, shaking inside.

"Then you shall die," Drax hissed.

His lips peeled back, and his mouth stretched forward into a long muzzle. She screamed as the mighty dragon inhaled and opened his mouth. A long, licking flame rushed toward her. Sparks flew from the leading edge, igniting the trash.

"You will give it to me," Drax roared.

Cassandra stared in horror as the fire approached in a terrifyingly slow-motion way, illuminating the alley in a surreal reddish-orange glow. She stumbled backward and landed flat on her ass.

"No!" she screamed, throwing an arm over her face.

The motion wouldn't stop her from burning alive, but at least she wouldn't have to watch the flames rush at her like that. She could hear the greedy crackle, sense the change in air pressure as the fire sliced through the alley. She cringed, waiting for a blistering, burning sensation.

Then a second roar split the air. A furious, alpha roar accompanied by the crackling sound of fire. She stared, then ducked again. It was Silas, fighting fire with fire.

The flames raged closer, yet all she felt was heat. No agonizing pain, no blistering skin. She opened one eye and saw a strange orange glow.

"What the..." she murmured, peeking out between her fingers.

The inferno was still raging, but she was crouched behind a protective wall.

Not a wall, her overwhelmed mind realized. *A wing.* Silas was sheltering her with his wing.

Her breath caught. Whoa. Silas was protecting her?

Flames crackled and roared all around, and all she could do was duck as a dragon fight raged around her. Spits of fire erupted, one after another, each accompanied by piercing bellows.

Then came a deafening roar of pain that made her want to cry. Silas was hurt — all in the name of protecting her.

She slapped her hands over her ears, wishing she could tell Silas to stop. To tell him he barely knew her, and she wasn't worth it. That she wasn't sure she'd have the courage — or conviction — to do the same for him.

Yet Silas refused to fold back his wing or take flight. He stood his ground, protecting her. A tear slipped down Cassandra's cheek. Silas was risking his life for her.

Then, in the brief silence between fiery volleys, a woman's voice rang out.

"Idiots. What are you doing? Stop! Stop!"

There was power in that voice. Confidence. Cassandra popped up her head and peered back down the alley.

"Tessa?" she croaked, though no sound came out.

"Silas. Drax," Tessa called urgently. "Not here, you idiots. Not now. We're in the middle of the city, for goodness' sake."

Cassandra ducked as Drax belched more flame then backed away.

"Maybe not now," Drax roared. "Maybe not here. But soon. I will find the Spirit Stone, and I will kill you all."

Cassandra looked up, shocked to see him morphing back to human form. Only a silhouette at the end of the alley, but just as pompous and angry.

32

Moira appeared behind Drax, throwing a coat over his shoulders, and Cassandra nearly scoffed out loud. Did that woman always watch from a safe distance while the men around her warred? Or had Moira been lurking, looking for the right moment to pounce? Drax might have the firepower, but Moira was scarier in a way. Like a cobra that bided its time, waiting for exactly the right moment to spit her venom.

Their footsteps echoed down the alley as they disappeared from sight.

"Silas," Tessa cried, running up from behind.

Cassandra scrambled to her shaky feet. Silas hunched before her, favoring his left side. He was back in human form, spitting words through clenched teeth.

"Fucking Drax."

The curse was a little clunky, as if he were too refined to utter a word like that. But it was full of hate and pain, so Cassandra stepped closer.

"Oh!" Her hand flew to her mouth.

Silas was naked. Totally naked.

A man ran up, unbuttoning his jacket as he came. The minute he threw it over Silas's shoulders, Silas groaned.

"Help him up, Kai. We have to get out of here." Tessa bustled them along. "Quickly."

Cassandra started following then hung back. Wait a second. Her whole goal had been to avoid dragons, right?

"You're safer with us than without," Kai said, seeing her hesitate. "So choose, and choose quickly. Come with us and live, or strike out on your own and die. Because Drax will be back. I guarantee you, Drax will be back."

"Hurry," Tessa said, waving her along.

Cassandra's eyes locked on Silas's. He hadn't spoken a word, but his expression said the same thing. *Come with me. Come with me and live. Please.*

"Choose," Kai thundered, taking two bristling steps toward the main street.

Tessa led the way out of the alley, and Kai guarded the rear. Silas only followed after a sharp glare in Drax's direction, as if he were more inclined to stay behind and fight all over again.

To fight for her all over again? Cassandra gulped. Silas sure as hell hadn't been protecting the diamond.

She looked left and right, weighing her choices. She could cower against the alley wall and watch them go or...

She reached for Silas's unhurt arm and helped him along. "Come on. Let's get out of here."

The glance Silas shot at her was full of wonder, and a moment later, he nodded through a grimace of pain.

"Yes," he murmured. "Let's get out of here."

Chapter Four

Silas dug his fingers into the armrest of his seat while the private jet executed a shaky takeoff. He was going to kill Drax. Slowly.

We should have killed him in the alley, his inner dragon grumbled, watching the Manhattan skyline as the aircraft rose. *Better yet, we could have fought him in the air like in the olden days.*

Silas made a face. The olden days were a bygone era, many centuries before his lifetime, when dragons still roamed openly. Nowadays, all shifters were bound to secrecy. Which meant no aerial duels, at least not where humans might see.

One way or another, we'll get revenge, his dragon insisted.

That he would. But right now, it was time to regroup and calculate his next steps. Luckily, the jet had been ready for a quick exit, so all their things were on board, along with a few items he'd taken from his uncle's penthouse. Silas had been able to change from Kai's overcoat into his own clothes too, but damn it all. He'd been hoping to head back to Maui with the diamond.

We have Cassandra, his dragon purred in spite of the pain in his arm. *That's the important thing.*

He took a deep breath. Damn dragon, running away with all kinds of impossible ideas.

She's not hurt, is she? his dragon asked in a softer voice.

Silas sighed. The creature had a mind of its own, and it was a constant struggle to keep that side of his soul leashed — and to keep it from hollering in his head all day.

When it came to the woman, his inner dragon hadn't let up since he'd laid eyes on her in the auction room. Even now, the beast was trying to get him to crane his neck and check on her. She was sitting in the row behind him, so near yet so far.

Near. Want her nearer, his dragon complained.

Silas cradled his injured arm and frowned. Back in the alley, he'd acted on instinct instead of being rational. His dragon side had just ripped out of him, taking foolish risks to protect a woman he barely knew.

He grimaced through the throbbing pain in his left arm — the side that had taken the brunt of Drax's fire blast. Dragon hide provided some degree of protection against fire, but no one was fully immune.

"You okay?" Kai asked from the seat next to his.

Silas hid a wince by putting his chin on his hand and watching the view. Pretending to, at least. The pain came in bursts like storm waves on the shores of Koa Point, telling him how severe the injury was. Sooner or later, he'd have to shift to dragon form and treat the burn. But for now, he'd remain in his human body and hide the worst.

He forced himself to concentrate on the scene below. The grid of streets. The dark lines of rivers hemming in Manhattan from all sides. The lights of ships in the harbor. Or were those spots dancing in front of his eyes?

He blinked, trying to focus. Somewhere down there, Drax was plotting his next move. What would it be?

Silas closed his eyes. What would his own next move be?

Home. Take the woman home, his dragon promptly replied. *Win her over. Make her our mate.*

Which just went to show how limited a dragon's thinking could be. This was about much more than a woman or a single gem. This was about the future of dragons and the shifters of Koa Point.

Kai leaned back and muttered under his breath. "Fucking Drax."

Silas squeezed his lips together. Drax was the root of so much evil in the world. Moira too. He hadn't seen his ex-fiancée in years, but she'd had the gall to call recently, asking how he was — and oh, did he happen to know anything about a missing Spirit Stone?

She'd asked sweetly, innocently, but he'd seen through that.

Moira didn't have an innocent bone in her body. She'd been after the Waterstone — the Spirit Stone Cruz and Jody had put their lives on the line for. The sapphire was secure at Koa Point, but now, the Windstone was on the line.

"I half expected Drax and Moira to show up at the auction," Kai grumbled. "But to shift right in the middle of the city like that..."

Silas was glad to have brought Kai and Tessa on this trip. It never hurt to have two dragons guarding your back, especially when tangling with the likes of Drax.

His supporters are mercenaries. Ours are family, his dragon said.

Silas made a face. Technically, Drax was family, too — a third cousin, to be precise. But the shifters of Koa Point felt like true family. The five men had grown as close as brothers in their Special Forces days, and the women who'd joined them over time had each proven her determination and grit. He'd fight to the death for any of them, and they would do the same for him.

Which was the problem. He didn't mind laying down his life for his family, but he'd be damned if one of them died for him. Now more than ever, he needed to keep his head screwed on straight.

"Maybe Drax shifting in the city is a good thing," Kai mused. "It shows he's more desperate than we imagined. We have four spirit stones. He has none."

Silas shook his head. That didn't ease his worries one bit. Drax had been seconds away from outbidding him at the auction. If Cassandra hadn't come along and halted the sale...

For the hundredth time that night, his mind spun over the hows and whys of her involvement. Why had fate brought an innocent woman into a dragon fight?

It's destiny. She's our destined mate, his dragon said, lashing its tail from side to side.

Silas was about to shake his head when another burst of pain shot through his arm.

The gem, he ordered himself. *Focus on figuring out how to get the gem before Drax does.*

What do we care about one gem? his dragon protested.

At that moment, it was hard to care. The world kept fading in and out of focus, no matter how sharply he ordered himself not to feel the pain.

"So now what?" Kai asked.

Silas didn't answer right away. Defeating Drax would be a game of chess, not a round of speed poker, and every decision could affect a dozen other moves down the line. And, damn. He could barely see straight, let alone think straight.

"We go home. Regroup. Think this through," he mumbled as another wave of pain raked his nerves.

"And what about her?" Kai whispered, gesturing back toward their guest. "She must be hiding the gem somewhere."

Silas held the elbow of his injured arm tightly. That was the crux of the problem. They'd come to New York for the Windstone but failed to secure it. The only good news was that Drax didn't have it either.

The real good news is she's not hurt, his dragon slipped in.

That was a near-miracle, considering she'd nearly been roasted alive. But that didn't mean Cassandra was safe, or even comfortable. He'd seen her wrap her arms around herself at the jetport, trying to be brave. She was the only one with no luggage, the only one who wasn't heading home. She hid it admirably, but he'd caught a glimpse of fear in those beautiful brown eyes.

You can trust me, he wanted to beg.

One row back, Tessa was chatting with Cassandra, and Silas distracted himself by listening in.

"Are you hungry?" Tessa asked.

Good old Tessa, the chef. She could work her way into anyone's heart through food.

"Not hungry, thanks," Cassandra said in a flat tone.

"You sure? I bet I could whip something up."

"Thanks, I'm fine."

Silas would bet Cassandra was about as fine as he was, not that she'd admit it.

"What line of work are you in?" Tessa asked.

Cassandra hesitated, and he wondered if she was formulating a lie. "I'm a bartender."

He wished she would keep talking. There was something soft and mesmerizing in her voice — a sonorous alto he could listen to all day.

"Nice plane, huh?" Tessa said next.

It was, and thank goodness for that. They'd flown to New York on a commercial airline, but doing that now would have been hell on his injured arm.

"Is it your jet?" Cassandra asked.

Tessa laughed out loud. "I wish it were ours. Kai has friends in high places. No pun intended."

Kai grinned and thumped his armrest. "G550. Great ride. A pilot buddy of mine owed me a favor, so I called it in."

Tessa stretched out her legs and sighed. "I have to say, it's going to suck to ride economy after this."

Silas shifted slightly, trying to find a more comfortable position. Tessa was right. They had all agreed not to throw money away when an airline served just as well but, shoot. He might have to rethink that the next time around.

Next time? his dragon protested. *Next time we fly on our own wings.*

A bing sounded, and the seatbelt light went out as the pilot announced cruising altitude and the flight plan.

"Maui?"

Cassandra's yelp made Silas turn and look back. She wasn't just surprised about their destination. She was alarmed. Why?

"Anything wrong?" Tessa asked.

"No," Cassandra squeaked. "I've just never been that far before. Ten hours, huh?"

She was fibbing, and he knew it. The question was, why?

"Yep, including a refueling stop," Tessa said.

Silas gritted his teeth. It was going to be a long flight, but he couldn't let himself drift off — not yet.

He motioned to Kai, and they both swiveled their seats to face the women. Another advantage of a private jet, he supposed. He did his best to ignore the pain in his arm and templed his fingers exactly the way his great-uncle used to do — a signal of *we're getting down to business now,* and *I am the boss.*

"Miss. . . " he started, then waited for her last name.

She waited too, obviously not one to give in to any demands. Finally, she replied. "Nichols. Cassandra Nichols."

She said it with a daring, *Bond. James Bond* intonation, and he had to admire her pluck.

"Miss Nichols," he said. "What exactly did you do with the diamond?"

She grinned and flicked her palms up. "What diamond?"

Tessa hid a smile. *I like her already.*

I like her too, his dragon murmured, nodding vigorously.

He ignored both of them and glared at the woman. "The diamond you walked out of the auction house with. The one Drax so desperately wants."

Cassandra arched an eyebrow. "You mean, the one *you* so desperately want?"

Damn it, he didn't want anything desperately. He was cool and controlled all the time.

Except around her, his dragon pointed out.

Kai and Tessa were watching him, and he'd never felt so on the spot.

"I don't want it desperately."

"No? Could have fooled me."

Damn it. He hadn't expected this at all. He'd expected a blubbering, tearful mess. Most humans reacted that way at their first sight of shifters. And judging by Cassandra's reaction in the alley, it had been her first sight. He was sure of that.

"What do you know about the diamond?" he asked, trying to gain some headway.

"I know it's mine. Eloise left it to me."

"Eloise who?" Kai scribbled on a notepad.

"My aunt. She told me to guard the diamond with my life. And you can bet your ass, I will."

Silas stared. Did nothing scare her?

Oh, she's scared, all right, his dragon murmured. *But damn, does she handle it well.*

"Guard it against whom?" he asked, getting back on track.

One side of her mouth crooked up. "Dragons, of course."

He sat back a tiny bit. "Listen, I only want to help."

"I don't need help," Cassandra insisted.

Tessa leaned in, thank goodness. "It's more than just a diamond, you know."

Cassandra made a face. "Yes. It seems to have a magnetic effect on dragons."

Silas tried a different tack. "We'd be more than happy to pay you for it. No need to pay the auction house a commission. More money for you."

She crossed her arms. "Maybe I'm not interested in money."

Everyone is interested in money, Kai murmured into his head. *Try again.*

Silas ignored him. "So what are you interested in?"

"Keeping it out of the hands of dragons," Cassandra said as if that were obvious.

Silas snorted. "Believe me, I'd be happy for you to do that. But now that the diamond has attracted Drax's attention..."

"Yours too," she pointed out.

Somehow, she had a knack for taking the wind out of his sails. And for stirring every one of his senses. His dragon was restless, sniffing wildly, taking her in. There wasn't a hint of city in her clean, clear scent. Just the fragrance of lavender and dandelions. If he closed his eyes, he could picture little white tufts floating across endless fields, someplace way out in the country where problems seemed far away.

But he couldn't close his eyes, no matter how much he wanted to. He had to remain alert and wary.

"My goal is to keep others from abusing its power," he assured her.

"And who will prevent you from abusing its power?"

Silas pursed his lips. He'd considered that very question himself. The Spirit Stones were notoriously difficult to control

— a little like his inner dragon. If the five jewels were reunited, who knew what influence they might try to exert over him?

He wished he could state the truth: that he would have preferred the Windstone to remain lost to the shifter world. That he didn't want anything to do with it. But it was too late for that. Duty called, and he would answer.

"You can trust me," he said.

"Can I?" She crossed her arms.

Tessa lifted one eyebrow and looked at him. *She has a point, you know.*

He nearly said, *You have no choice but to trust me,* but something told him that wouldn't go over well.

"Silas did save you from Drax's fire, you know," Kai pointed out.

Cassandra's eyes didn't stray from Silas for a second. "Why exactly did you do that?"

"I'm starting to wonder myself," he muttered as another burst of pain shot through his arm.

"Speaking of which, let me have a look at that injury," Tessa said in an authoritative, *I'm changing the subject now* tone. She stood and signaled for him to lean forward.

He leaned away. "I'm fine."

"Great. Then show me," Tessa insisted.

Silas made a face. He was alpha of a powerful shifter clan, and he would not be bossed around.

But Tessa put her hands on her hips and crooked an eyebrow just the way his mother used to do when he was a kid.

He sighed and gave in. That was the problem with strong-willed women who didn't shy away from pushing the boundaries of clan hierarchy from time to time.

In the good old days... his dragon started before he shut it up.

The good old days were a myth, and he would never want to live a different life, even if he could.

Tessa plucked the jacket off his shoulders, and he slowly worked the buttons of his shirt down, grimacing the whole time. He must have been on an adrenaline high when he'd put the shirt on, because it hurt like hell to remove, especially where the cotton scraped against burned skin.

"On second thought," he said, ready to give up.

"Come on already," Tessa said.

He took a deep breath. *A good alpha never shows any sign of weakness,* his father had always insisted. It wouldn't be wise to reveal his injury to Kai, Tessa, and worst of all, Cassandra.

We can trust her, his dragon insisted.

How could the beast be so sure?

She trusted us enough to board this plane.

He considered for a moment, then slowly twisted and peeled the shirt off.

"Ow," he muttered when Tessa reached in to help.

"Don't be such a— oh." Tessa gasped, seeing the extent of the burn.

The skin on his forearm was blistered and bloody. The skin around his elbow, where he'd taken the brunt of Drax's flames, was black and charred. His bicep area was a mess, and his shoulder—

Kai's jaw dropped, and Cassandra's eyes went wide. "Oh my God..."

"It's fine," he insisted.

Tessa reached out, and he jerked away.

"There must be a first aid kit on board," she said, scurrying off.

"Shit," Cassandra whispered, staring at his arm.

Yes, that about summed it up. But feelings weren't meant to be shared, so he kept his mouth shut.

Cassandra's eyes grew morose, and her uncompromising voice changed to a softer, mournful one. "I'm so sorry. That's my fault."

"Not your fault. It was Drax," he corrected.

And I'd do it all over again for you, his dragon added.

A flash of her eyes made him guess she was reliving the firefight in the alley. Her fingers clutched the hem of her shirt, and her lips moved, though no sound came out.

"Shifter healing will take care of it," he said, trying not to wince at the next burst of pain.

43

"Shifter..." Cassandra murmured, backing away. But a second later, she stopped herself and leaned closer, her face brave and resolute. "Let me have a look."

He wanted to turn away, but somehow, he couldn't. He just sat there, helpless, while she lifted his arm. Gently, like a goddamn Florence Nightingale with a magic touch. It barely hurt. Well, it hurt, but not any more than it already had.

Nice, his dragon hummed inside. *Nice to have her help.*

Except he didn't need help. He was an alpha dragon, for goodness' sake!

Tessa came back with a pouch and rooted around, but Cassandra waved away the ointment she offered. "No good. Not for a burn."

"Are you sure?"

Cassandra nodded firmly.

"What, then?" Kai asked.

"Just leave it alone," Silas growled. Really, he only meant Kai and Tessa. Cassandra's attention, he didn't mind. Just having her there was...comforting. Nice.

I trust her. I like her, his dragon said.

Kai shook his head. "Shifter healing is all well and good, but how long do you want to be out of commission, especially if Drax comes flying along?"

Okay, he had a point there.

"Give me one second," Cassandra said, heading to the galley.

Tessa followed, while Kai poured a stiff drink from the bar.

"Old-fashioned pain killer," his cousin murmured, pouring a second whiskey for himself.

Silas started bringing his drink to his lips, but when Cassandra came back, he got sidetracked again.

"Can you check in the bathroom for lavender?" she asked Tessa. "And aloe. I could use some aloe." She was like an emergency room nurse who knew exactly what she needed and expected it, stat.

Silas frowned at what she'd brought — a couple of tea bags soaked in...milk? "I thought you were a bartender."

A little smile played at the corners of her mouth. "In my crazy family, we have home remedies for everything."

"How crazy?" Kai muttered under his breath.

Tessa came back with two little jars. "I found this..."

Cassandra studied the labels then discarded one. When she sprayed the tea bags with the second bottle, the scent of lavender filled the cabin.

Kai looked alarmed, but Silas let his eyes slide shut, allowing the scent to take him to a different place and time. The south of France was alive with that scent in spring. He'd loved that as a kid. He saw rolling fields of purple flowers — rows and rows of them, hemmed in by stone walls and ancient monasteries. He pictured butterflies, buzzing bees, the warmth of the Mediterranean sun...

"How's that?"

He glanced down to find Cassandra crouched before him, holding the tea bags against his arm. When he looked up, it was right into her eyes, and he just about lost himself there. His ears filled with a roar, and his heart thumped.

"Fine," he whispered. "Just fine."

Time stopped. The buzz of the engines faded. The pain too. Cassandra's eyes brightened. His dragon hummed, and for a moment, the whole world seemed at peace. It was just him, her, and a warm, satisfied feeling he hadn't experienced in... years?

Ever, his dragon breathed. *Haven't felt like this, ever.*

His breath caught. Her cheeks flushed. Did she feel it too? The swirl of energy, the pulsing force that made him lean closer?

Destiny, his dragon murmured. *And yes, she feels it too.*

Maybe she did. Her lips cracked open in surprise, yet she kept perfectly still.

Then Kai spoke — shouted, it seemed like — and the magic bubble Silas had been drifting away in burst.

"How does that feel?"

Silas blinked a couple of times, trying to pull together an answer. *Good* wasn't the right word. Neither was *great,* because the pain was still there, though dulled. But *right* was a good fit. It felt right, surrendering to Cassandra's touch. Trusting her.

"Fine," he bluffed, fighting to maintain an expressionless face. His shifter friends were so tuned in to him, they might pick up on the emotions coursing through his veins. He had to focus on something other than Cassandra. He had to put the diamond above everything, even his possible mate.

Not possible mate. Definitely my mate, his dragon growled.

"Maybe you should rest a little," Tessa suggested.

He nodded. Yes, rest sounded good. He was tired. So tired, his senses weren't working properly.

Not tired, his dragon protested as Cassandra helped him over to the couch. *Not of this human. Just tired of some things.*

He put his feet up and tried to let his mind drift, but it kept coming back to the same theme.

Getting tired of being tired, his dragon moped.

He wasn't tired of responsibility because he'd been born to lead others through the worst of times. Just the *alone* part of leading. The too-quiet, empty feeling that hit him at the end of most days. Kai, his younger cousin, had been a reliable confidant when they'd first moved to Koa Point. But these days, Kai had Tessa to talk to and spend time with. One by one, the other members of their shifter clan had found their mates too. In some ways, their group bond was tighter than ever. But in terms of company, it was either everyone together or Silas alone, and nothing in between.

Well, Keiki, the kitten, always brought a smile to his face, but that wasn't the same thing.

Something soft rustled over his chest. A blanket? The leather of a nearby seat squeaked as Cassandra sat down, tucking her heels under her body as if settling down on a lawn. Making herself comfortable for the long ride.

She didn't say anything for a time. Eventually, she glanced toward Kai and Tessa, who had cuddled together in the forwardmost pair of seats, and then looked back at him.

"Are you really all right?"

He took a deep breath. Not really, but yes at the same time.

"I'm fine."

She twiddled her thumbs before going on. "I'm sorry. I guess I thought dragons would be impervious to fire."

He allowed himself a bitter chuckle. "That would be nice."

"You put yourself in danger for my sake," she whispered. "Why?"

He rolled his head to look at the ceiling, avoiding her eyes. "Maybe I wanted to save the diamond."

A lie, but what the heck.

"You knew I didn't have the diamond," she said in the same quiet undertone.

"But you know where it is." He studied her reaction.

"Yes, I do. But I won't give it to you. I won't give it to anyone."

He watched his own chest rise and fall before answering. "Maybe I plan to follow you to the diamond and rob you."

She raised her eyebrows. "That's your master plan?"

He couldn't help grinning. Pretty much nothing had gone to plan so far. "I'm improvising."

She laughed. "Well, I'm not dumb enough to lead you to the diamond, you know."

"That I know."

"So maybe you should just give up." She twirled the ends of her long chestnut hair.

He shrugged apologetically — well, as best as he could with the one shoulder and lying down. "Dragons never give up."

"Then you'll be waiting a long time."

Was she teasing or warning him? Both?

I can wait a long time if it means waiting with her, his dragon said. *Talking to her. Waiting for her to realize she's my mate.*

"I'm a patient man." His voice dropped an octave, giving the words a subtle undertone he hadn't intended.

"Hmpf. I guess we'll see."

She was throwing down the gauntlet, he sensed. Issuing a challenge. Or was he just imagining things?

47

Either way, she didn't sound like she would bolt at her first chance or poison his next drink.

Of course, she wouldn't. His dragon grinned like a fool, gleeful at the prospect of spending more time with her instead of rationally working through what to do next.

Silas sighed. He was too tired to plan. So he closed his eyes, tipped his chin back, and for the first time in a long time, released his worries, if only for the next few hours.

"I guess we will," he murmured as a blanket of sleep eased over his body. "I guess we will."

Chapter Five

"Welcome to Maui," Tessa said, leading Cassandra out of the jetport.

Cassandra followed with stiff steps. It had been a hell of a long trip. But now, she was wide awake – and not quite believing where she was. Of all places — Maui?

Yes. Maui. Aloha, all the twinkling stars in the impossibly indigo night sky said. The air was thick with the scent of lush foliage and open ocean, the balmy temperature just right. So right that Cassandra had to remind herself the situation was all wrong. She'd had no choice but to leave New York with Silas and his dragon shifter friends. Luckily, they hadn't tried anything sneaky — yet.

In part, she was tempted to play along. As Eloise had once said, *To conquer your enemy, you must know him. Intimately.*

Which gave her libido all kinds of inappropriate ideas now that the strapping Mr. Llewellyn was part of the equation. But another part of her was dying to run for her life.

"Great. Well, thanks for the ride." She took two steps to the right. "I'll just be going now..."

Kai cut her off and stood glowering over a cardboard box they'd brought all the way from New York. "Going where?"

"Are you saying I have no choice?"

Silas looked so tired she almost felt sorry for him. But this might be her last chance to test the limits, so...

Silas waved one weary hand toward the exit. "Of course, you have a choice. But your chances are far better with us than on your own, given what Drax is capable of."

His eyes were so sincere, she nearly gave in. But just in case, she walked past Kai, heading for the exit while listening for rushed footsteps behind. She made it all the way out to the sidewalk, where she peeked in the reflection of a car window. Silas and the others had turned right and headed for a boxy silver car.

Huh. They really were letting her go.

Cassandra let another full minute tick by while Silas and Kai loaded the box and their bags into the back of the car. Then something swooped by in the air — a bird? A bat? — and she found herself scurrying over to them, trying to salvage her pride.

"Maybe I will accept a ride, after all."

When Silas turned, she fully expected him to laugh. But his eyes glowed in what looked like relief — genuine relief — and he quietly motioned her ahead.

Tessa picked up without missing a beat, introducing her to a big bear of a man with a beard and a friendly smile.

"Hunter, this is Cassandra."

Cassandra blinked. Wait a minute. Was he just a bear of a man, or was she facing another shapeshifter?

Hunter murmured his greeting and opened the door to a Rolls-Royce. An honest-to-God Rolls-Royce that made Cassandra's jaw drop all over again. When the vehicle hummed into motion — really hummed, like a musical instrument — she ran her finger over every perfect leather surface. She spent most of the drive like a dog at the window, sniffing the air. Brooklyn had salt air too, but heck. It had a lot of nasty smells, as well. Maui's air was purer. Cleaner. More promising.

She marveled all the way across the island to Silas's estate. Yep — an entire estate, or so Tessa had said. Not that there was a hint of much when they turned off the main road — just a modest mailbox and a crooked blue receptacle that said, *Maui News*. But then the Rolls coasted down a gravel road and came to a huge wooden gate carved with an intricate design.

"Welcome to Koa Point," Silas murmured as the gate slid open.

Cassandra shivered at the thought of entering the enemy's lair — one part of her fearful, the other part inexplicably thrilled.

As the car rolled down the winding driveway, she couldn't stop swiveling her head left and right. There was a stable-like garage with one bay after another, each sheltering a different exotic car. To the left was a wide patch of perfectly manicured lawn, dotted with just enough shrubbery to hide what lay ahead.

"Koa Point," she murmured when she stepped out of the car, trying to take it all in.

It was nighttime – perhaps not in the time zone she was accustomed to, but here on Maui – and a quarter moon shone through palm trees with fronds that flickered and swayed. Tiki torches illuminated a snaking path through bushes bursting with purple and pink flowers. Each inhale carried the rich scent of ginger to her lungs.

She snuck a peek at Silas, who held his shoulders high, walking without any hint of injury. Was that due to sheer toughness, shifter metabolism, or her herbal remedy?

A second later, she snorted. Right. Who was she kidding? She knew nothing of witchcraft, so it had to be his stoicism or shifter healing. When he winced slightly, readjusting the bag on his good shoulder, she had her answer. Pure toughness, it seemed.

"That's our *akule hale*." He pointed ahead. "The meeting house."

A couple stepped out from the thatched building, waiting to greet them. The interior of the structure was lit brightly, and she saw all the furnishings of a living room and open kitchen. But that was one hell of a living room — one without walls and with a constant sea breeze.

She looked at Silas. "What does koa mean?"

He nodded. "It's a tree native to Hawaii."

"The toughest kind of wood," Tessa added with a wink. "It's also the word for an elite class of warrior."

Casandra mulled that over. Tough wood? Elite warrior? Both fit these men to a T.

"Hi." A sandy blond man smiled broadly and extended one hand. The other he kept firmly around the waist of the woman at his side — a brunette with an equally friendly smile. "I'm Boone."

"I'm Nina," the brunette chimed in, shaking Cassandra's hand as if she were an old friend.

Silas appeared at her side and stood close. Nearly as close as Boone stood to Nina, but Cassandra didn't shy away. In fact, she had to resist the urge to snuggle closer. Damn it, what was it about Silas that made her brain turn off and her ovaries turn on?

"This is Miss Nichols," he said.

Boone laughed. "You just spent how many hours on a flight with her, and you're still not on a first-name basis?"

"Ten hours," Cassandra murmured, giving Silas a pointed look.

In spite of everything — the fight in the alley, the injury, and all that time in close quarters — he had remained formal and reserved. She wondered if he had been brought up in exclusive boarding schools that had taught him exactly the right way to behave. But his eyes shone the way a little boy's would, and she sensed a man waiting to break free from a cage.

Tessa brushed past them, heading toward the kitchen area. "Well, come on in already. Can I get you a drink, Cassandra?"

"That would be great, thanks." She was beyond resisting. Tessa had shown nothing but kindness and humor throughout the long trip.

"Would anyone like a snack?" Tessa called.

"Me." Boone stuck up his hand.

"You're not the one coming back from a long trip," Nina chided.

"I'm speaking for Silas, who'll never admit he's hungry." Boone winked. "Plus, I can always eat, especially if Tessa is the chef."

Cassandra followed the others into the meeting house, looking around. Every time she thought she was too exhausted to process any new impressions, a fresh detail would catch her attention. Like the sand-over-concrete floor covered in woven rugs or the peaked ceiling that rose high overhead. A bird flitted between the thick support beams, and two ceiling fans swirled in slow circles. Extra-large leather couches set in a square lent the air of a man den to the place, but there were feminine touches as well. A throw pillow in the shape of a heart. A vase of flowers. Photo frames made of seashells over the fireplace. There was an entire kitchen area to one side with a stainless-steel refrigerator covered with pictures and news clippings. One article she spied said something about a helicopter crash, and another showed a picture of a grinning surfer accepting a trophy.

So much for the cold, clammy dragon's lair she'd been imagining.

Kai and Tessa flopped right down on the couches and leaned back. Cassandra didn't intend to do the same, but she ended up doing just that. Between the auction, the alley, and the flight — whew. It was all starting to sink in.

Nina handed her a glass of lemonade, and Cassandra swirled it around, making the ice cubes clink. How had she ever gotten into this mess? How would she ever get out again?

"To coming home," Tessa said, raising her glass.

"To home," everyone echoed.

Cassandra looked at her feet. Home? She wasn't particularly attached to the tiny unit she rented in Brooklyn, but it was hers. When would be the next time she felt at home?

The others settled in with satisfied sighs, each couple in a world of their own. Boone slid one arm around Nina's shoulders and the other over her protruding belly, giving a little pat. Cassandra tried not to look too hard, but yes — Nina had to be expecting. Meanwhile, Tessa had cozied right up to Kai. Hunter — the big guy who'd picked them up at the jetport – had disappeared the second they stepped foot on the estate, murmuring something about his mate, to which Kai had chuckled something about bears and hours of sleep.

"So good to be home," Tessa sighed.

Cassandra looked around. Was home a person or a place?

She glanced at Silas, half expecting a gorgeous supermodel type to appear, cry, *Darling, you're home,* and rush into his arms. But he sat still as a statue, alone and aloof.

When he glanced up, Cassandra looked down. The couples snuggled, unaware of anyone else. The love and camaraderie of the place were obvious, but she couldn't help thinking it would be a lonely place for the odd man out.

Her eyes drifted to Silas again — and damn it, he mirrored her. But instead of tearing their gazes to neutral territory, their eyes remained locked. Like an invisible magnet tugging her his way or a silent wind blowing at her back, something made her lean in his direction. The shift of a tectonic plate, maybe, sliding her toward him in super-slow motion. The sound of distant waves and swaying palms faded until all she heard — or thought she heard — was the steady beat of Silas's heart.

His nostrils flared, and his fingers dug into the armrest. A muscle in his cheek twitched, though he remained otherwise still.

She'd only known Silas for a matter of hours, but her mind flipped through a slide show of little moments she'd shared with him. The solid curve of his wing, sheltering her from Drax's firestorm. The fury with which he'd roared at Drax, and the anxious look he'd turned on her afterward that said, *Please. Please tell me you're all right.*

Then the slide show rushed onward. She remembered his skin heating under her touch when she'd treated his wound. The vulnerable way he'd looked at her when he was stretched out in the jet, and finally, the shine in his eyes when he watched her discover the estate.

Then a calico kitten jumped on the back of Silas's seat and purred, making the slide show halt.

Silas shook his head as if to free himself from a spell and turned to the kitten.

"Keiki," he murmured, lighting up.

And, wow. If she'd had a camera to add one more image to the collection, she would have snapped a shot to capture the first glimpse of open emotion Silas had allowed himself in the past hours. Possibly the first show of affection he'd allowed himself in a long time, judging by how quickly he slipped a mask over his face.

"Keiki has been staking out your house, waiting for you to come home." Nina laughed.

Cassandra knotted her fingers in her lap, wondering what other shifters were in the room. Wolves? Bears? Lions?

One thing was for sure. None of the horror stories Eloise had frightened her with matched the scene here. All she saw — even as the mood turned somber during Silas's debrief of the events in New York — was love, joy, and devotion. The couples showed it every time they locked eyes, and that extended to the group as well. Clearly, this was a unit. An extended family. People who stuck together through thick and thin.

Love and devotion. A sea of it all around her, making her ache. Back in New York, she usually felt like the lucky one — no overly complicated relationships, no job woes, no wayward kids. But here. . .

She scratched her toes against the woven mat under her feet. Here, she couldn't help but notice what her life lacked. A true friend. A partner. A lover.

And just like that, her eyes slid over to Silas and drank him in.

"Good thing you got away safely," Nina said.

"Good thing," Silas whispered, looking straight at Cassandra.

She gulped her lemonade, wishing it had a little vodka mixed in. Did dragon shifters have their own kind of magic or was that particular to Silas?

"Well, it's been a long day. Make that, a long night." Tessa yawned and offered a hand to Kai. "Shall we head home?"

Kai stood immediately, pressing himself to her side as if an inch apart were too much. His arm slipped around Tessa's waist, and her flashing green eyes hinted that she might have something other than sleep in mind.

"I'll show Cassandra to the guesthouse," Boone said. He hadn't moved an inch from Nina's side throughout the entire discussion of the auction, the diamond, and Drax. "Ready?"

Before Cassandra could open her mouth, Silas leaped to his feet and growled, "I'll take her."

Cassandra's blood rushed, and she couldn't decide if that was arousal or fear. But she just nodded and tossed her hair as if she were at work behind the bar. She had dealt with plenty of men in her time. Some came on strong, some flirty, and others who were flat-out drunk. She could handle this guy.

Or so she hoped.

"This way," Silas said, motioning down a footpath.

"Good night," she called to the others, trying to keep the tremble out of her voice.

"Good night," Tessa said.

Nina waved. "Sleep tight."

Boone chuckled. "Don't let the bed bugs bite."

She substituted *dragons* for *bed bugs* — and immediately gulped.

Silas led the way, and she followed, doing her best not to notice the neat box of his ass or the bulge of his shoulders. He held up a vine of coral-colored bougainvillea, and she ducked under it, coming far too close to his body in the process. She'd never seen or smelled a koa tree, but she guessed that's what it would be like: strong, oaky, dependable. It should be illegal for a man to smell that good after all they'd been through.

"Thanks." She power-walked forward, reminding herself what she was doing on the estate and why. She'd been tasked to protect a special diamond — one that could be abused by exactly the type of man she was with now.

"Not far now," Silas said.

The murmur of waves over pebbles and sand grew louder, and when Silas led her out onto a beach, she stopped short. A row of white breakers shone under the light of the quarter moon. The dark hulks of neighboring islands slumbered on the horizon like turtles, and a bird soared overhead. The guesthouse was part of that view too, and it blew her away.

"Amazing," she breathed.

Amazing started at the rainbow hammock strung between two trees and continued to the cozy structure beyond it. A curved roof started low on the ends and swept high at the top, as if an admiral had tossed his hat upon the most beautiful beach he'd come across in all his travels and declared, *Build me a cottage here.* The low porch started where the sand ended, and two lounge chairs angled toward the sea. She could already picture herself sitting on a colorful towel, sipping a coconut-shell drink.

A breaker rolled, and she turned back toward the sea. Stars glittered across an indigo sky. Crickets chirped from the dunes, and the scent of roses wafted from a nearby bush.

Silas pushed a sliding screen door aside. No squeak, no rattles, no bangs. Yellow curtains stirred lazily in the sea breeze, and the blue bedding practically fussed over her like a mother hen.

Come in, come in! You must be so tired, but now you can relax. Catch your breath.

Which would have been much easier if Silas weren't there, taking up so much of the doorway that she didn't dare edge past. He tapped a supporting beam with his palm.

"We just replaced the roof and completed a few other repairs." There was a hint of pride in his voice, and Cassandra guessed that the *we* who sweated over that job might just have been him.

He struck a match and lit a giant white candle set on the porch table. It flickered and danced within a cylinder of glass.

"It's gorgeous," she said, ascending the last step.

Her feet stalled out, and she paused an inch away from his chest. For a second, she stood there, barely breathing, barely able to think. What was this crazy feeling that took over her when she got close to him?

She glanced up and couldn't quite meet his eyes, because his gaze had dropped to her lips. His mouth cracked open as if to say something – or even better, to kiss. On instinct, she leaned in closer, holding her breath, yearning for *his* kiss.

She tilted her chin up, unable to think of a single reason why not to kiss. It seemed perfectly natural, especially given the honeymoon setting of the place. But then a palm frond swept over the thatched roof of the guesthouse, almost giggling, and she snapped back to her senses.

"Goodnight, Miss Nichols," Silas whispered, jerking away.

Miss Nichols. Would she ever break through his defenses? And, yikes. Did she really want to?

She watched him go, aching inside, and replied in a slightly husky voice. "Goodnight, Silas."

A second later, he was gone, and she flopped down in a chair, staring out over the sea. Eventually, she sighed and puffed out the candle. Then she sat in the dark, watching wisps of smoke twist and turn in the pale moonlight.

"Goodnight, Koa Point," she whispered, hugging herself.

Chapter Six

Days passed, and though Cassandra was on guard against the type of evil Eloise had described, nothing happened. Nothing bad, anyway.

She'd half expected spartan barracks with dragon firing ranges and straw figures to incinerate, but there was no such thing. No cruel, domineering dragons. No blasts of fire or sudden transformations into snarling, slobbery beasts. Just four quiet, sunny days in a peaceful corner of paradise.

The estate was amazing. The guesthouse opened onto a scoop of golden sand where turquoise water washed in and out. There was an entire garden of exotic flowers, from delicate hibiscus to bold torch ginger and fiery bird-of-paradise — not to mention plain old roses she couldn't help but sniff on the way past. Tessa and Nina fixed her up with all the clothes she needed. And before long, she started to grow comfortable with a daily routine among the shifters of Koa Point.

Too comfortable, really.

She would wake up early, still on East Coast time, and linger on the porch, gazing over the pink-hued horizon. The stars would dim, and the outline of Molokai would gradually take shape. Not that her mind spent much time considering the neighboring islands. More like musing over her enigmatic host — or worse, fanning herself to dispel the aftereffects of hot fantasies she'd started dreaming at night. It was almost as if Silas had visited her and done all sorts of wickedly good things. Things her body — and soul — needed.

Desperately.

Of course, the moment she woke up — well, maybe a drowsy minute or two later, once she'd relished the feeling — she would snap back to her senses and lecture herself with echoes of Eloise's words.

Never trust a dragon. They are vile, cruel creatures. They are the enemy.

But that grew harder to believe with each passing day. Especially once she showered and wandered to the meeting house, where she would pour herself a coffee and exchange pleasantries with the residents of the estate as they wandered in alone or in pairs.

Dawn — a bear shifter/police officer — was usually the first up and about with a bleary-eyed Hunter practically glued to her side.

"Bears are late risers," Dawn explained, giving Hunter's boulder-sized shoulder an affectionate pat. "I'm a night owl, myself," she added with a wink.

The moment Dawn left for her job, Hunter would head to bed for a nap. Later, he would get to work maintaining the estate's fleet of luxury cars. The others wandered in and out throughout the morning, some rushing off to jobs, others taking it slow. Kai and Tessa would head straight to the kitchen, while Nina would flop down on a couch and let Boone massage her shoulders.

"Morning sickness," he explained, part proud father, part pained partner who couldn't stand to see his mate suffer.

The concept of a *mate* had struck Cassandra as barbaric the first few times she'd heard the word. And when she overheard that Silas had once been betrothed to Moira, the word *medieval* popped into her mind — along with a wave of jealousy she couldn't entirely explain. Why should it matter to her who Silas had been with in the past?

It mattered, though. More than she wanted to admit.

But the more she observed, the more she came to like the idea of having a mate, especially if that meant having a man treat her in the same adoring manner as the men of Koa Point showed. Boone scurried around, doing everything he could to relieve Nina's misery, from foot massages to compresses to homeopathic drinks.

"Have you tried hibiscus tea?" Cassandra asked. "Hibiscus with a touch of ginger and a spot of honey."

Boone looked up in surprise. "I thought you were a bartender."

She shrugged. "I mix all kinds of things. I haven't been able to help myself, ever since I was small."

"What, like potions?" Boone joked.

Silas came in at exactly that moment, and he froze upon hearing those words. Cassandra froze too. Maybe she really did have some witch characteristics. And, oops. If witches considered dragons mortal enemies, was the feeling mutual?

A moment later, Silas headed for the coffee machine, looking more lost in thought than angry. Cassandra mixed the tea, which Nina sipped tentatively. The next morning, Boone trotted over to the *akule hale* to fix the drink at first light.

"Did it work?" Cassandra asked.

He gave her a hearty thumbs-up. "Maybe not a miracle cure, but it helps a lot, so thanks."

"See you," Kai said, giving Tessa a long, lingering kiss before heading for his helicopter.

A dragon who flew a helicopter. It made her mind spin.

Soon, thoughts of escaping receded to the far corner of her mind, replaced by a wary curiosity to learn more about shifter life. When she called her boss at Tony's Bar to beg for an extended break — for family issues, she'd fibbed — she'd ended up asking for a few extra days. There was so much to discover, to study, to learn.

Lunch, like breakfast, was a relaxed, come-and-go affair, but dinners were communal. Everyone came together as the sun set, and they made amiable conversation while Tessa whipped up dish after mouthwatering dish. She hadn't been kidding about being a good chef. Nina bustled food and plates to the table as if serving was in her blood, and Cassandra couldn't help but admire her style. If only the waitresses at Tony's Bar hustled that way.

"Ah, Tessa. You've outdone yourself," Kai would announce at the end of every meal.

It was at about that time that Cassandra would look around in wonder, reminding herself who — or what — they all were. Dragon, wolf, and bear shifters. Apparently, a pair of tiger shifters — Cruz and Jody — rounded out the gang at Koa Point, but they were away at a surf competition. She could barely keep track of it all.

But the details didn't matter, because one thing came through loud and clear. This was a community in the truest sense of the word. A close-knit family of kindhearted, loving people who appreciated every gift fate sent their way. Boone was building a nursery for the twins he and Nina were expecting, and Hunter was helping, making sure those babies would have a safe, comfortable home. Tessa was experimenting with new recipes for Nina, and Kai had shouted out in glee when Cruz called with news of Jody's first podium finish on the pro surf tour. The men goaded each other as only close friends could, each of them tough as nails until little Keiki wandered by, bringing out their quieter, softer sides — even Silas, who didn't have a trace of *soft* anything.

The women, meanwhile, were welcoming and kind, and each member of that special sisterhood had a way of keeping the guys in line. Tessa did it with exasperated comments like, *Seriously, Kai?* and thought nothing of slapping away a wolf shifter's hand if he tried to sneak a sample of what she was preparing. Nina did it more subtly, with a constant stream of goodwill. Dawn was a tough police officer, feminine yet unrelenting when circumstances called for it. She had just served Boone another speeding ticket, in fact.

"The law is the law," Dawn chided sternly when teased about it.

"Yes, ma'am," Boone replied with a grin. "I'll do my best to repent."

"Try harder," Dawn sighed in reply.

The only female resident Cassandra hadn't met was Jody, though she had no doubt the surfer would be as independent, sharp-minded, and tough as the others.

"Can I get anyone a drink?" Kai asked, stepping to the wet bar on the second night.

Cassandra watched him scoop ice with a glass — a rookie move that made her teeth grind — for all of ten seconds before dashing over.

"Can I help?"

Kai didn't look too enthusiastic until he saw her deft movements. Then he backed away, murmuring, "Be my guest."

"Nothing for me, thanks," Nina called, patting her belly.

Cassandra shook her head and started on an alcohol-free drink.

"Pineapple ginger sparkler," she explained. "I have the feeling you'll like it."

Nina loved it, as it turned out. Tessa loved her Bushwacker, and Boone joked about a Sex on the Beach, at which point Silas growled.

"Between the Sheets?"

The growl grew louder.

"Blue Hawaii would be great," Boone hurried to correct, hiding a grin.

"What about you?" she asked Kai.

He grinned. "Backdraft."

She raised an eyebrow. It figured a dragon would choose a flaming cocktail.

"Kai," Tessa warned.

He laughed. "Sorry. Just kidding. But I wouldn't mind a Lava Flow. You know how to make those?"

"Bet your ass, I do," she murmured — too loudly, as it turned out, because everyone laughed.

Between the drinks and her familiar position behind a bar, Cassandra felt in her element for the very first time.

"What can I get you?" she asked Silas, suddenly self-conscious again. Had he been watching her the whole time?

But, no. His eyes were focused somewhere far, far away, and he gnawed on a thumbnail.

"Glenfiddich," he said in a low, emotionless tone, as if it was imperative he never showed anyone the real him.

Cassandra reached for the whiskey bottle, waiting for someone to say something. Anything. To pep Silas up with some-

thing like, *Don't worry, we'll figure out what to do about Drax.*
Or, *Come on, Silas. Take the night off from worrying.*

But no one seemed to notice — except little Keiki, who
wound between his legs.

"Here you go," she murmured, giving the ice cubes in his
glass a swish as she handed it to him.

"Hey, Cassandra," Boone called, yanking her attention
away. "What's the craziest thing anyone ever ordered in your
bar?"

Funny how it made her ache to leave Silas sitting alone.

She forced a smile on and turned her attention back to the
others. "Where do I start?"

Everyone laughed.

"Well, there was a guy who wanted our best cognac mixed
with cola."

Kai made a face. "Did you give it to him?"

"No way. Then there was this lady who wanted a martini
with an olive on the side. I gave it to her, though I didn't see
the point."

"What's the wildest thing you ever overheard?" Tessa
asked.

Oh, she had a lot of those. So she shared her best — and
worst — stories, not just that evening, but over the next few
days.

And gradually, with every bite of every meal, with every
round of good-natured laughter, Cassandra started asking herself whether Eloise had been wrong. Were all shifters monsters
or just some?

That was the question that led her to the library, where she
started spending most afternoons. When Silas had first mentioned the library, she thought he meant the public institution
in town.

"No, I mean the library," he said on the third afternoon,
pointing uphill. "In my house."

Her eyes had grown wide, her steps shaky. Surely that
meant the end. Silas's patience had grown thin, and he was
luring her to his place where he would attack or torture her,
right?

Cassandra put on her toughest New York walk and followed, ready for anything — or so she thought. The slope grew steeper, and the path folded into a series of stone steps that aimed toward a cleft in the cliff. Then they rounded a corner and—

"That's your house?" She halted in her tracks.

Up to that point, her focus had been on the winding flagstones that paralleled a cheerily gurgling creek. But the moment she spotted the house, her jaw dropped.

"That's it," Silas said, continuing as if it were any other structure with four walls and a roof.

But it wasn't. Cassandra couldn't even count the number of walls or roofs, it was such a sprawling, curved, multistory place built entirely of...

"Bamboo?" she whispered when she finally got her feet in gear.

He nodded. "My uncle designed it."

The comment niggled at a corner of her mind, telling her that detail was significant, somehow. But she couldn't do anything more than stare.

There wasn't a straight line in the building, for starters. It seemed to grow up and out of the cliff, climbing and spreading as it rose so that the upper stories were wider than the base. A magical, Disney Castle meets *Jungle Book* meets Sydney Opera House kind of place with open balconies and graceful, curving lines. There wasn't a single pane of glass — the house was as open to the breeze as the meeting house — or anything like a door.

"This is amazing," she breathed.

"It is something, isn't it? Not to everyone's taste, I suppose. My aunt hated it."

"How can anyone hate this?" Cassandra said, running her hand over the smooth bamboo handrail of the sweeping staircase.

Silas paused at a huge, open balcony with breathtaking views, and Cassandra's jaw dropped again. "Holy crap." She slapped a hand over her mouth. "I mean, wow."

Silas cocked his head at the view. "I suppose it is nice."

"You suppose?"

He'd said it in a way that suggested he'd never had the time to pause and drink it all in.

"It is beautiful," he admitted. "I remember my uncle Filimore saying he could see whales breaching from here. Not just one or two but a few every day."

She scanned the ocean, though all she saw were whitecaps. "How long have you lived here?"

"Nearly three years."

She stared. "And the whales come every year?"

He nodded. "For calving season, in the spring. Or so I've heard."

"You're kidding. You've never spent an hour just looking out? Fifteen minutes? Five?"

Silas looked at his feet and stuck his hands in his pockets, and suddenly, she could picture him at age eight or nine, being chastised for a minor offense.

She lightened her tone. One thing the man did not need was more stress, that was for sure. "Maybe we should swap places. You can take my apartment in Brooklyn, and I could house-sit for you here."

Silas looked up with what started as a wry grin. But the moment their eyes met, he grew serious again, and his eyes began to glow. Not the angry red but the homey brick color she'd spied once or twice, and her heart thumped harder.

Maybe you should stay here with me, she imagined those eyes saying.

And hell, wouldn't that be a Cinderella story. *Dashing billionaire falls in love with New York bartender and lives happily ever after on exclusive Maui estate.*

Cassandra hit the brakes before her imagination came up with an even more absurd idea. He was a dragon shifter, after all.

"So, the library?" she prompted, trying to get back on track.

"The library," he said, clearing his throat.

He led her up another few turns of the staircase, passing an eagle's nest of a living room, a cozy den with yet another balcony, and the world's loftiest kitchen. None of which she paid half as much attention to as the outline of his firm ass.

Okay, okay, so he was part dragon. It wasn't her fault she couldn't overlook the *man* part. The refined, muscled, mysterious—

"Say again?" she stammered in response to whatever it was that Silas had just said.

A tiny smile played at the corners of his mouth as he motioned her forward. "This is the library. What do you think?"

Chapter Seven

"You're welcome to read anything you like, any time," Silas said.

Cassandra stepped into the room and turned in a breathless circle. She'd been expecting bookshelves, but the floor-to-cathedral-ceiling collection was beyond her wildest dreams. Shelves of ancient, leather-bound volumes rose on three of four sides of the trapezoidal room. The widest side opened to yet another balcony with a view over a wide swath of the estate. She turned to the shelves and ran her fingers over spines, some lettered in indecipherable script, others printed in neat block type with glittering gold trim.

Silas stood in the open doorway, arms crossed over his chest, and she wondered about dragons and treasures. Legend said that dragons loved to amass great riches. Did books fall into that category as well?

Silas wasn't looking at the books, though. He was watching her. Frankly, she enjoyed watching him too, at least from the corner of her eye. Her dirty mind, meanwhile, spun with images like using the solid wood table for more than just reading books.

She cleared her throat and tipped one book, then another sideways.

"*Shifting Through the Ages?*" She squinted at the title. "*Weres, Wolves, and Whims: A Glossary of Shifters Through Time.* Are these all shifter books?"

"That section is." He waved to a different shelf. "Over there are normal books, I guess you'd say. History, geography, that kind of thing. The parts humans know about, at least."

Was that a tease in his voice? Cassandra eyed the shifter section again. She would definitely be checking those out soon.

She pulled a book out and reshelved it two spots down, tsking. "*Modern Medicine, Ancient Traditions* is out of alphabetical order. Mr. Llewellyn, I expected better."

He put his hands up. "Don't look too closely. You'll find more."

She did look closely — at him — as he went on.

"Believe me, there are a lot of out-of-place books in my life."

He tapped a cardboard box with his heel — the one he'd brought from New York. More books? Still, his tone suggested books weren't the only aspects of life he wished could be neater, tidier.

"You like things organized," she said. A statement, not a question. "Under control."

Her voice went a little husky on that last part as her mind galloped into forbidden territory again.

The glow in Silas's eyes flared, and she had the distinct impression it wasn't him peering out so much as his dragon. And somehow, instead of freaking her out, the notion made her nipples peak.

She turned quickly, hiding the flush in her cheeks. It had been ages since she'd flirted with a man, simply because no one interesting had come along. But Silas was beyond interesting. He was fascinating. Powerful, yet understated. Solitary, yet part of a tightly knit group. A simmering volcano, a force kept rigidly under control.

"*Dragons of Wales: Noble & Common Lines?*" She rifled through a few pages.

Silas gave an apologetic shrug. "Some shifters are a bit hung up on old ways."

"*Some* shifters?"

He chuckled. "So I've heard."

She pulled out a smaller book with red leather binding that carried the scent of centuries. "*A Reason, A Season, A Lifetime.*"

Silas nodded. "That's a good one."

"*Mates, Myths, and Legends?*"

"That must have been my great-grandmother's. She loved that stuff."

"And what do you love, Mr. Llewellyn?" She turned, surprising herself with her boldness.

He bit his lip, serious again. A long, thoughtful minute ticked by before he spoke. "Call me Silas."

Her pulse skipped as if she'd just been called forward for a prize.

"Silas." It came out a husky whisper, and Cassandra started to wonder if she had her own animal side.

His eyes traveled up and down her body, and his fists clenched at his sides.

"History," he murmured. "Philosophy. Shakespeare."

She snorted. He was testing her, just like she was testing him.

"I didn't ask what you were *taught* to love. I asked what you love."

His eyes sparkled, and she gave herself a bonus point. Was she the first to take the trouble to understand the real him?

He looked out over the vast Pacific. "What do I love? Koa Point. The people as much as the place." He lifted a hand and absently drew a curve in the air. "I love flying at night. Pushing against the trade winds, then gliding home."

Home. The word had a yearning, wistful quality that made her wonder what need this luxury estate failed to fulfill.

She closed her eyes and focused on the play of the breeze in her hair. What would flying be like? Could a person ride on the back of a dragon, or would that be beneath such a fabled beast?

When she opened her eyes, Silas was studying her. His lips moved as if to add one more item to his list, though no sound came out.

"And what do you love, Miss Nichols?" he whispered at last.

God, he was close. Close enough to kiss, if only she could work up the nerve.

"Call me Cassandra," she breathed.

He hesitated then spoke so quietly, she barely heard.

"So what do you love, Cassandra?"

She kept her eyes on him. "Sunsets. Quiet city streets at night. Alto saxophones."

His eyebrows jumped up. "Alto saxophones?"

She nodded. "I love the sound of an alto sax. And I love mixing drinks."

Keiki strode in, rubbing against the doorframe and mewing for Silas to pick her up.

"Hey, little one," he murmured, nestling her against his chest.

Cassandra reminded herself it wasn't nice to be jealous of a kitten.

A muscle in Silas's cheek twitched, and his voice dropped. "Mixing drinks or mixing potions?"

She'd been holding her breath, and she let it out slowly. So Silas knew about the witch part of her blood. He'd openly admitted that he and several of the others were private investigators, and it made sense for him to have investigated her. But, damn. She had only found out the witch thing a few weeks ago. Did Silas have some kind of secret network of spies?

Moments ago, he'd been warm, open, almost intimate. Now, his face was an impassive mask, impossible to read.

"Mixing drinks," she said firmly. "I'm an expert in that."

"And what about potions?"

She made a face. "Total amateur. I didn't even know until recently."

"You didn't know about your father?"

Her fists tightened on reflex. "I knew he was a cheating ass who left me and my mother when I was three. I guess that's why my mother never told me about witches. I'm not sure she even believed in them. And anyway, one-eighth witch doesn't count for much."

He looked at her with a *maybe yes, maybe no* expression.

"And Ms. Vedma — Eloise?"

Her eyes widened. Wow. Silas really had been digging into her life.

72

"I always thought she was just a neighbor. I had no idea she was my father's sister." She took a step toward him, bristling. "She was killed by a dragon a few weeks ago. Did you know that?"

To Silas's credit, he nodded. "I know. I'm sorry." His voice was pained, as if he knew exactly what it felt like to have someone violently ripped from his life.

Keiki reached up and pawed Silas's chin, asking why he'd stopped petting her. Silas stroked his fingers over her fur absently.

Cassandra stared at him as an ugly thought crossed her mind. "Did you do it? Did you kill Eloise?"

No self-respecting murderer would come out and admit to his crime, but she'd be able to tell by his expression. Years of working in bars had taught her to spot liars.

He shook his head immediately. "It was Drax. Or rather, one of his henchmen, according to my sources."

"And where were your sources that night she was attacked?" she all but spat.

He caught her hand, and she stared, surprised to find it winding back to slap him.

"What witches do is not my concern. For centuries, dragons and witches have left each other in peace — an uneasy peace, for sure. But peace all the same." His voice caught on the word *peace* before growling out the rest. "My sources were purely focused on Drax and his men. What he was up to, where, and when."

"Too bad they were too late to help Eloise."

"I'm sorry. I'm truly sorry." He leaned over to put Keiki down and stayed crouched for a moment. Avoiding her? Giving her a moment of reprieve?

Cassandra stepped back, collecting her nerves. Silas really did sound sorry, and she couldn't stay angry at him no matter how hard she tried.

"Witches and dragons are enemies, then," she said, slumping against a bookshelf.

He straightened, reminding her how tall he was, and nodded. "For the past five centuries, at least."

So what does that make us? she nearly asked, though she could guess the answer.

"Why did you bring me here, Silas?" she asked instead. At least she'd get that much into the open.

His shoulders slumped, and his voice grew weary. For a short time, the two of them had escaped reality. Now, the outside world was crushing down on them again.

"As I said. For your own protection from Drax."

"And the Spirit Stone?" Her voice wavered, taut as a spring.

She waited for his eyes to drift toward the window, avoiding the truth. But those deep, dark eyes stayed focused on hers, tired yet honest.

"I would feel better if I could protect it too. But believe me, I know enough about stolen property to respect what's yours as yours."

Her chest warmed, her fists unclenched, and part of her mind strayed. What stolen property was he talking about?

"Do you think Drax will seek out the diamond?" she ventured at last.

An angry red tint shone from the center of his eyes. "I know he will."

"It's safe," she assured him, but damn. How could she be sure? Still, she forced herself to meet his searching eyes.

"I hope so."

A sea gull cried as it swooped outside, and they both stood in brooding silence.

"So where does that leave us?" Cassandra asked, wishing she could go back to lighter, teasing topics. Wishing they could both loosen up and have some fun. And for one brief second, she saw the same wish in Silas's eyes. More than a wish, maybe. A desire. His eyes dropped to her lips, and his nostrils flared.

"That leaves us..." He trailed off as if losing track of his own words.

Cassandra was losing track too because, holy cow. Somehow her hand had wandered over to his chest, and she stepped closer, feeling like a marionette. Like someone else had taken over the controls and was walking her over to him.

74

Silas's eyes narrowed, and the glow intensified, flaring and swirling like twin bonfires.

Her throat went dry, her mind blank. What was happening?

Destiny, an ancient voice whispered in her mind. *Destiny.*

A word loaded with meaning for shifters, but one she was only starting to understand. Did destiny have something awful in store for her, or was it showing her the path ahead?

His lips moved, and no sound came out. But sound wasn't the point, because suddenly, her lips were moving too. Not to speak, but to kiss.

To what? one tiny compartment of her mind protested.

The rest of her felt awash in a sea of bliss. Sure and steady, as if kissing Silas *needed* to happen. As if the world would end if she failed in that one simple thing.

She sidled closer, heart thumping madly. Her eyelids drooped as she leaned forward, intent on one thing.

Destiny, the voice echoed as her lips met his.

Soft. Warm. Comfy. Her eyelids fluttered. Wait a minute. Since when was Silas any of those things?

Her lips moved, finding more of the same — plus an intensely masculine flavor that made her inner vixen purr. A low, throaty voice rumbled in her mind, and somehow, she wasn't alarmed.

Mine. You are mine.

She hung on to his body before she started swaying unsteadily. That sounded a hell of a lot like a dragon, and it was in her mind.

I want to love you. Protect you. Honor you to the end of my days.

The words melted her, but *the end of my days* sounded ominous. How far away did he mean?

One side of her mind floated in the dreamtime of the kiss, while the other exploded with impressions from an unfamiliar scene. There were roars. Bursts of flame. A dark, charred landscape where shadows raced. A life-or-death battle that somehow involved her.

None of it made sense — except the kiss. That warmth, that connection felt exactly right. She clutched his shirt and pressed closer.

Destiny, the ancient voice growled one more time.

What part was destiny? The kiss hinted at timeless love, but the other scene promised desolation and destruction.

Both, the ancient voice declared.

Her hands tightened on Silas's shirt as she struggled to push the dark images away. One tiny kiss against all that evil — but it worked, because a minute later, the desolate scene was gone, and all that remained was warmth and desire.

Her nerves tingled. Her cheeks flushed. Her soul sang. The way Silas gripped her shoulders made her wonder if it was the same for him.

Then Keiki meowed plaintively, and they eased apart. Cassandra blinked, looking around.

Bookshelves. Arched, bamboo walls. Silas, staring at her. Her eyes went wide. Holy shit.

"Hell of a kiss," she mumbled, hiding the wobble in her knees, if not the shake in her voice.

Silas looked positively dumbstruck, and she barely heard the one word he uttered.

"Destiny..."

He looked so stricken, she wanted to throw her arms around him and squeeze the worries away. To say, *I want to love you. To protect you. To honor you to the end of my days.*

But instead of getting closer, they grew farther apart. Silas stepped away, his face creased with concern.

"I'm sorry," he murmured.

I'm not, she wanted to say, but somehow, the words wouldn't come. What had just happened between them? And why did it have to end?

Silas was cold and cool as ever, though his voice was hoarse when he waved around the library, picking up where they'd left off a moment before.

"Use your time here well, Cassandra."

He sounded so sad, she wondered how soon she would have to leave.

76

"Read and learn — though you might not want to believe every word. Our ancestors had their own agendas, and their words reflect that."

Agenda. She was tempted to ask Silas what his was, but then she caught herself. That part of Silas was easy to read. The man had *duty* and *honor* stamped all over him. Duty, honor — and self-sacrifice. Even if he did feel what she did — a powerful *something* she wasn't entirely ready to examine herself — he'd never, ever let it get in the way of his duty. And doubly so if witches and dragons were sworn enemies.

So where did that leave her?

"You really don't mind me reading your books?"

He shook his head.

She plucked a book from a shelf and showed it to him, testing again. "None? What about this one?"

He nodded slowly. "*Herbs & Healing Spices.* As I said, you're welcome to explore. The books on witches and witchcraft are over there."

She stepped over and ran a finger along the spines. Did Silas really trust her to that extent? She loved reading, though she rarely found the time. Of course, now that she was confined to a private Hawaiian getaway for an indefinite period, she had lots of time for *Highland Hexes* — or better yet, *Witches & Warlocks.*

"Seriously?" she asked, turning back to him.

He nodded. "Of course. You have a right to know about your ancestry, and you might learn a thing or two."

She raised an eyebrow. "Like spells against dragons?"

He stuck his palms up. "You won't need them against me. But it wouldn't hurt to know a spell against...other dragons."

She filled in the gap. *Like Drax.*

Silas ran a hand through his hair. "If there even is such a thing. But the more prepared we all are, the better."

She stared at him, thinking of the battle she'd envisioned. "Prepared for what, exactly?"

"For trouble."

"What kind of trouble?"

He sighed and stared out over the sea. "I wish I knew."

Chapter Eight

Another three days passed, though, to Cassandra, time flew. She spent hours in the library, poring over books. Surreptitiously trying out spells, and when those failed — as they inevitably did — she snuck over to the shifter shelf and indulged herself in a little private investigating of her own.

She started with *Dragons of Wales: Noble & Common Lines,* impressed to discover just how prominent the Llewellyn clan was. But that was pretty staid reading compared to *Weres, Wolves, and Whims,* and she thumbed through every page in the shifter glossary, amazed at what she found. Apparently, there weren't just dragon, bear, wolf, and tiger shifters. There were lions. Boars. Mermaids, even, though those were considered extinct. There was even a mighty feline called a *liger* — a tiger-lion cross said to possess incredible power, even by shifter standards.

According to the book, most shifters benefitted from accelerated healing powers, which made her wonder about Silas's burns. Had he recovered fully yet?

She looked in the direction of his office, then ordered herself back to the witchcraft section. But that was frustrating as hell because no matter what she tried, she couldn't get a single spell to work. Not the levitate-a-candle spell, nor the ignite-a-flame-with-a-snap-of-the-fingers spell.

"Damn it," she muttered after the twentieth try.

She ended up lighting the damn thing with a match and trying the extinguish spell, but that failed too.

"Damn it all," she muttered, blowing the candle out like the mere human she was.

She slammed the spells book closed and sat back, crossing her arms over her chest. It was just like her brief lesson with Eloise, in which the old woman had tried everything, only to throw her hands up in frustration.

Can you not cast any spell?

No, she couldn't.

Cassandra bit her lip. Obviously, she just didn't have enough witch blood to make a spell — any spell — work. Only enough to make her enjoy playing around with the human version of potions — home remedies and stiff drinks. It was a damn good thing she had sent the diamond to a safe place.

But, shit. The place she'd sent it to wasn't so remote, after all.

Her eyes drifted to one of the maps hanging on the wall between shelves — a chart of the Hawaiian Islands hand-drawn way back in whaler days. The thing was probably worth a fortune in itself. There was Maui, with Lahaina featuring prominently — a town not far down the coast. Tessa had taken her to a market there. But when Cassandra's eyes strayed across the Alenuihaha Channel to the Big Island of Hawaii, she grimaced.

"Not far enough," she murmured then looked around in alarm.

Whew. No one to overhear her because, shit. She could picture the conversation from there. Like Silas, asking, *Not far enough for what?*

God, what would she say? *Too far to visit, I mean.* She would have to come up with a lie like, *I've always wanted to see the Big Island.*

She rubbed her eyes. If only there were a spell for stretching distances, but hell. She would probably fail at that too.

Her gaze fell back to the bookshelf. She really ought to look up Spirit Stones. But she desperately needed a break from witchcraft, so she headed to the shifter shelf instead and ran her finger down the row, looking for something new. And there it was — a smaller, newer volume called *Shifter Mating Rites*.

She blushed just reading it and looked up. What if Silas caught her reading that?

She turned her back to the doorway, peeked inside the book, and read. A moment later, her eyes grew wide, and she snapped the book shut.

Wow. Apparently, there was a shifter equivalent to the *Kama Sutra*, and the author hadn't shied away from sordid details — or illustrations. And judging by those, shifters preferred to screw in human form.

She glanced at the empty doorway and opened the book again. Just a crack, because she was only going to peek briefly before putting the book away.

Ten minutes later, she was still reading and holding the book wide open.

Bear shifters are reputed to be gentle lovers, in spite of their size. Males are utterly devoted to their mate's pleasure, often spending hours...

She turned the page. No wonder Dawn always looked so goddamn radiant.

Wolf shifters, like most shifter species, will let nothing keep them from their destined mates. Unlike their canine relatives, these shifters find satisfaction in a number of different positions, and they are known to couple at any time of day.

So that explained the giggles Cassandra heard drifting out from Nina and Boone's seaside cottage.

She leafed through the book until she found dragons and took a deep breath. A peek at the doorway showed the coast clear, so she read on.

Dragons are the most passionate, possessive lovers. It takes a strong female, indeed, to express and act on her own desires.

She gulped and looked out the open window. Boy, it was hot in that library.

While some males prefer harems, most dedicate themselves to a single mate, often waiting years for the right woman to come along.

She closed her eyes and listened to the breeze whisper through Silas's huge, practically empty house.

While dragon courtship may take decades—

Decades? she nearly blurted out loud.

—once a male dragon claims his mate, he dedicates himself to her for the rest of his life. The mating rite consists of intense copulation, at the height of which one dragon claims the other with a bite...

She blanched at the illustration that depicted a woman tipping her head back while her partner leaned over her neck. Wasn't that for vampires?

Apparently, the bite wasn't about drinking blood. But when she read about the mating brand — a part of the mating ritual in which a dragon exhaled a puff of searing heat into their partner's veins — she snapped the book shut. She pushed it back into the shelf — far back — not sure if she found that incredibly arousing or an absolute no-go.

For the next few minutes, she stood with her arms wrapped around her middle, chastising herself. She was getting way too far ahead of herself. She ought to stick with witchcraft and—

Her shoulders drooped. And remind herself of all the skills she lacked? Maybe her deadbeat dad was to blame. He was only one quarter-warlock, after all, which made her a mere eighth of a witch. Maybe that was too little to stir any magic.

Magic is everywhere. You only need to learn to harness it, Eloise had said.

Cassandra made a face. She didn't have the power to harness anything.

There are levitation spells. Fire spells. Spells for invisibility...

Invisibility? Cassandra had shrieked at the time.

Eloise just shrugged. *Don't worry about that one. We've been avoiding it ever since cousin Louis... well, never mind. There are weather spells, transformations, lure spells...*

Cassandra looked back over to the witchcraft books. She really ought to research the latter. Eloise described the lure spell as weaving a dream and pushing it into someone else's mind, making them act as if upon their own idea.

An incredibly effective spell if you can master it, Eloise had said. *They were once used to lure in unicorns — or draw enemies into a trap. I've been working on one myself.*

Cassandra wondered what that might have been, and whether it had succeeded.

She sighed and went back to the G-rated book on unicorns.

Unicorn shifters went extinct not long after pure unicorns...

"Damn shame," she murmured.

For a minute, she allowed sadness to consume her, just as she did every time she read about orangutans losing habitats or dolphins caught in nets. But then again, it was only a few days ago that she'd discovered the world of shifters who lived carefully concealed double lives. Who knew what else might exist?

She looked out the window and sighed. It was getting late, and she was going cross-eyed from reading. Time to go.

She put away the books spread across the table — most of them decoys to cover up the witchcraft books she'd been studying, in case Silas walked in — and clicked off the lights. Then she turned to the remaining candles and hesitantly snapped her fingers.

"Damn it," she cursed then puffed them out in exasperation.

Her eyes followed the smoke as it meandered with faint air currents that had been invisible until then. Could dragons read air movements as light as those? She supposed they did, like birds.

Then she remembered Tessa wanted to see her about something, so she straightened and strode out of the library, ending another long day. Crickets chirped outside, and the sky was a rich indigo. Her steps slowed as she passed Silas's study, and her pulse skipped.

Dragons are the most passionate, possessive lovers.

He was working his usual late night, and Cassandra paused at the doorway without realizing it. The view was amazing — at least, that was the excuse she used. A princely view of the moon glittering over the channel between Maui and Molokai. The house was so high up, the view might as well have been from a plane — or a dragon's-eye view. Was that why Silas spent so much time there?

Keiki was there, winding around his legs. Silas reached down, petting the kitten absently. Was shifter healing fast enough for him to be fully recovered from the terrible burns? Or was he okay on the outside but messed up on the inside?

She frowned. That described Silas, for sure, and not just in terms of his arm. But really, what did she know? Even after reading and researching for days, she'd only come to understand how little she really knew of the supernatural world. All her failed attempts at spell-casting rushed back into her mind, and she frowned.

You just have to believe.

Maybe Eloise really was batty. Maybe all this was just a dream. Any minute now, she'd wake up to the sound of Brooklyn at night — rolling traffic, distant sirens, the voices of late-night revelers...

Her nostrils flared. Dreams didn't smell of night-scented jasmine or heady plumeria or any of the other stunning tropical flowers that flourished all around. Flowers that seemed twice as fragrant after dark, like the huge angel's trumpets she spotted outside.

She looked at Silas's broad back. The man had shoulders an Olympic swimmer would die for — except, of course, all that muscle didn't come from swimming. It came from *flying*. The man could turn into a dragon. Why didn't that scare her to death?

Somehow, it didn't. Not when it came to Silas, at least.

Silas scratched his arm as he scribbled on a notepad, so deep in thought, he hadn't noticed her. Piles of paper cluttered his desk, some tall enough for Keiki to hide behind. Most of the office was neat as a pin, giving her the impression he'd recently been engulfed by an overwhelming new set of problems. And yes, even a man with the talents and power of Silas Llewellyn could be overwhelmed. She'd seen plenty of examples from behind the bar — successful businessmen or top athletes who took to hitting the hard stuff and confiding in her because they didn't dare show any sign of weakness to their closest friends.

But weakness, she knew, could lie in failing to recognize one's limits. Strength often meant asking for help.

One side of her mouth curled up in a half grin. That was true of humans. Did it apply to dragon shifters too?

"Hey," she whispered before Silas caught her peeking.

He turned, flashing a weary smile. "Hey."

Which just went to prove that the mysterious Mr. Llewellyn wasn't as aloof or proper as he often seemed.

"You doing okay?" she asked, though she could guess what his answer would be.

"Fine." His smile grew in size but not in sincerity. "And you?"

She laughed. The truth or not the truth? "I get these how-the-fuck-did-I-get-here and what-will-I-do-next moments—"

His grin was genuine, and he nodded as if he knew exactly what she meant.

"—but in between, I look around and think, hey, I can handle this." She gestured out at the view.

She gulped and added, *For now, at least.*

Silas followed her hand. His chest rose on a deep inhale, and for one instant, his teeth caught his lips in a wistful expression. Then he smiled at her. "It is nice, isn't it?"

She nodded, smiling brightly. Silas had his studly moments, but this — this vulnerable, titan side of him — was just as appealing. The real him?

Of course, Eloise had another warning about dragons, and it ghosted through Cassandra's mind.

Be careful, my dear. Dragons have a way of seducing fair maidens.

She had snorted that off at the time, because she hardly qualified as *fair* or a *maiden.* But considering the way she was starting to feel about Silas...

She tapped the doorframe with her knuckles, reminding herself she'd better go.

"Goodnight, Silas."

He was so formal, so careful to keep his distance at times. And now that he'd had a moment to collect himself, she half expected him to say *Goodnight, Miss Nichols.*

"Goodnight, Cassandra," he whispered.

She smiled then forced herself to turn and pad down the stairs.

Chapter Nine

Silas sat in his office, looking out over the sea. Over a week had passed since his return to Maui — an exhausting week of long hours spent trying to track Drax's movements and the diamond. A week brightened only by his encounters with Cassandra, even if she often mystified — and even defied — him.

"Spunky, huh?" Kai had commented after the dinner in which Cassandra had taken over the bar.

She was more than spunky. She was strong. Confident. Alluring. In short, dangerous in ways he'd never anticipated.

Still, he tapped his fingers on the huge oak desk, counting his problems.

Drax. The missing Spirit Stone. The death of his great-uncle, which had created a power vacuum in the dragon world. A vacuum Drax — and others — would be all too happy to fill. And on top of all that came the usual issues of being a shifter in a human-dominated world. Rumors were swirling around Maui about an anonymous investor intent on developing Koa Point and the adjacent property into yet another luxury resort.

The problem with rumors was that they often stemmed from the truth, and he genuinely worried for the future of Koa Point. Rumors also drew the attention of outsiders, and sooner — not later — he'd have to make some kind of public statement to dispel them. Not only that, but those rumors had reached the shifters of Koa Point, and while he hated keeping the truth from his friends, he was bound by oath to do so, at least for the time being.

He stared into the distance. His problems were like the whitecaps frothing up the surface of the Pacific — line after line of them, whipping in an angry wind.

Pacific. Peaceful. His dragon snorted. *What fool came up with that name?*

Magellan, he said. *Or wait. Was it Balboa?*

His dragon's ears popped up, seizing the opportunity. *We can go to the library and see.*

Silas gripped the edge of his desk. No, he couldn't, because Cassandra was there.

Right there, down the hall, his dragon murmured, tempting him.

He kept his eyes aimed steadfastly out over the view. Cassandra was the swell underlying the whitecaps, making them crash upon the shore. Yet another complication at the worst possible time.

My mate is not a complication, his dragon growled.

Silas clenched his jaw. Those very words defined *complication.* Now more than ever, he had to calculate every step carefully. Everything was at a tipping point, and one misstep — one distraction — could have terrible consequences. It was no time to allow emotion to cloud his judgment and lead him on detours he absolutely, positively couldn't risk.

Yes, she was his mate. His dragon knew it, and his human side recognized that too. It was undeniable, the pull she had on him. A pull infinitely greater than the laughable influence Moira had once had over him. But he had to deny the attraction. Somehow. If he didn't concentrate fully on Drax, he risked everything he loved — even Cassandra.

Love her, his dragon growled. *Need her. Can't live without her.*

He made a face. He'd always figured he was doomed to a long and lonely life, but maybe fate had put him down for short and lonely instead.

Keiki hopped into his lap. The kitten had a knack for finding him when he was at his most agitated and settling him down.

Cassandra does that too, his dragon pointed out.

She did, which was part of the problem. Having her nearby filled the emptiness that threatened to make him a bitter old man long before his time. But her proximity excited him too — and worse, his dragon.

She excites me, all right. His dragon grinned.

She'd spent the past days in the library, burying her nose in books, muttering to herself at times. Trying out spells?

He couldn't help but feel a twinge of pride at the idea of Cassandra mastering new skills thanks in small part to him. But he could practically hear the tortured sounds of his ancestors rolling in their graves.

Why would you want a witch to increase her power? Who knows how she might abuse it?

"Just one-eighths witch," he whispered to no one in particular. And judging by the way she banged her fist on the table at times, she wasn't making much progress.

"Fuck!" Cassandra shouted, right on cue.

He chuckled in spite of himself. Delivered in her faint New York accent, her curses always made him grin. She could swear like a sailor — or a no-nonsense bartender, he supposed.

A second later, she threw out a quieter, "Sorry," and his smile grew. She was just as aware of him down the hall as he was hyperaware of her. The question was, did she feel the undeniable attraction too?

Keiki purred, demanding more attention.

"You've been helping Hunter, I see," he murmured, wiping a patch of grease from Keiki's back.

She closed her eyes in a feline *yes.*

He looked down over the estate. So much at stake there. So much he had to protect.

His dragon murmured in agreement, not even swiveling its ears toward the secret cave where his modest treasure hoard lay hidden away. If he'd learned anything over the past years, it was that the most precious things had no monetary value at all.

He picked up a pen with his free hand and tapped at his long to-do list.

Eloise Vedma — contacts, background. He crossed that one out. His informants on the East Coast had sent him a dossier with everything they could find on the witch, which wasn't much.

Call lawyer. He made a face, thinking of his uncle Filimore's will — the parts he knew about, at least.

Prep for meeting with zoning committee. Although he'd been assured local zoning laws would prevent an underhanded investor from developing Koa Point, he wanted to triple-check for any loopholes that someone else might exploit. Someone like Drax.

Charity gala Saturday. Tux. Speech. Date.

The *Tux* and *Speech* were crossed out and ready to go, but *Date* still glared at him.

He'd rather avoid the event — and the attention it was sure to bring — but Maui was a relatively small island, and speculation was already rife about the inhabitants of Koa Point. Making occasional appearances at public events was the best means of keeping gossip mills satisfied with the kind of inconsequential tidbits they craved — who was wearing what, saying what, being seen with whom. That way, people had something to talk about but not *too* much to talk about.

Still, walking into those events felt like running a marathon across a minefield. And bringing a date — or not — was the biggest issue of them all.

He frowned, looking at the calendar. It was already Saturday, and he still hadn't decided on whether to go with a date or alone. Appearing alone would advertise his status as an eligible bachelor and open the floodgates to every man-eater on Maui — and there were plenty of those, all looking for a fine catch.

Not an eligible bachelor, his dragon snarled. *I found my mate.*

Silas shut the thought away.

Appearing with a date — which would be easy to arrange, even this late in the game — had a way of focusing the attention on the woman. Who she was, what she was wearing, how heavily she was involved with him. Which had its advantages and disadvantages. The difficulty was finding a date who would be satisfied with one evening and nothing more — no candlelight dinner, no meaningless sex, no relationship. None of that had ever interested him.

Except now. Now, he could picture it perfectly — walking up a red carpet with Cassandra's elbow hooked around his. Surprising her with dessert at one of Maui's best restaurants afterward, where he would have called to arrange the best champagne and a rose-strewn tablecloth. Leading her up to his bedroom at the end of the night and never letting her go.

Never letting her go, his dragon murmured dreamily.

He grimaced. None of that was going to happen. He couldn't let it.

Why not? We need a date, and Cassandra is perfect, his dragon said. *We could take her.*

Oh no, he couldn't. No way.

Why not? his dragon shot back.

Because he was far too attracted to her, and they were getting dangerously closer every day.

Images flashed through his mind. Images of Cassandra's fingers wrapped around his. Gripping tight at the height of sex. Soft and relaxed the morning after. Tickling him as he woke, telling him how good she felt.

My mate is perfect, his dragon insisted.

He snorted. Perfect. Right. So perfect, who knew what he might be capable of?

I'll be a perfect gentleman, his dragon said, nodding eagerly.

That, he had to see.

What he really needed was Ella — the desert fox shifter who had been the only female member of his Special Forces unit. Ella was single, pretty, and best of all, there was absolutely nothing between him and her other than the mutual respect each member of their unit had always had for one another. She'd even flown in from Arizona a few times for that reason, joking that a boring night out with him was still worth the week she spent on the island afterward.

But he hadn't thought far enough ahead, so he was still stuck.

Cassandra. Cass-an-dra, his dragon said, breaking her name into syllables to get the idea through his thick head. *A woman we actually love. One dinner out would be perfect. She'll get to know us better. To trust us.*

Which made sense until he remembered he didn't trust himself, not when it came to her.

He pushed himself out of his chair and started pacing down the hall. No matter how he played it, getting close to Cassandra wasn't an option he could afford. It didn't matter how the idea made his heart jump up and down, or that she put an achy lump in his throat every time he saw her. For her own sake, he had to resist his mate.

But we need her, his dragon pleaded.

Of course, he needed her. She was the only one who knew the whereabouts of the diamond.

What do we care about the diamond? the beast roared.

Truthfully, he didn't. But keeping the Spirit Stone away from Drax was his duty. Only that would secure peace for the shifters of Koa Point — and for dragons everywhere. He had to keep the big picture in mind.

But all his dragon saw was a thousand pleasant pictures of him and Cassandra courting. Loving. Living happily ever after.

He kicked the floor as he walked. Wishful thinking. And oops — he nearly kicked poor Keiki. She had taken to following him and doing her best to mimic his moods. At the moment, that meant lashing her tail and glaring ferociously at everything in her path. Then she looked up at him, sweet as can be, as if to ask, *Did I get it right?*

His chest tightened. Some role model he made. He scooped her up and tried tenderness instead.

We could have kids, his dragon mused. *With Cassandra. They would turn out great.*

He steeled himself against the suggestion. Destiny was just testing his resolve, seeing if he had the backbone to be the dedicated leader the shifter world so sorely needed. And a strong leader made personal sacrifices for the greater good.

Fine, his dragon huffed. *We still need a date for the dinner, though.*

No, he didn't. He could damn well go alone. So what if that made him go all hollow inside?

The clock down the hall ticked, setting off a countdown.

And so it went for the rest of the miserable afternoon. He went through the motions of showering, shaving, and putting on his tux, trying to keep his mind blank. Then he walked down to the garage, mentally dragging his feet, if not actually scuffing his leather shoes. It was just like his father used to say: life was full of unpleasant business, and great men — and dragons — proved themselves by enduring such tests.

He avoided the meeting house where the others were ready to spend the evening in a much more pleasant way — at home, with people they knew and trusted, just being themselves and having a good time.

"Hey, Silas!" Tessa called. "Aren't you forgetting something?"

He patted his pocket, wondering what she meant. His wallet was right where it should be, and the key to the car would be hanging in the garage. So what did she mean? He turned around, and—

His breath caught. Not at the sight of Tessa walking toward him, but at the woman at her side.

A woman with glossy brown hair done up in an intricate twist. The late afternoon sun glinted in her brown eyes, making them sparkle and shine. Her sleeveless chiffon dress hinted at every glorious curve without revealing much skin, because she was too classy for that. The fabric swayed in the breeze as if inviting him to dance. And damn — he nearly took her hand and did just that.

"Cassandra," he murmured. Well, he did on the inside, even if he couldn't actually push a sound past his lips.

Then he noticed the color of her dress and stopped short. It was black with a hint of red, exactly the color of his dragon.

Destiny, his inner beast breathed.

Her shoes were black, and the shawl thrown over her arm was ivory.

"We drew straws for who would have to go out with you tonight," Tessa said with an exaggerated sigh. "Guess who lost?"

Cassandra's eyes sparkled as if she'd won, and something inside him swelled.

"What do you think?" Tessa prompted. "Nice dress, huh?"

It was an amazing dress, but he couldn't think. Not with his dragon turning cartwheels in his head. Cassandra was beautiful. Well, even more beautiful than ever. Classy. Perfect. And she was coming straight for him. No hesitation. No sign of regret.

The closer she got, the harder his heart thumped. Her lips parted slightly, but she didn't release his gaze.

"Ready to go?" she asked, as if they had a date or something.

You do have a date, you idiot, his dragon bellowed into his mind.

He blinked a few times. No, it wasn't a dream. And yes, she really was holding his hand.

"We told Cassandra how often you get stood up by your dates, and she felt sorry for you," Tessa winked as if that had ever been a problem. "Isn't it nice of her to fill in this last-minute?"

"Very nice," he agreed.

With a click and whirl, the gears of his mind creaked back into action, and he realized Tessa had set it all up.

Wait a minute, Tessa. What have you done? he barked into her mind.

She grinned and stepped back into the shadows, leaving him and Cassandra alone.

Me? Nothing much. Just doing what a powerful alpha can't manage to do for himself.

"If you don't want me to come..." Cassandra said, lowering her eyes.

His hand shot out and grabbed hers. "I'd love for you to come."

Cassandra looked up, beaming, and he nearly had to take a step back from the effect she had on him. It was ridiculous for a grown man to get so excited over one night – and over a woman who'd been strong-armed into being his date. But okay, he could live with being ridiculous, as long as she was his.

She is mine, his dragon growled. *My destined mate.*

Slowly, breathlessly, he turned toward the garage and stuck out his elbow. And slowly, gingerly, Cassandra wove her arm through his.

Heat rushed through his veins as she nestled closer, and his dragon cooed.

"Have fun!" Tessa called, obviously pleased with herself.

And off he and Cassandra went on a real date.

"Are you sure you want to go?" he murmured, giving her one last out.

"Oh, don't worry," Cassandra chuckled. "I do this all the time. Going out with desperate men, I mean, just to make them feel good."

"Well, I don't do it every day," he whispered, leaving it at that. Let her read between the lines. Let her puzzle out how special this was to him.

He walked her to the center bay of the garage then to the left side of the car. "It's a right-side drive," he explained, lengthening his stride to get to the passenger-side door before she did.

"Mercedes 300 SL, right?" she asked as he popped the gull wing door up. "1954?"

He stared at her. "1955."

"Ah, of course," she said without missing a beat. A moment later, her eyes flashed merrily. "I used to work in a bar with a classic-car theme. You can quiz me on the way."

He would rather quiz her on every facet of her life. To get to know her better. To fill in all the years he'd missed sharing with her. Sure, his East Coast sources had reported everything they could find, but so much was missing. Her interests. Her passions. Her favorite jokes, flavors, and poems. All the important things.

"Thank you," she said, gliding gracefully into the car.

"My pleasure," he murmured, trying not to stare at the long, bare leg that appeared between the side slits of that elegant dress.

Normally, he would bang the door down without a second thought, but this time, he placed both hands on the edge and lowered it with a careful click. Then he paced around to the driver's side and slid in. They drove the first few minutes in silence, and he wondered what was going through her head.

"So, do you do a lot of these events?" she asked in a voice that gave nothing away.

"Too many," he admitted, looking straight ahead.

She tilted her head at him. "Then why do you go?" She took a printed leaflet off the dashboard and squinted as the car rolled down the coastal road. "Are you really that committed to the... um... "

"The Society for the Benevolent Protection of Native Hawaiian Wildlife? Three Paws Rescue Center?" He shook his head. "Don't get me wrong — the causes are great. Of course, if I could just send in a check, I would. But events bring attention to those organizations and raise public awareness, which brings in more money, more volunteers, and helps change mind-sets. I just wish the same could be accomplished without the media attention or the crowds." He tugged at his collar.

She laughed. "And here I was thinking you were a philanthropic James Bond."

He snorted. "Not that glamorous, believe me."

He wished he could explain it. Yes, he had a healthy bank account, and yes, he was lucky to live on an amazing estate. But he would be just as fine – even better off, maybe – living a simpler life in a smaller place. A smaller world, if that made any sense.

And a mate, his Dragon added immediately. *I could live anywhere as long as I had my mate.*

The Mercedes zoomed down the Honoapi'ilani Highway, and he pointed to the right. "There. See that food truck?"

She nodded as they flashed past a boxy, silver truck parked in its usual spot at Puamana Beach Park.

"I'd rather have a seven-dollar dinner at a place like that then the thousand-dollar feast tonight."

She looked at him. Really looked at him. "So why not do it? Why not just go?"

He stared through the windshield, wishing he could explain what crushing duty felt like. The obligation to carry on the family legacy.

And anyway, it was too late. The food truck was already far behind, and he had a gala to get to on the other side of Maui. He checked his watch.

Plenty of time, his dragon whispered in his mind.

And just like that, his mouth started watering for a good old-fashioned Maui *poke* bowl or a fish taco. Something straight and simple he could eat with chopsticks or his bare hands rather than picking exactly the right silverware for each course.

He revved the engine higher as they reached the low saddle of land that united the two halves of Maui. Haleakala rose to the right, wearing her usual crown of clouds, and the jagged West Maui mountains poked up to the left. The windows he'd had retrofitted to the fixed frames were open, and the wind whipped his hair. Cassandra rested her head against the head-rest, soaking in the views.

"It's beautiful," she whispered.

He looked from side to side, taking in the magic of Maui as if for the first time. The scraggly, abandoned fields of sugarcane. The patchwork colors on the mountain slopes. The rich, humid scent of the tropics. Funny how having Cassandra enjoy something made him appreciate it too.

"Cassandra," he ventured. "Why did you agree to come with me tonight?"

"Maybe I'm keeping an eye on you. The way you've been keeping an eye on me."

He tried joking that off. "Funny, I thought I was just being a good host, giving you the run of the estate."

She nodded. "You have been a great host. Gracious, polite, considerate."

His gut warmed, hearing that from her.

"And you've been keeping an eye on me," she added.

Okay, so he had — sometimes too closely for his own good. But hell, she'd been doing the same to him.

"We used to have a rule against allowing humans on the estate," he said, as if that explained anything.

"Humans?" she snorted. "Dragons are what worry me." He shot her a critical look, and she backpedaled. "Well, maybe not all dragons."

His dragon grinned. *I knew she liked me.*

"But wait a second," she said. "You had a rule against humans? What changed?"

He ran a hand over his chin, thinking back. "Well, Tessa came along and ended up staying with Kai. Then Nina was in trouble, and we couldn't turn her away." He laughed. "Boone *definitely* couldn't turn her away. Then Dawn and Hunter finally got together, and Cruz found Jody..."

He trailed off. Somehow, the changes at Koa Point had snuck up on him. Changes for the better. One by one, his shifter brothers had found their destined mates. He never believed it might happen to him, but now...

He held his breath and looked into her shining eyes.

I believe, his dragon said in a reverent hush.

Did Cassandra believe? Did she even know what she was getting into with him?

Sugarcane stalks waved from the roadside like scarecrows, mocking him. A car beeped from behind, and he wrestled his gaze back to the road.

"Anyway, we dropped the rule," he finished, and they both left it at that, drifting into silence again.

A tour bus had pulled over, and people stood on the side of the road taking pictures of Haleakala in the saturated afternoon light.

"Oh. I should warn you there will be cameras at the gala. Reporters, I mean." His heart thumped harder. Damn it, she'd balk for sure, and his date would be over before it really began.

Cassandra just nodded casually. "Tessa told me."

Silas made a mental note to get Tessa a bouquet of flowers. Better yet, a basket of fancy cooking oils or herbs that might help her develop new recipes for the cookbook she was working on.

"And you're okay with that?" He looked at Cassandra.

"Drax already knows I'm here, right?"

Silas's jaw went hard. He gave a curt nod and tried shooing hate out of his heart, at least for one night.

"All right, then." She waved a hand and winked. "Just make sure they get my good side."

You only have a good side, his dragon said.

And just like that, the tension eased out of his body again. So much so, he was tempted to turn down the coastal road to Hana, just to stretch out the trip. As in, stretched out by hours and hours.

We could stay out all night. His dragon nodded eagerly.

Of course, he did no such thing. All too soon, they reached the outskirts of Kahului, and he dutifully turned into the left lane to head for the Arts and Cultural Center where the gala was scheduled to take place.

Cassandra pointed ahead. "What's that way?"

"The beach," he said, a little too wistfully.

So close, his dragon whispered.

"Oh. Nice." Cassandra said in a perfectly neutral voice.

He drummed on the steering wheel, waiting for the signal to turn green.

Still plenty of time for a little detour, his inner beast purred.

But a detour wasn't part of his plan. The plan was to attend the dinner, get it over with, and then go home.

Of course, that was before he had Cassandra as a date.

Live a little, his dragon said.

Silas had lost track of how many times in his life he'd ignored that advice. He never lived a little. He always stuck to his plan.

The car behind him beeped, and Silas glanced up to find both lights green — the left turn and the one straight ahead. He pulled slowly forward, then...

He grinned. Maybe he would live a little for a change.

He gunned the engine and cut into the next lane, driving straight through the intersection instead of making the turn. Cars beeped in protest as he sped ahead.

That's my boy, his dragon cheered.

Cassandra chuckled. "Oh, is this the back way to the Arts Center?" she asked in a faux-innocent tone.

No, it is not the back way, he chastised his dragon. *This is the way to the beach.*

And with any luck, to one of the best food trucks in Maui, the beast snipped back.

He checked his watch and finally gave in. "I guess you could call it the scenic route."

Sure can, his dragon said, looking over at his date.

Chapter Ten

Cassandra laughed, and her voice was music to Silas's ears. "Scenic route. I like the sound of that."

He shook his head at himself but drove on. In for a penny, in for a pound, he supposed. And really, they did have a little time for dinner before the event truly kicked off. All he needed to do was show up at some point, shake a few hands, speak a few words. That didn't mean he had to spend the entire evening there.

The smooth roll of tires over asphalt changed to a rumble as he turned onto the side road to Kanaha Beach Park. Silas leaned forward, as excited as a kid at Christmas. Would the food truck be there, or would this whole detour expose what a lost cause he was?

The sun glinted off a metal surface ahead, and his dragon cheered inside.

"There it is," he said, casual as can be.

"Jenny's Hawaiian Mixed Plate?" Cassandra asked a little skeptically.

He nodded. "They have the best *poke* bowl on Maui." Then he rushed to add, "At least, according to Boone."

Cassandra laughed. "So you hardly ever come here, right?"

She looked right at him, and he grinned. In truth, he rarely ate at Jenny's. Somehow, he never found the time.

You have to make time, his dragon said.

Which, he supposed, was exactly what he'd just done.

He parked the Mercedes between a dented pickup and a decades-old green Nissan with a surfboard on the roof. Then he stepped from the car to help Cassandra out. The minute she stood, she linked her arm through his and smiled. They made quite the sight — what with him in his tux, Cassandra in her stylish dress, both looking spiffed up enough for a red-carpet reception in Hollywood even though Jenny's was a bare-feet-in-the-sand kind of place. But Silas didn't care what he looked like. He cared what he felt like.

I feel good, his dragon murmured. *Really good.*

So he strode right up to Jenny's food truck and nodded to the Asian woman at the counter. "Two *poke* bowls, please."

The woman didn't even bat an eye at her overdressed customers. "Drinks?"

"What do you recommend?" Cassandra asked.

He nearly laughed, picturing her fingers drifting over a wine list.

"The guava-papaya iced tea sounds good. If you can handle that stiff a drink," he joked.

Cassandra nodded firmly. "Bet your ass, I can." She turned to the woman in the truck, holding her fingers up. "Make it two, please."

And so it was that, instead of stepping into the midst of a stiff and stuffy reception at the Maui Arts and Cultural Center, Silas found himself swinging a leg over the bench of a picnic table in the sand. Cassandra wiggled into the narrow slot and took a seat by his side.

"It's beautiful," she breathed, looking at the ocean.

Beautiful, his dragon agreed, peeking at her.

His nostrils flared, picking out her lavender-dandelion fragrance from the background scents of the ocean and beach. Salt air and *pohuehue* were everyday experiences on Maui, where Cassandra stood out like an exotic flower.

"Beautiful," he murmured.

Their eyes met for an instant before jerking apart. Their legs were nearly close enough to touch, and he could feel her heat at his side.

"So, ready to dig in?" she asked.

He poked at his Styrofoam bowl with his plastic fork and frowned. "The ladies of the Dunes, Wetlands, and Coastline Trust would lynch me if they saw this."

Cassandra patted his hand, setting heated sparks through his veins. "Maybe every once in a while, you're allowed." She stabbed her fork into her dish. "What is this exactly?"

"*Poke* bowl. Marinated fish. It's a traditional Hawaiian dish."

Their legs brushed under the table, but Cassandra didn't pull away. In fact, she kept hers nudged up against his.

Nice, his dragon hummed, filling his mind with all kinds of inappropriate images — like her bare leg, winding around his. A horizontal leg, with both of them lying down...

He cleared his throat and took a hasty swig of his iced tea.

"Well, then," Cassandra said. "I guess I have to try it."

His mouth went dry just from the sight of her bringing a forkful to her mouth. He loved seeing her let her guard down. Being a normal woman and treating him like a normal man, with none of the shifter/witch/Spirit Stone complications that had clouded his world for the past week.

Cassandra held her fork in her mouth and squeezed her eyes shut, making a little groaning sound. "This is so good."

Silas scuffed his leather shoes in the sand and clutched his cold glass, desperately fighting off a hard-on.

Cassandra was on her third forkful by the time he tried his first. When he did, he closed his eyes too. He'd forgotten how good food truck meals could be. And he'd never imagined how temptingly sensual it could be, simply watching a woman eat.

Their elbows touched, and the heat of her thigh warmed his. Her scent seemed to wrap even closer, weaving around his body.

"Not bad," he murmured, waging a losing battle to focus on the food.

Cassandra pointed her fork toward the line of breakers rolling over Maui's windward shore. The sky was a rich pink, the beach practically glowing in the slanting evening light. Somewhere behind them, the sun was setting on Maui's West side.

"Not bad?" She snorted. "I'd say it's pretty damn good. Good food. Good view." She paused as if weighing up her words and finally added, "Good company."

103

It was almost an afterthought, and she spoke so quietly, he nearly missed it.

"Good company," he agreed.

He turned to look at her, and when their eyes locked, the sunset didn't matter any more. Neither did the crashing breakers or the rice on his fork. Nothing seemed to matter except her.

Beautiful, his dragon breathed, staring into her eyes.

Rich, brown eyes that shone and sparked. His heart thumped a little harder, and he clamped down hard on his glass. Her eyes dropped to his lips, and he held his breath.

Kiss me, his dragon whispered, practically begging Cassandra. *Please.*

She leaned a tiny bit closer, and his pulse skipped. The kiss in the library had been the best of his life, and this was sure to be—

Bang! The lid of a pot slammed inside the food truck, and Jenny yelled out.

"Last call!"

They shot apart as fast as a couple of teens caught in the act, and Cassandra's face went pink. Silas could feel his cheeks heat. But hell, even that was nice. When was the last time he'd felt so alive?

Cassandra looked at him — really *looked* — and her lips twitched. "Oh, what the heck." And a second later, she kissed him.

A kiss that was somewhere between *peck on the lips* and *quick smooch,* but it set him on fire. He hung on to it, drawing out the joy as long as he could. He was just sliding a hand up her arm when she broke away.

"Nice," she whispered, two inches away from his lips.

He dreamed of tugging her back for another one. Of her nuzzling his ear, whispering all kinds of dirty things. Of holding her much closer and much tighter and—

Cassandra leaned back, nodded in satisfaction, and raised her glass in a toast.

"To..." she started then trailed off, stuck.

To stolen kisses, his dragon filled in. *To destined mates.*

"To back roads and scenic routes," he suggested instead.

Cassandra's smile stretched. "To back roads, scenic routes, and lunch truck meals. Thanks for bringing me here."

"Thanks for coming," he murmured.

Cassandra went back to her *poke* bowl, and he did too, sneaking peeks at her. He wouldn't have minded another kiss — a lot more kisses, actually — but this was nice too. Just sitting beside her, feeling like a normal couple. Getting to know her better, and best of all, knowing she was interested in him. He yearned for more — more time together. More dinners at food trucks. More sunsets.

Unfortunately, time was slipping away from him, the real world closing back in. Cassandra hunted down the last grain of rice in her bowl and licked her lips. She swigged down the rest of her iced tea then grasped his wrist and turned it so she could see the time.

"Damn." She sighed. "Time to go?"

He didn't want to look at the watch but, yes, it was time to go. But he got to leave with Cassandra and stay with her for the rest of the night.

The rest of the night, his dragon purred.

The greedy bastard. Because Silas hadn't been thinking *that* far into the night.

Ten minutes later, he pulled the car up to the valet parking at the Arts and Cultural Center and handed the keys to the attendant.

"I guess there is one advantage to arriving late. No line for parking," he tried.

"We're fashionably late," Cassandra decided. "This way?"

He grinned. It was supposed to be him showing her the way, not her bolstering him through an unpleasant duty. So he rolled his shoulders, hooked his elbow firmly around hers, and strode toward the entrance, ready to play his role.

A camera flash exploded from the left followed by another from the right, capturing the two of them. Silas groaned inwardly. That picture was sure to make the society pages the next day. Was Cassandra really okay with that?

She didn't waver in the slightest. In fact, she smiled like a champ and strode along as if she'd walked red carpets a hundred times before. She did whisper out of the corner of her mouth, though.

"Do you always get this kind of reception?"

Another flash blitzed. "Mr. Llewellyn! This way, please!"

"Mr. Llewellyn!" another man called.

Silas walked straight ahead, tightening his squeeze on her arm a little bit. "Just ignore them," he whispered. "This happens all the time."

"Sure," she chirped. "Happens all the time."

"Mr. Llewellyn, what's your favorite charity here?" a reporter asked.

"Mr. Llewellyn, who is the lovely woman tonight?"

He coughed into his hand, hiding a growl.

None of anybody's business except mine. His inner beast emphasized the last word then repeated it a few times. *Mine. Mine. Mine!*

"Mr. Llewellyn, what do you have to say about the proposed development on the west side?"

That one stopped him cold.

"If that proposal is a legitimate one, I can assure you that I will fight it to my dying breath." He glared.

The reporter looked a little taken aback, the poor man. Clearly, he had no idea of the evil forces behind that proposal.

Cassandra touched Silas's arm, and the rage abated as quickly as it had come.

When they reached the top stair, she exhaled. "Whew. Quite the gauntlet."

He shook his head and motioned ahead. "Out of the frying pan and into the fire."

Getting past the reporters was one thing. Surviving the shark tank of the event itself was another.

"Not quite what I expected," Cassandra murmured, looking over the scene.

Silas grinned. "It's a gala for the Coalition of Maui charities, but the event is organized by the animal rescue group, so..." He motioned over the crowd.

A three-legged Chihuahua snarled at a German Shepherd three times its size, while its owner strained at its leash. "Down, Apollo!"

The Chihuahua bounced like a bunny, but the second it sniffed Silas, the little spitfire backed down, as most dogs did.

That's right, little guy. I'm the boss here, his dragon growled.

A yellow parrot squawked from a woman's shoulder, whistling and making kissing sounds.

"Fortune! We're in public!" the woman hissed.

"Cute name," Cassandra whispered.

Some of the pets were groomed, some scrappy. Others were dressed for the occasion, like the Jack Russell terrier sporting a fox stole. When a police siren sounded in the distance, a pair of Alaskan Malamutes began to howl.

"Olaf! Elsa! Quiet down!" the owner admonished.

"How exactly did you decide to support these charities?" Cassandra asked.

He motioned around. "The owner of the estate let us decide, so the guys voted."

She chuckled. "And who exactly owns the estate?"

"A very private man."

"So I've gathered. My question was, who is he?"

He pointed to a waiter. "Would you like some hors d'oeuvres?"

"You're a master of avoiding questions, aren't you?"

"The shrimp looks good..."

She laughed, and thank goodness for the little Pekingese-Shih Tzu mix that trotted past next.

"Oh my gosh. So cute! Is he friendly?" Cassandra asked, kneeling to pet the dog.

"Sure. That's Cujo," the proud owner said.

Silas could swear the dog purred. And who could blame it, given the attention Cassandra lavished upon the little fur ball.

Unfortunately, it wasn't long after that the next wave of guests spotted him and pounced.

"I'll just get us drinks, shall I?" Cassandra said, escaping to the right with Cujo and his owner.

Smart woman, his dragon sighed, reluctantly letting her go.

The women of the Botanical Society got to him first, bemoaning invasive species and the recent orchid blight. He pledged his full support, as usual. They were good people — the real heroes of these good causes who fought on behalf of Maui. He could relate to that.

Still, his eyes kept drifting to Cassandra as she picked her way through the crowd. His blood pressure rose as one after another man turned his head.

Mine! his dragon roared, wishing he could take flight and burn every one of those assholes to a crisp.

But Cassandra just danced past them with her firm, New Yorker step. She did stop for the animals, though, like a Labrador-Staffordshire mix that seemed intent on licking her face.

"Lany, heel!" the owner insisted. "Lany, down! I'm so sorry. She just loves to meet new people," Silas overheard.

Cassandra kneeled to pet the dog, laughing. "Aren't you a friendly girl?"

"Silas," a deep voice said, dragging his attention around.

"Mr. Mayor, Mrs. Tang," Silas said, shaking hands. "Good to see you."

He meant it. The mayor and his wife chaired several charities, and they were potential allies in the ongoing zoning issues that threatened the area around Koa Point. Not that Silas would address that directly at this venue, but every meeting helped build a working relationship.

"So happy to see the state park reopened," he said.

The mayor gave a little bow. "So happy to have had your support."

"It was the least I could do."

Donating time and money really was the least he could do, because the park road had been damaged in a flash flood caused by a shifter fight — the fight in which Cruz and Jody had fought for their lives. The two freshly mated tiger shifters had rolled up their sleeves and pitched in with restoration efforts before leaving for the last events of the pro surfing season.

Then the mayor got to chatting about the latest wind power movement, and Silas did his best to listen. But his mind — and his eyes — kept sneaking over to Cassandra. She was waiting for drinks at the bar, and every gesture she made took his breath away.

Want her. Need her, his dragon insisted, drowning out all other sounds.

Cassandra spent a moment chatting with the bartender, a beefy Kanaka — swapping tricks of the trade, perhaps. But then a tall, athletic man leaned in to say something right in her ear, and Silas's vision went red. The wide smile Cassandra had been wearing disappeared, replaced by a weary, *What the hell do you want?* expression. She looked the man slowly up and down, taking in his slicked-back hair, haughty eyes, and tailored suit.

Slick, rich, and arrogant, Silas's dragon huffed. *Entitled son of a bitch.*

For a split second, he touched his own tux. Did he come across the way that ass did?

His dragon shook his head. *Slick? Okay, maybe a little. Rich?*

Silas sighed. That remained to be seen. But really, who cared about money? Peace was far more important. Love, too — and neither of those things could be bought, no matter how rich a person was.

Are we arrogant? His dragon continued the checklist. *No way.*

Silas decided *entitled* didn't apply to him either. He'd lost too much and worked too hard ever to take anything for granted. Still, he scrubbed a hand over his chin and made a vow. More lunch trucks, fewer galas — no matter how much duty called. More sunsets on the beach, fewer hours in the office his buddies jokingly called the throne room.

He grimaced. Who was he kidding? Until Drax was defeated, he couldn't do any of those things.

Cassandra waved two glasses in the man's face, making it clear she had a date, and sidled away from her would-be suitor with a firm stride. Clearly, she'd had a lot of practice brushing men off. And she needed it, because she was absolutely stunning tonight.

She's always stunning, his dragon grumbled.

Every man in the room turned his head as she passed. Several moved to intercept her, but she brushed past each one, keeping her eyes — and smile — firmly on Silas.

His chest swelled a little as his dragon crooned. *Me! She wants me!*

"So, location remains an issue," the mayor went on.

Right, the wind farm. Silas tried to drag his attention back to the conversation he'd usually be all ears for — but all he wanted to do was spit flames and announce to the world that Cassandra was his.

The mayor went on for a while, until he, his wife, and a clutch of innocent bystanders were bulldozed aside by the true Rottweilers of the crowd — a phalanx of young, aggressive, *I-take-what-I-want* types not the least bit interested in charities.

"Excuse me," the mayor winked, clearing the hell out of the way.

A towering blonde in stiletto heels race-walked over, beating three other women to Silas and grasping his arm.

His bad arm. He hid a wince.

"Silas. So good to see you again," the woman announced at the top of her lungs.

Silas couldn't recall ever having seen her before — and he certainly never had engaged in any of the dirty deeds her sultry tone implied.

"Good to see you," he said in a perfectly neutral tone, trying to place her.

Keeping his eyes on her face was a struggle, though, because the plunging neckline of her dress created one of those optical tricks that just about forced a man's gaze to the generous cleavage on display. She even dipped a shoulder and leaned forward, trying to give him a bonus peek.

"Finally, we'll have a chance for that drink you promised," she said, tiptoeing her fingers over his skin.

Silas had never promised any such thing, and she knew it.

"Another time, perhaps," he said, turning to a passing caterer. But then he caught the mayor looking at him. Beseeching him, almost.

Don't piss her off, the mayor mouthed.

He tilted his head.

The mayor's lips formed a name. *Penelope.*

Shit. Penelope Whatshername — the fabulously wealthy, thirtysomething widow of a real estate mogul who had been three times her age. The husband had supported many of the island's charities as a tribute to his late first wife, and Penelope continued to support them — mostly to keep her name in the press. But if Silas pissed her off, who knew how long her support for important charities might last?

Silas looked around. Surely there was another taker among the nearest men, but they all backed off, ceding her to Silas. He wanted to snort. As if he was the least bit interested in anyone but Cassandra.

Involuntarily, he turned to find his date, but Penelope whipped a hand out and turned his chin back to her.

His dragon growled. *One little puff and you're ash, sweetheart.*

Silas removed her hand in one icy, *don't ever do that again* move.

Penelope smiled, apparently unable to tell the difference between turning him on — no chance — and pissing him off.

"We can go for that drink right now," she purred, looping her arm around his. She dipped her right shoulder, letting her dress strap slide, revealing a field of creamy skin. "In fact, we can go somewhere where we can be alone."

He cleared his throat and slid away, making the hand she pressed to his chest drop away.

"Actually, I'm here with a date." He tried to keep the gloat out of his voice. But damn, it felt awfully good to be able to say those words.

Never have to be alone again, his dragon cheered. *Not as long as I have my mate.*

Penelope's look turned into an icy glare. "Well, you absolutely must introduce me to the lucky girl. . ."

...so I can tear her hair out, her murderous eyes finished the sentence.

Something tugged on his right arm, and Silas spun around to find Cassandra.

"Oh, there you are, honey." She winked.

And just like that, the tightness in his brow eased.

Honey. His dragon lit up. *I like the sound of that.*

Silas silently thanked the fates that had brought him this woman.

"Hello there." Cassandra smiled, showing her teeth to Penelope. She stepped forward so firmly that the blonde took a step back.

She'd make a great dragon, his inner beast purred.

"Don't you want to introduce us, honey?" Cassandra said.

Not really, no. He wanted to get the hell away from that man-eater, pronto.

"Allow me to introduce..." He stirred the air with his hand, struggling with the name.

"Penelope van Buren," the blonde hissed, extending a stiff hand.

"This is Cassandra Nichols, my..." Silas trailed off.

Mate, his dragon filled in.

Penelope's penciled-in eyebrows arched, waiting for the answer.

"Date," Cassandra said brightly, taking Penelope's hand.

Silas worried that one of them would deliver a death grip. But luckily, a border collie rushed between them, snapping at a passing fly.

"Abby, wait!" the owner cried, dashing after it.

"So cute," Cassandra smiled, patting the dog's back as it went.

Penelope sniffed and wrinkled her nose. "Adorable."

"Well, I'd love to chat..." Cassandra said, patting his chest.

Unlike Penelope's touch, that pat made him go warm all over and squeeze closer to Cassandra's side. His mind went completely blank.

"...but we have to go," she finished.

We do? he nearly asked, not quite catching on.

We do! We do! His dragon nodded eagerly.

Cassandra squeezed his hand, and he followed without thinking. Without breathing, almost.

"But—" Penelope protested.

He barely heard, though. In fact, he barely heard the hubbub in the room. Because Cassandra was smiling at him — really smiling, and her eyes shone. Her lips quirked, and all his attention zoomed there. His heart beat harder, and a low thump filled his ears as if an entire row of native drummers had lined up on the stage and started pounding a sultry beat.

Destiny, a hypnotic voice whispered in his mind. *She is your destined mate.*

His eyes focused on the dip in the middle of her upper lip. A heartbeat later, the world seemed to tip gently on its axis, making him lean closer.

Cassandra did the same, and her smile faded to a more serious look. Her lips parted, and her tongue ran over her teeth.

Kiss her, his dragon whispered.

Silas took a deep breath, trying to fight the need.

No more denying. No more pretending, his dragon insisted. *Kiss her.*

Silas dug deep, searching for the power to resist — and came up empty. His mind emptied too, and all the compelling reasons to keep away from Cassandra vanished into thin air.

She wants it too, his dragon insisted. *Kiss her.*

So he did. Or maybe she did, because their lips met halfway and pressed together in a perfectly balanced kiss.

His eyes slid shut, and he turned off all his senses except those in his lips. The rest of the world ceased to exist, leaving just him and her there in a moment he'd never forget. A perfect moment — one of the very few of his life. The kind he knew would become a lifetime highlight even as it was happening. His arms wound around her back, and zaps of lightning zigzagged through his veins, making every tight muscle unwind.

Tastes so good. Smells so good, his dragon hummed.

Cassandra's hands smoothed over his shoulders, and her chest pressed against his. As if they were on a dance floor, and the music was slow. As if they'd been together for a lifetime and knew exactly how to fit together, how to give and take. But there was the thrill of the unknown at the same time, and fireworks went off in his mind. Bright, sparkly ones that might have been little heart shapes for all he knew.

A camera flashed, but neither of them looked up. Penelope muttered and slunk away, but nothing was interrupting him now, damn it.

Cassandra's chest expanded in a soul-deep sigh that traveled through her body, into her arms, and over to him.

So good, his dragon agreed. *My perfect mate.*

Her mouth opened under his, and she tilted her head, pushing closer. And just as he kissed her deeper, desperate to taste more, a dark cloud pushed in at the edge of his consciousness, setting off a dozen warning bells.

Silas snapped his head up, sucking in an angry breath.

"Well, well. What do we have here?" two voices tsked at exactly the same time.

Every muscle in his body coiled, and every hair on the back of his neck stood. He stepped forward, shielding Cassandra as a single word dropped from his downturned lips.

"Drax."

"Moira," Cassandra grunted, equally displeased.

Chapter Eleven

If Silas hadn't held Cassandra back by the elbow, she might have slapped Moira. His hand tightened around hers, reminding her just who that was.

A dragon — two dragons — who could spit fire.

For a moment, Cassandra couldn't care less. She could sense Silas's hate for the pair, and she'd seen and heard enough to hate them too. They were at the root of Silas's late nights and proverbial gray hairs. Both embodied every negative characteristic of dragons that Eloise had warned her of.

"Yes — what do we have here?" Drax puffed on a cigar in flagrant violation of the building's *No Smoking* rule. "Consorting with the enemy, Silas?"

Cassandra bared her teeth. So Drax had found out about her witch blood. Apparently, he'd also found out how thin that blood was, because he didn't show the slightest concern.

"Believe me, I know my enemies," Silas growled.

His fingers squeezed hers, promising he didn't mean her.

Cassandra wanted to wipe the smirk off Drax's face — and off Moira's too. But who was she kidding? She was just a lowly bartender who couldn't get her spells right. Moira was a dragon.

A dragon who had slept with Silas. Cassandra blanched, overcome by a wave of disgust. Okay, that might have been a long time ago, but still, it hurt. What had Silas ever seen in Moira?

A sidelong glance reassured her, because Silas looked disgusted too. His fingers flexed, taking the shape of claws, and she softened again. Everyone had a past. The important thing was the future. But, crap — what future did she have with the likes of Drax and Moira staring her down, clearly intent on harm?

Silas stepped farther forward, protecting Cassandra with his body. But she stepped right back into the open with her chin held high.

"Why, Silas. You told me this is a charity event. I can't imagine what these two are doing here," she snipped.

Drax uttered a humorless chuckle, and Moira's lips turned down.

"Actually, I'm in Maui to check on some property." Drax exhaled a long plume of smoke and leveled a knowing look at Silas.

Cassandra nearly yelped as Silas squeezed her hand, tensing at Drax's words. His jaw clenched, but otherwise, he held still. Frighteningly still.

Cassandra's mind raced. What was Drax talking about?

Moira brushed a nonexistent speck of dust off Drax's lapel and sighed, feigning boredom. "Yes, we thought it was high time to check on Filimore's properties. Perhaps even develop a few. They're so underused."

Cassandra didn't dare look at Silas, even though she was dying to ask which properties those might be. Koa Point? The neighboring place? Something else?

"Underused? Try peaceful," Silas growled.

Drax laughed. "Peaceful? You're going soft, Silas."

Every muscle in Silas's hard body tensed, showing he was anything but.

Drax leaned forward. "Better not make yourself too comfortable, my friend." His lips slithered over *friend*, making it a threat. "My lawyers are at work, you know."

"Lawyers. Is that the best you can do?" Silas looked as if he'd like to duke out their disagreements with fists, fangs, or fire.

Cassandra nudged Silas. Drax was purposely baiting him. Didn't he see that?

But it was too late. Silas's face was red, and his eyes were glowing — the angry shade of crimson. His pulse pounded visibly at his brow. Shit. Was he about to shift?

Silas, she cried silently, wrapping her fingers around his, trying to calm him down. She'd never seen Silas so close to losing control.

"Spare yourself the noble effort, cousin," Drax said, dripping disdain. "Give me the diamond."

"I don't have the diamond," Silas shot back.

Drax grinned and motioned at Cassandra, making her stomach turn. "Then give me the woman."

"Never!" Silas barked, making the nearest twenty people turn in surprise.

Cassandra turned too, surprised at the vehemence in his voice. A warm rush went through her veins, and she wished she could hold on to that feeling instead of the urgent need to defuse things, fast.

"Is this how you operate?" she sneered at Drax. "Taking whatever — whomever — you want?"

Drax laughed, shooting a look at Moira. "Believe me, they come willingly."

The she-dragon's tight features twitched, and Cassandra wished for some poker-playing experience to figure out what the hell that meant.

"Maybe some do, though I can't imagine why," Cassandra sniffed. "Others will fight you with every weapon at their disposal. And believe me, that's when you need to watch out."

She raised her hands and let her fingers dance in the air at Drax, copying some of the moves she'd seen in Silas's books. Any self-respecting witch would have groaned at her sloppy version of the *turn-into-a-frog* spell, but hell. It was pretty damn convincing, even if it would never work. Silas's eyes went wide, and Moira shuffled back an inch.

A second later, though, the she-dragon collected herself and scowled. "I see this little witch has cast her spell on you, Silas. You could do so much better."

By *better*, Moira meant herself, of course. Cassandra almost hurled a retort, but Silas snorted first.

"Be civil, Moira."

She raised a plucked and painted eyebrow at him. "Oh, I'm not calling her a bitch. But a witch — yes. She's been playing you all along."

"The way you played me?" Silas's voice rose.

Moira winked and leaned closer, allowing the folds of her dress to split and give Silas the full benefit of her meaty boobs. *You and I can still have it all,* her flashing eyes seemed to say. *Come with me, and you'll have everything you want.*

Cassandra narrowed her eyes. Moira was plotting something behind Drax's back, for sure. Not that Drax seemed to suspect, judging by his indulgent expression.

"Well, it's too late now." Moira sighed theatrically. "She'll soon have doomed herself."

Cassandra's blood went cold. What the hell did Moira mean?

"Moira." Silas glared. "What have you done?"

She laughed. "It's not what I've done. It's what she's done with that spell of hers."

What spell? Cassandra wanted to shake Moira. She couldn't extinguish a candle, let alone cast a spell that could influence future events. But then she remembered Eloise's parting words.

A lure spell, Eloise's voice ghosted through her mind. *I've been working on one myself.*

An image flashed through Cassandra's mind. One second, it was there — the scene of a blackened landscape, torn with great blasts of raging fire and shadowed by battling dragons — and then it was gone.

Cassandra clenched her hands into fists before she started shaking. Whatever a lure spell was, it packed a powerful punch.

"Maybe you're the one who's doomed," she forced herself to retort.

Drax sent out another long plume of smoke, silently appraising her. Cassandra wrinkled her nose as the tendrils wafted in the space between them, moving slowly in the still air. Then she puffed, sending the smoke right back the way it came. Moira put a hand over her mouth and coughed, shooting murderous looks at Cassandra.

But again, Cassandra didn't care. Dragons might be pretty damn imposing, but they needed to get one thing straight. She was not to be fucked with. One way or another, she'd foil their sinister plans — whatever those might be. Surely, she'd find something among the books in the library. An anti-dragon potion, maybe. A fireproof magic spell.

And, yes. She would look up lure spells the second she returned to the library. But first, she had to end this confrontation before it escalated.

She ignored the urge to retreat and clapped twice.

"Now isn't that wonderful!" she announced in a loud, clear voice. "You want to make a donation to the Coalition of Maui charities?"

Half the people in the ballroom stopped in their tracks. Drax frowned.

Cassandra motioned the mayor closer. "Well, that's wonderful news. Silas, won't you introduce the mayor to one of New York's most generous philanthropists?"

Silas's mouth twitched in a tiny smile. The mayor scurried forward, as did Penelope van Buren. She wound her Copper-toned arm around Drax's and batted her eyes.

"Penelope van Buren. How do you do?"

If looks could kill, Moira would have been booked for homicide there and then. But what really irked Cassandra was the way Drax reached out to clamp a hand over Silas's arm. Silas's bad arm.

"See you soon, baby cousin," Drax growled.

Cassandra wove her fingers around Silas's and subtly pulled him away. She didn't know much about battles, but it seemed like this was a time to make a strategic retreat.

Silas remained silent, but she could swear he was cursing Drax in his mind. So she borrowed a page from the shifter playbook and did the same, focusing all her energy on pushing a thought over to Drax's mind. The dragon might not have heard her, but it felt good to get her two cents in.

See you never would have been nice, but she figured that was wishful thinking. So she settled for the next best thing, putting as much venom into the thought as she could.

See you soon, asshole.

Chapter Twelve

Cassandra sat very still as Silas accelerated the car down the highway. He held the gearshift so tightly, his knuckles turned white, and his jaw formed a hard line.

Cassandra peeked in the rearview mirror. "You think Drax will follow us?"

She placed a hand on his leg without thinking, because she needed it — that contact, that warmth. The reassurance that somehow, everything would be okay.

Maybe Silas needed it too, because he gently covered her hand with his.

"No, not really. But he is getting bold, coming to Maui like this."

He gunned the engine, letting the car rush through the night. Traffic was sparse, and Highway 380 was an open road, hushed but for the hum of the vintage car's purring engine.

"You mean he's never been here?"

"I guess he's never deemed it worth his while."

"And Koa Point? He won't attack there?"

Silas shook his head. "Dragons never pick a fight on an enemy's home turf. They prefer to lure each other out."

Lure. The word stuck in her mind as the tires raced over the even road.

"Plus," Silas added, "We have our own watch rotation. Hunter's on duty tonight."

She gaped. "All night?"

Silas shrugged. "It helps to have a group of shifters all eager to roam in animal form for a few hours."

So she hadn't been imagining soft footfalls or distant howls over the past couple of nights.

121

"So, no attack from Drax," she concluded.

Silas frowned. "Not at Koa Point, anyway."

Another silent minute passed, and the air grew so thick with Silas's anger and frustration, she could have scooped a handful and tossed it at the scenery blurring outside. Silas hit fifty-five, sixty-five, and was heading toward seventy in a forty-five zone. The car felt twice as fast from her vantage point on what ought to be the driver's side.

Luckily, the right-hand drive setup gave her access to Silas's left arm. He'd whipped his jacket off on the way to the car, but his shirt still covered his skin. Now that she thought back on it, he'd been wearing long sleeves all week despite balmy temperatures.

"Let me check that," she said very quietly.

Silas tucked his elbow against his ribs, keeping it out of reach. "It's fine."

She put a hand on his leg. "You can't be strong for everyone all the time."

"There is no one else."

The hard edge in his voice made her want to say, *There's me.*

"Just a quick look. Please."

"No need."

She sighed. "You know, I once talked Eloise's cat down from a tree, and it didn't take as much convincing."

Silas kept his lips sealed for a long minute before answering. "Black cat?"

She threw up her hands. "You're changing the subject again."

"Okay," he murmured.

"Okay — you're changing the subject?"

He shook his head and slowly swung his elbow out from his side. "Okay, you can check it. If you want."

Right. Like it was her hobby to examine burns or something. But she played along. "It would make me feel better. And yes."

"Yes, what?" he grunted as she gingerly removed his cuff links and folded back his sleeve.

"It was a black cat."

Really, she just wanted to distract him, and it worked.

"See? It's fine," he grunted.

It didn't look as ghastly as she feared — more pink than puckered or scabbed — but Silas had failed to hide a couple of telltale winces and the twitch in his jaw.

"I'll put something on it when we get home," she said, letting him off easy.

He looked at her, and oops, she caught the slipup too. Koa Point wasn't home. Not for her, anyway.

Silas's eyes shone, making it far too easy to dream.

A second later — or maybe a minute — she dragged her gaze back to the blurring asphalt of the road and cursed his stubbornness.

But truthfully, that stubbornness was part of what fascinated her. That tenacity — it was all part of a complex man she found herself more and more attracted to. Silas moved something in her that no other man ever had — not the handful of chiseled athletes, not the wealthy businessmen, not even the cute construction-worker types she'd met over the years. She'd listened dutifully to their problems and woes, but she'd never wanted to help a man so badly. Which was ironic, because Silas didn't want help. But then again, what man ever did?

She snorted. If she were honest with herself, she didn't just want to help Silas. She just wanted him, period. For days, her body had been yearning for his, and the out-of-nowhere kiss back at the gala had ignited a bonfire. Jesus, what had she been thinking?

She knotted her hands tightly and took a deep breath. Maybe if she helped Silas get through the problems of the present, they could have a stab at a future together.

"Drax mentioned an uncle and some property. What's that about?" She looked straight ahead, in case looking at Silas *and* asking at the same time was too much an invasion of his comfort zone.

Silas bared his teeth and formed a few silent curses. "Drax's uncle is my uncle. Our great-uncle, really. Filimore."

"The one who died in New York?" Her eyes went wide.

"One who was murdered in New York," Silas grunted. "Drax poisoned him. I'm sure of that."

Her mind raced. Eloise had fallen victim to a dragon attack. Silas's uncle too. Apparently, Drax didn't let anything stop him — not even his own kin.

"His uncle... your uncle..." She thought it through.

Silas made a face. "Drax is my third cousin on my mother's side. His line is older than ours by almost a generation, though."

"Ours?"

"Kai and I. We're first cousins."

She did her best to map the family tree in her mind, putting Drax way out on a crooked branch and Kai closer to the center with Silas.

"How long do dragons live?" she whispered, trying to recall what she'd read.

Silas flexed the fingers of his right hand over the steering wheel. "A couple of hundred years." Then he shook his head ruefully. "If they die of natural causes, that is."

Cassandra remembered hearing that Kai was thirty-one, which had to put Silas in roughly the same age range. Neither of them had ever mentioned parents, siblings, or other cousins. How much warring went on in the dragon world? Were family sizes naturally small?

So many questions. So few answers. Should she venture there tonight? She decided to focus on Drax for the time being. And dang, even that was a lot to swallow.

"Drax mentioned property," she said, leaving the sentence open-ended for Silas to fill in.

The Mercedes whizzed under a set of streetlights, and she caught a brief glimpse of Silas's tight features and deep frown bathed in yellow light.

Another minute passed by, and still, he didn't answer. Should she push him? Shouldn't she?

"Silas," she whispered, running her fingers lightly over the fabric of his slacks. Begging him to unwind just a tiny little bit. "Are you really going to solve this on your own?"

He gripped the gearshift harder. "Honestly? That was the plan."

She wanted to scream. Didn't he know asking for help wasn't an admission of weakness? That many hands made light work?

"Well, if you won't tell me, at least talk to the others. Kai is your cousin. The other guys are PIs. Dawn is a policewoman. Tessa is supersmart, and Nina is good at thinking outside the box. Any of them could help you figure things out. Did you ever hear of two heads being better than one?"

He drove on in stubborn silence.

She crossed her arms over her chest. Fine. If he wanted to keep everything bottled up inside, she'd let him.

But a moment later, he spoke — so quietly, she barely heard. "They don't know."

She sat very still, waiting for more, but Silas remained mute, working his jaw from side to side.

"They don't know about Drax? Tessa and Kai were in New York, so—"

He shook his head. "They know about my relation to Drax." He grimaced. "And about Moira. Everyone knows." His voice was laced with bitterness and regret. He ran a hand through his hair, pulling at the strands.

Without thinking, she put her hand over his and tugged it down to the steering wheel. "So what *don't* they know?" she asked.

Silas sighed and motioned vaguely. "They don't know about the owner of the estate."

Her mind whirled over the cryptic exchange between Silas and Drax.

Better not make yourself too comfortable. My lawyers are at work, you know.

Her pulse quickened as she worked up the courage to ask the million-dollar question. She might prove herself an idiot, but she might just prove right.

"Does Drax own Koa Point?"

Silas floored the gas pedal to pass a lone truck. The engine roared, and wind buffeted the car. Memories of her encounter with Drax in a New York alley rushed through her mind, and she squeezed her eyes shut. Jesus. How did she ever get mixed up with dragons?

That is your destiny, Eloise had said.

She looked over at Silas. What if Eloise was slightly off the mark, and fighting dragons wasn't her destiny? Maybe forging peace between dragons and witches was. Or would she fail as miserably at that as she had at every spell she'd attempted?

She glanced at Silas out of the corner of her eye and gulped at another possibility. What if Silas was her destiny?

Chapter Thirteen

Silas steered the car back into the right lane, still quiet, so Cassandra tapped on his leg and tried again.

"Silas — Does. Drax. Own. Koa. Point?"

"Sort of. Kind of. Not really..." He stopped and started, discarding his own words.

"Sort of?"

He tapped on the gearshift, then slowly, cautiously turned his palm up to clasp hers.

"My uncle Filimore — the last of the great dragons — was the owner of the estate."

He exhaled long and hard with a *There, I said it* kind of relief.

"The uncle poisoned by Drax owned the estate?"

Silas nodded. "Filimore hired me as caretaker. He also made me promise never to tell anyone."

"Why?"

He made a face and shrugged. "Dragons. What can I say? The older generation lives under an archaic code of conduct."

She nearly laughed and pointed out Silas's penchant for coffee brewed properly. For dressing with style. For keeping a library of leather-bound books...

"Everything is a secret," he went on with a hint of bitterness. "Everything is hidden."

"Every problem is solved alone," she added.

"I suppose so." Then he cast a sideways glance at her. "Am I that bad?"

She laughed. "Yes. But hell, we all have our weak points."

"Weak points?" he grunted, clearly displeased.

She poked his leg. "Sometimes strength can be a weakness, you know." Then she flapped her hands, going back to where he'd left off. "Filimore made you promise not to reveal that he owned the estate. But now that he's gone..."

Silas made a face, as if every vow he made was for life. "The real issue is his will."

Her heart thumped as much out of anticipation as appreciation that Silas was finally opening up to her. Trusting her the way she'd come to trust him.

"The will leaves the estate — and most of Filimore's holdings — to two principal heirs."

Cassandra sat perfectly still.

"Me." Silas pointed at himself. Then he scowled and jerked a thumb over his shoulder. "And Drax."

Her eyebrows shot up. "Holy shit."

Silas nodded. "Couldn't have said it better myself."

"Why would your uncle leave anything to Drax? Didn't he know how corrupt Drax is?"

Silas shrugged. "Who's to say I'm not the corrupt one? Sometimes, I can't tell any more."

She grabbed his hand and drummed it on the gearshift, emphasizing her words. "I say. Drax reeks of evil. You don't have to be a dragon to know that. But you? You are honorable. Principled. Loyal."

He stared at her.

"Okay, and stubborn too."

He chuckled, finally giving in. "I suppose everyone has their weak points."

"I could go on, you know. You're way too uptight. Too formal. Too shuttered off. What you need is a couple of good, long walks on the beach. Barefoot."

He attempted a stern look. "Finished?"

She grinned. "Only just starting. But maybe I'll lay off for tonight. And by the way, you have a few strong points. Maybe I'll tell you about them sometime."

He broke into a smile then brought her hand to his cheek. Briefly, he closed his eyes and pressed her hand close. The emotionally challenged dragon's version of a hug, she supposed.

A second later, he turned his eyes back to the road. And a second after that, he kissed the back of her hand.

She hid a happy sigh. As far as intimacy went, that gesture might not be much — but the fact that it came from a tough, alpha type made it special. Really special, making her tingle right down to her toes. And damn, that was just a kiss to the back of her hand — possibly the least intimate spot ever. What would it be like to really get it on with this man?

Mind-blowingly good, she decided. If only she weren't hurtling down the highway, discussing life-and-death issues with him.

"Thank you," Silas murmured, looking at the road, keeping hold of her hand.

She ran her fingers over his and gazed out over the driver's side of the car. Silas took up the foreground view — furrowed brow and all. They were almost across the central valley, and the Pacific was opening up before them. All that space, all that sky. The glittering, moonlit sea went on and on to infinity. Impassive. Unstoppable. A lot like destiny.

Destiny. Where did hers lie?

She mulled the question over for the next ten minutes, then noticed the signs. They would be coming up on Lahaina soon, which meant Koa Point wasn't too far away. The second they got there, Silas would probably close up again.

A light turned red, and Silas coasted to a stop, tapping his fingers on the steering wheel. Then he caught himself and put his hand on her thigh.

"Cassandra," he murmured, tilting his head toward hers.

She leaned in until their foreheads touched and shut her eyes, closing the world away for a heartbeat or two. She couldn't see it, but she swore Silas's chest rose and fell with a sigh.

She sighed too. If this was what destiny felt like, she'd embrace it — the good and the bad.

Silas tilted his chin upward, placed the world's gentlest kiss on her forehead, and mumbled sadly, "Light's green."

She straightened slowly, reluctantly, bolstered by the fact that Silas kept her hand firmly in his when he drove on.

She took a deep breath. So much to make sense of, so little time. And if she was serious about helping Silas, she needed to understand his problems, not just think about herself.

"So your uncle left the estate to both of you? What about Kai? Wouldn't he be mad?"

Silas laughed. "A few years ago, he might have been. But now, he's got everything he wants."

Silas didn't have to elaborate for Cassandra to understand. Kai had Tessa. A nice home. A bright future. Funny, how much that suddenly appealed.

"I think Kai is glad to stay out of it," Silas explained. "And anyway, he understands dragon traditions. Everything goes to the oldest in each family line."

She pulled on her lip. "Fine, but I still don't get it. Did your uncle expect you and Drax to kiss and make up?"

Silas snorted. "More like, *May the best man win.* Like I said, old dragon ways..."

She thought that over. "Do old dragon ways mean you can't enlist help?"

"There's an honor code—"

Now it was her turn to snort. "And you expect Drax to respect that? I can just see him calling in his buddies — if he has any. Plus, Moira is sure to sneak in a few low blows from the side. She seems to specialize in that."

Silas gave a resigned sigh and — true to form — shied away from one topic by focusing on another. "Drax doesn't have buddies. He does have an army, though."

Cassandra froze. "You mean an *army* army?"

Silas tilted his head from side to side. "A dragon army. I guess it's more like a platoon by human standards. But that's still a hell of a lot of firepower."

She jabbed his side. "Pun intended?"

He managed a weak smile. "I wish. But no. I mean literally."

She shoved her feet flat on the floor so her knees couldn't shake. "Okay, Drax has an army. So do you. There's Kai and Tessa, for starters. Then you've got — what? Wolves. Bears. Tigers..."

He shook his head immediately. "I don't want to involve them. Can't you see?"

She tilted her head at him. All she saw was an overly proud man trying to take on the world alone.

"The guys have all served their country. They've fought enough," he said in a hush.

So did you, she wanted to say, but he rushed on.

"They've made a new start in life. A *good* life with women they love. They're starting families... Families that deserve stability and time for each other." He shook his head sadly. "The whole time I was growing up, my father came and went. A battle here, a feud to settle there. He'd come home injured and angry — sometimes so angry, no one could approach him. And just when we'd ease back into something like normalcy, another conflict would flare up, and he'd be off again." Silas had started out tapping the dashboard with each word, but the motion grew closer to successive bangs. "My father's father died when he was six. I was thirteen when my father died. I don't want that for Boone's kids — or Kai's, or Hunter's, or the rest."

Cassandra pictured Boone hugging Nina's baby belly, then Kai lifting a tiny child with Tessa's red hair and green eyes, giving the child a little toss and an exaggerated catch the way playful dads did. She pictured herself and Silas walking down the beach with a little girl between them, counting *One, two, three!* and swinging her in the air—

Her breath caught. Her heart pounded. Where did that image come from? She could hear the child's laughter, see Silas's smile. She could sense the soul-deep contentment and, above all, the peace.

She turned her dumbstruck face away just in time to avoid Silas's gaze. Real-time Silas, not the one in her vision.

She sucked in her lips and rocked a tiny bit. That was just some kind of hot flash, right?

"If I can find a way to engage Drax one-on-one..." Silas continued.

She tried to get her mind back on the topic: a power vacuum in the dragon world. Two opposing forces, free-falling toward conflict that could plunge the shifter world into chaos. Dang. Maybe Eloise was right.

Dragons are vile, dangerous creatures. Medieval, almost.

"And you're sure Drax would stoop low enough to poison your uncle?"

It was just like Eloise had said. *Never trust a dragon. They're all greedy and heartless.*

But that description fit Drax, not Silas. She remembered Silas tossing a ball of yarn to Keiki. Stirring his coffee quietly in the meeting house, mulling over problems he didn't want to burden anyone else with. She pictured him in the alley in New York, thrusting out a wing to protect her despite the pain he endured.

If she could have marched right over to her aunt's house and hammered a fist on the door, she would have. *You were wrong, Eloise. They're not all greedy and heartless. I know.*

"That's the dragon world," Silas sighed. "Constant upheaval. If a powerful dragon lord rises to power, a few generations may enjoy peace."

She snorted. "Why can't I imagine peace in a world dominated by Drax?"

Silas frowned deeply. "Oh, there would be peace. Right after he annihilates his enemies and makes the survivors cower."

They drove on in silence, each caught up in their own thoughts. Cassandra looked up into the dark, hulking mountains of West Maui, though her mind was elsewhere. Koa Point. The way laughter drifted over the lawns. The peaceful lap of waves over sand. The quiet rhythm of daily life. Friends coming and going, each with their own cozy home and an unspoken devotion to one another.

Her fingers tightened over an invisible jewel. The Windstone. Might that help Silas overcome Drax? Had she been foolish to hide it from him?

"And you blame me for being uptight," Silas joked, pulling his hand out from under hers. "That's a hell of a grip."

She forced a smile, but her mind was spinning. Silas. His shifter friends. The Spirit Stones. Drax. Were they all pawns on a chessboard, or did they command their own fates?

She thought about herself. Where did a one-eighths-witch with no magic power fit in?

"Silas," she whispered, not quite sure what to say next.

His rueful expression said he knew the feeling. "Believe me, I know it's foolish to take on Drax alone. But if I can find a way to do that without involving the others — to lure him into a fair fight as tradition dictates..."

Cassandra looked up at the stars, thinking. *Lure. Dragon. How to lure a dragon...*

What you need is a good lure spell, Eloise had said.

She scratched her dress in frustration. What she needed was some magic. Soon.

And air, damn it. She needed fresh air.

She leaned toward the open window, undoing the twist in her hair. She felt Silas's eyes on her as she combed the long strands with her fingers, but when she looked over, he looked away.

Mr. Denial. Mr. Duty. Would he ever allow her in?

"You ever wish you'd gotten the convertible version of this car, just so you can feel the wind in your hair?" she asked.

He ran a hand through his neatly cropped hair — so much for the liberating feeling of hair whipping in the wind — and murmured, "We have the convertible too."

She laughed aloud. "Of course. In silver, like this one?"

"White."

Part of her wanted to follow up on the *we* part — she still couldn't get her head around his uncle's crazy will — but her thoughts ran away with the whipping wind, the indigo sky, the pinpoints of stars above. "Do you ever fly at night?"

He looked over sharply, and she leveled her gaze at him.

"I thought you hated dragons." His resonant baritone cozied right up to her bones.

"I'm starting to realize there are good dragons and bad dragons. That maybe Eloise had just as many preconceptions as some of my other relatives did. The human ones, I mean."

"And what preconceptions were those?"

She shook her head, almost embarrassed to say. "You name it. One of my cousin's neighbors were from Pisa, and after forty years of living harmoniously side by side, her mother finally admitted they weren't bad — for Italians, of course."

Silas chuckled, so she went on.

"We made sure not to get her started on other ethnic or religious groups. Her discovery of the century was always something like, 'You know, they're actually nice.' She drove us crazy with her closed-minded, old-fashioned ways. But I guess she grew up in another time, another place."

Silas nodded. "Believe me, I know the type."

"So, yeah. I'm starting to think Eloise might have been the same way, just with dragons. She let something slip about vampires too."

Silas's nose wrinkled. "Never trust a vampire."

She slapped his thigh. "Listen to yourself!"

"It's true."

"Well, Eloise said the same thing about dragons."

Silas spoke so softly, she had to strain to hear. "And what would you say about dragons?"

She smoothed her hands over her dress. Was she really ready to share her thoughts?

"Maybe they're not all that bad," she murmured.

He chuckled, waiting for more.

"They hardly ever belch smoke," she said, trying to rile him up.

He flicked a speck of dust off his sleeve. "Hardly?"

"They don't seem to prey on innocent virgins," she went on.

Silas's head whipped around. "Innocent what?"

She laughed. "I mean, judging by the company dragons keep. There's Moira…"

He grimaced.

"…and me. And seeing as neither of us is innocent *or* a virgin…"

He shook his head, finally catching on to the fact that she was toying with him. "And here I was, thinking you were a fair maiden."

"Ha. Think again."

They both laughed, and somehow, her hand found its way over to his leg again.

"What else do you think of dragons?" His voice grew huskier.

She took a deep breath. Was she really ready to flirt with a dragon? Silas had a way of taking everything seriously. Really seriously. Who knew where things might lead?

Her girl parts cheered, eager for a steamy outcome.

"Well, there's this one dragon in particular I've come to know..." she started.

He coaxed her along with a nod.

"A little reclusive. Kind of eccentric, you might say."

"Eccentric?" He made a face.

"Well, he does live in this crazy house. He's got the world's coolest library..."

She caught him smiling at that.

"...an unusual group of friends..."

"Unusual?" he protested.

"...who are really, really nice. And you know what they say about friends..."

He tilted his head, waiting for the punchline.

"You can judge a person by their friends."

That drew a tiny smile from him, so she went on.

"And there's this really sweet kitten he's very kind to."

"You never know," he warned. "It could all be an act."

"I thought so at first. But then I saw him — all those late nights. All that stress he bottles up inside."

"Dragons don't stress," he insisted.

"This one does. About his home, about his friends. About the future. It's a big, bad world out there, and he's trying to conquer it all on his own."

He looked straight ahead, mum.

"He does everything for everyone but nothing for himself. And that's what I love about him."

His eyes darted to her then bounced away. God, the man was like a teenager, fascinated by but unable to talk about love. Had Moira burned him that badly?

"Love?" he growled.

135

She tried to play it cool. "Could be a figure of speech."

He nodded, very businesslike.

She tightened her fingers over his leg and leaned close to his ear. "Could be not."

His eyes glowed a warm brick color in the darkness, and her inner furnace heated by about twenty degrees. Silas's heat reached out toward her, coaxing her closer. Inviting her to think all kinds of dirty thoughts, like unbuttoning his shirt and sliding a hand across his chest.

The car slowed and swung into a turn, pushing her body away from his.

"Home," Silas murmured as they drove up to the gate of the estate.

Home. She turned the word over in her mind. Where was home? Where did she fit in with the chess pieces destiny seemed so intent on arranging?

The gate slid open, inviting them in. A pity Maui wasn't bigger — she would have preferred to drive for another few hours. Because the moment Silas set foot on the estate, she'd bet he would head straight to his office and lock himself in with his problems.

The car pulled up to the garage — back where they started in some ways, but much further along at the same time. When Silas came around the car and offered her a hand out, she had to resist the urge to pull him in and drive back out the gates. But she let him walk her toward the guesthouse in silence.

A firefly blinked in the darkness, the sole light between tiki torches that had burned low. A bird fluttered through the trees. The meeting house was dim and lifeless, the others long since scattered to their homes. Everything was serene and safe, but her feet felt heavy as she walked toward the inevitable goodbye. Silas had opened up to her on the drive, but the most she could expect from him was a polite peck on the cheek and a whispered *Good night.*

Minutes later, they were at the porch of the guesthouse, peering over the waves. Cassandra closed her eyes, replaying the kiss they'd shared at the gala. A kiss that had come out of

136

nowhere and turned into a force of its own. One she had never wanted to end.

Silas cleared his throat, and she braced herself. This was it. Silas felt the same longing for *more* as she did — she was sure of it — but he would lock it away.

"Cassandra," he whispered.

At least there was that — he'd quit calling her Miss Nichols. A small victory?

She faced him, refusing to utter a word. Determined to make parting as hard for him as it was for her.

When he continued, Silas's voice was croaky. "Can I take you up on that offer?"

She blinked. "What?"

He motioned behind him, still weary, yet hopeful, somehow. "That long walk on the beach. Would you mind?"

Her eyes went wide, and for a moment, she couldn't speak. But when Silas stuck his elbow out, she threaded her arm through the gap and nestled close to his side.

"That would be very nice," she managed, feeling the heat rush back to her core.

Chapter Fourteen

It had been a long time since Silas had taken a walk anywhere. When a dragon shifter needed to blow off steam, he went flying. That was just the way things were done. So he'd done a lot of that lately, though it hadn't really seemed to help.

But a walk, as it turned out, was just what he needed. And yes — he even did it barefoot. Just ten steps down the beach with Cassandra made the knots in his shoulders unravel and the pinched feeling in his brow ease. He wiggled his toes in the sand, tilted his head back, and took in the stars. Maybe there was more than one way to go about things in life — other than dragon style.

Which was akin to sacrilege, but hell. Other than Kai and — he grimaced — Drax, he was the last of his family line. Maybe he didn't need to stick to tradition quite so closely any more. Some traditions were good, of course. They reminded him who he was and made him feel connected with the long line of dragons he'd come from. But other aspects, well. . .

Maybe Cassandra is right, his dragon considered. *But I still like flying. Maybe we can take her someday.*

As far as relaxing forms of distraction went, flying with Cassandra would probably rate an eleven out of ten. But walking on the beach with her. . . That was still a ten.

The light play of her fingers over his, the warmth of her body against his side, the tickle of her hair on his shoulder. She made him feel alive in a way he hadn't felt for a long time. A little too alive, even. His dragon had been screaming all kinds of ungentlemanly suggestions into his mind throughout the evening, and it was growing worse now.

Must have my mate! Must mark her. Must claim her.

No matter how game Cassandra seemed to be to get closer, he had to keep control of his inner beast.

But she's so perfect! his dragon cried.

Technically, he knew no one was perfect. But, damn. Cassandra came incredibly close. Perfect for him, at least. Their bodies meshed as they walked, effortlessly matching strides. So perfectly that it was all too easy to imagine how they would mesh in other ways.

Oh, we'll mesh, all right. His dragon waggled his eyebrows.

"Nice night," Cassandra murmured, stopping to look out over the sea.

The sea breeze carried her scent over to him, letting it mingle with his, giving him all kinds of dangerous ideas.

He watched the moon ripple over the sea. The sparkling light bounced off waves in irregular patterns that were impossible to predict. It was magical, almost. Which made that aggravating twitch in his cheek go off again.

Never trust a witch.

Watch out for witches and their crafty spells.

Witches and humans are never to be trusted.

He shook his head, trying to dispel such nonsense.

Our mate wouldn't use magic on us, his dragon insisted. *This is a different kind of magic. Like Mom used to say — Love is magic.*

Of course, his father had scoffed every time his mother said so, but Silas was starting to wonder which one of them was wiser.

Look closely, his dragon said. *That's just nature's magic, not a witch's spell.*

He watched the sea, slowly relaxing again. The scene was beautiful. A different kind of beautiful than Maui's daytime splendor, filled like a vibrant watercolor painting with every hue in the rainbow. Nighttime muted everything to black, white, and countless shades of gray, and the contrast had its own beauty. Watching the sea from ground level was novel too. The rippling effect was different, for starters. From up high, the waves trapped lines of moonlight and held them tight. From the beach, moonbeams skipped over wavetops, unfettered and utterly free.

"Nice night," he agreed, slipping an arm over Cassandra's shoulders without thinking.

She patted his belly and spoke in a light, playful voice. "Almost calming, huh?"

He grinned. "It is."

She nodded. "You know what else is calming?" She was all-out teasing him now, but hell. He loved it.

"What?"

"This."

His eyes went wide as she kissed him full on the lips. Not so calming, really, because his heart rate tripled. But a second later, his eyelids drooped, and his mind went blissfully blank. Blank enough for him to wrap his arms around Cassandra and forget why she was supposed to be off-limits.

Her lips were honey sweet and pillow soft. Her hair was silky, her breasts soft against his chest. Her mouth opened under his, and he slid his hands over her hips. Moonlight might have been sparkling over the sea, but in that moment, she was the sunlight and he was the sea. Or maybe he was the moonlight and Cassandra was the sea?

Quit being a poet and just enjoy the damn kiss, his dragon barked.

So he did, and wow. Could a kiss really be that good?

Cassandra pulled back, leaving him smooching empty air for a second before his eyes snapped open and refocused on her.

A wave of anger shot through him. Was she playing games with him? Because Moira had done that, and—

"See?" she murmured through half-shuttered eyes — eyes so void of malice that his anger receded as quickly as it had come.

My mate doesn't play games, his dragon said. *She's not Moira.*

He could see the honesty in her trembling lips and innocent eyes — dazed, doe eyes that told him the kiss affected her as much as it had affected him. Her fingers pressed lightly against his chest, neither insistent nor forceful, and her breath came in uneven rushes.

So not Moira, his dragon crooned.

"I'm not sure I'd call that calming," he murmured, trying to stay cool.

She wants this. We want this. Don't stop now. His dragon egged him on.

"No?"

"More like the opposite," he admitted, running his hands around her waist.

She shrugged and inched closer. "That works too."

When they kissed again, a volley of fireworks blazed through his body. Big red, fiery ones that stirred his desire. Sparkly green and yellow ones that cascaded gently through his veins. Blue twinkles that started out like stars and exploded outward, taking all his cares with them.

The kiss grew hotter. Hungrier. More insistent — on both sides. Cassandra swept her tongue over his lips then more boldly over his teeth. He shuffled closer and let his tongue brush hers as he slid his hands lower, nudging her closer to his rapidly swelling cock. She ran her hands up and down his sides, driving his dragon wild.

He pulled her closer yet, and when she ground against his erection, he swallowed a groan. Then she whimpered into the kiss, blowing every fuse in his brain.

She is my mate. She is my destiny.

She's a witch, his father's voice echoed through his head.

He broke off the kiss, going red in the face. Even dead, his father had a way of butting into his life at the least opportune times.

She's my mate! his dragon roared.

Silas almost wished his father really were there so he could shout everything he'd never been able to express in real life. Things like, *I love and respect you, but I am not you. I will do things my own way. I will make my own decisions. Is that clear?*

By the time he finished that inner rant, his dragon's voice was a bellow in his mind.

He stood there panting, searching his mind.

"You okay?" Cassandra whispered, running her hands over his chest.

He checked every corner of his consciousness, every closet of memories until he'd made sure the specter of his father was gone.

"I'm good," he said, though his voice was hoarse as if he'd been shouting for real. "But listen..."

She shook her head wildly. "No buts. No ifs."

He grasped her by the shoulders. "Dragons don't do things halfway, Cassandra. If we go any further..."

Her grip tightened over his shirt. "I want to go further. Can't you see?"

"But witches and dragons have been enemies for centuries—"

Cassandra nodded. "Feuding like the goddamn Hatfields and McCoys. But that's not our feud, Silas. I get that now. Don't you?"

He did. He wanted her more than anything. But did she understand who she was tangling with? Did she really want to unleash his long pent-up desires?

"I don't want you to get hurt," he forced himself to say. "It would be safer—"

"I'm sick of playing it safe. I'm sick of careful."

He took a deep breath, deciding for one last try at sanity before he caved in completely. "You need to be sure before we take this too far. Before it's too late."

She cupped his face. "It is too late, Silas. And you know what?"

He blinked, trying hard to focus. But she was moving in for another kiss he desperately wanted, and he just couldn't summon the willpower to resist.

"The minute I met you, it was too late," she whispered. "And I wouldn't turn the clock back if I could."

In his mind, he stood perfectly still, shell-shocked by her words. His body, however, acted on its own and closed the remaining distance to meet her kiss. A hard, do-or-die kiss that had him pressing closer than before. He could feel her every curve, taste the desire on her tongue.

Don't even try to stop this now, his dragon growled.

He wouldn't. Couldn't. But after another minute of frenzied grappling on the beach, he did pull away for a lungful of air.

"I changed my mind," he murmured.

"You what?" Cassandra screeched.

He caught her hands before she could karate chop his windpipe. "How about a rain check on the walk, and we head to the guesthouse instead?"

"You..." she grumbled, though a smile crept over her lips.

"Sorry. Didn't mean to tease," he said, pulling her close again.

She'd only stepped away for seconds, yet it felt like a huge void. But the moment their bodies connected again, that sense of calm set in again. A calm within a storm, perhaps, because his body was still on fire.

She grabbed his hand, about-faced, and marched him back across the beach, covering the ground to the guesthouse in half the time they'd taken to stroll away. Then she yanked him up the three stairs and all but shoved him against the doorframe.

"Stay right there. And don't even think about changing your mind." She shook a finger in his face.

"Wouldn't dream of it. But—"

She shushed him with a kiss, then pulled away. "My turn to be a tease."

His lips moved, but no sound came out. What was she doing?

The space inside the guesthouse was compact, but the bed was big, and his dragon tracked her movements around it closely, already fast-forwarding through half a dozen positions he and she might—

Cut that out, he barked at the beast. How was he ever going to stay in control with the beast suggesting such things?

Who said anything about control? his dragon huffed.

Cassandra moved quickly, opening a drawer then slamming it shut in her rush. A match scratched on a rough surface, and the scent of sulfur filled the room.

His dragon breathed deeply. *I love the smell of a kindled fire.*

Silas followed the yellow glow of a match behind Cassandra's cupped hand.

"Now if I were any good as a witch..." she muttered.

What was that about?

She blew out the match, lit another, and proceeded to light a dozen more candles until the room was lit up like a chapel. Then she marched over to him and waved the last match in the air between them, extinguishing the flame.

Extinguishing that flame, his dragon chuckled. *Not the one inside me.*

"What do you think?" She cocked her head at him.

He opened his arms, and she slipped right into his embrace. Moonlight streamed past him through the open doorway, casting their shadows across the bed.

"I stopped thinking when we reached the end of the beach," he admitted. "But this is nice."

She nodded, obviously pleased with herself, and sidled closer until her hips were hard against his. "Your turf, by the way." She ran her finger over his lips. "You know, what with dragons being sensitive about territory and everything."

The last part of his mind capable of rational thought chastised him. Cassandra was the one out of her element, and yet she trusted him — unconditionally, it seemed.

So not like Moira, his dragon sighed.

He closed his eyes briefly, shuttering Moira out of his mind. This was his night with his mate, and he wouldn't let Moira butt in on his heart, mind, or soul ever again.

"Thank you," he whispered, kissing one of Cassandra's hands.

Her scent was concentrated around her wrists, together with that of a faint, exotic perfume, and the combination pushed him to the very edge of his control.

"Oh, you'll be thanking me soon enough." She winked. "I guarantee it."

"Still teasing, Miss Nichols?"

She shook her head, leaning forward until her lips brushed his. "Tease over. Let the fun begin."

Chapter Fifteen

Cassandra undid Silas's tie and drew it off slowly, letting the silk slide across his neck. His eyes flared, and the red glow intensified.

What exactly had gotten into her, she wasn't sure. But that hardly seemed to matter because she wanted him. Needed him. Now.

She kissed him — no, consumed him — while pushing his jacket back. The billionaire playboy look was a turn-on, for sure, but she wanted more. She had to practically wrestle the jacket off his shoulders, what with all that muscle trapped inside.

"Promise me when you take my dress off, you'll be a little more gentle," she murmured. "It's a loaner."

"Can't promise anything," he growled into his next kiss.

For a second, he was handcuffed in the inside-out sleeves of his jacket, and she chuckled. "You're at my mercy, dragon."

He turned that smoldering look on her. "I've been at your mercy from day one."

Her jaw dropped for a split second before she recovered. "And I thought you were the dangerous one."

She kissed his neck before he could answer and undid the buttons of his shirt, intoxicated by his scent — a natural cologne that carried a hint of sophistication with a splash of something completely wild. Silas tipped his head back, inviting her closer — another little fantasy come true. The kisses became nips, and Silas growled in warning. A real, animal growl, so unlike the refined man she'd grown accustomed to. But exactly like him too, because she'd seen past the carefully maintained exterior and glimpsed the real him — a mix of man and animal waiting to be let free.

And she was the one with the keys. She pictured creeping up to a castle tower, inserting a skeleton key, and slowly unlocking the creaky door to his soul.

A candle flickered in the corner of her vision, reminding her she was playing with fire. He was a dragon shifter, and she was part witch.

My dragon shifter, she told herself.

She let her mouth follow her hands, kissing her way down the chest she'd dreamed about. Pushing aside the sides of his shirt, she slid lower and lower until she was palming his cock through the pants.

Silas surged against her, and his eyes flared red. Not a scary red — a sensual scarlet that triggered every hormone in her body.

"Help me with this," she whispered, touching his pants.

He took her hands and guided them to his sides, stepping toward the bed. "Not a good idea if you want me to be careful with that dress."

She worked his shirt off, taking care around the sensitive skin of his left arm. As long as she didn't actually press down there, it seemed all right. Then she ran her hands over the back of his steely rear.

"I get the shoulders," she murmured, half to herself. He was a dragon shifter, after all. "But what do you need all this muscle for?" She patted his ass.

He grinned. "Takeoff. Landing. You know."

That's what he said aloud. But the glow in his dragon eyes said something more like, *The better to pleasure you with, my dear.*

She gulped then hurried to cover up with another kiss. "Right. Takeoff. Landing."

He ran his fingers over her shoulders and neckline, making her head tip from side to side. Then he turned the kiss sideways, broke it off gently, and guided her through a half turn, putting her back to him.

"I liked your hair up," he whispered, combing his fingers through the long strands. Then his voice dropped an octave. "But I love it down even more."

The needy bass made her wiggle in anticipation, and she groaned aloud when he parted her hair with his thumbs. He kissed her from behind, unzipping her dress at the same time. Every move smooth, stimulating. One side of her mouth crooked up as she laughed at herself. Silas could get her dress off so smoothly; she hadn't even been able to work down his fly. Well, the next chance she got, watch out.

"Pardon?" he murmured, touching the bare skin of her lower back.

"Nothing," she said, arching for more.

His strong hands gripped her hips and pulled her back against his cock. Then he eased away and bumped against her again, harder. A low, hungry hum came from his chest, giving her a hint of the beast within.

"Silas," she whispered, just about ready to bend over and do it right there. Who needed a bed?

On the other hand, she wanted to look Silas in the eye when he moved inside her. Somehow, she sensed that would be important if she were to maintain the delicate power balance they had.

Silas undid the clasp of her bra and pushed it forward. She moaned when he cupped her breasts, then sighed as he pulled the dress from her shoulders and let it puddle at her feet.

She turned, kicking the dress away, letting his eager eyes touch every part of her body. They roved over her bare breasts, her navel, the black lace panties. His mouth opened a tiny bit before he jerked his gaze upward again.

Oh, yes. Her dragon liked what he saw.

She hooked her thumbs in the panties and slowly wiggled them down. He made her feel beautiful. Desired. She lifted one foot then another to take the panties off, gripping his arm for balance.

A smile played over Silas's lips. Apparently, he knew as well as she did that that part was for show. She didn't *need* his help. But she liked it, for sure.

149

She let the panties drop to the floor and swung her hair back, standing half in moonlight, half in shadow.

Silas's cheek twitched again. He *definitely* liked what he saw.

"We need to even the score here," she said, beckoning him closer.

He arched an eyebrow, coming so close she had to tip her chin back to maintain eye contact. "Score?"

"One dress down, one pair of pants to go." She rolled forward on her toes, bumping his groin.

He beat her hands to his belt, quickly undoing the clasp, and together they pushed his pants and boxers down. Cassandra made sure to go extra slow, enjoying every inch of the journey.

"Dragons are known for patience, but..." he croaked.

"No ifs." She chuckled. "And no buts, except maybe this one." She patted his cheeks.

Then she rested her head on his chest and looked down, stroking his cock. Watching the tip glisten, feeling him harden. Silas's breath came in heavy huffs that stirred the hair at the nape of her neck. She cupped his cock with both hands and slid up and down, forcing herself to go slowly. He rocked into her hands, sliding his fingers along her ribs in an echo of the motion. Up and down, up and down, until she couldn't wait a second longer.

She backed up, meeting his eyes. When her calves bumped the edge of the bed, she held her breath.

Take me, she wanted to say. *Make me feel even better than I do now.*

Silas stood still, practically quivering under her hands. Then he leaned forward into a kiss that started as a light promise — an *I will take care of you* promise — and gradually unraveled into something deeper, hungrier. Wilder. So wild, she barely noticed the transition from standing to lying beneath him on the bed. Without breaking the kiss, he pushed her legs apart and pressed his weight over her, pinning her down. Then he pulled back from his kiss and met her eyes.

"Last chance," he murmured.

150

She bent her right leg, running it along the outside of his.

"Right," she deadpanned, rolling to open the bedside drawer. She'd discovered a packet of condoms there her very first night on the estate, along with a nail file and tissues. Everything a guest at this luxury estate might desire.

Literally, she joked to herself.

"What's so funny?" he asked as she handed him a condom and lay back again.

"Private joke." She tapped her hands on her chest impatiently. "Now, where were we? Oh, I know. Somewhere around here." She slid her hands under her breasts and slowly circled the nipples.

Silas smiled a wicked grin — a hint of the dragon within. Then he ripped the packet apart and slid on the condom. She helped him unroll it while folding her knees out of the way. Ready. Waiting.

"Last chance. For real," he warned.

"Not going anywhere, mister. And neither are you." She linked her legs around his waist.

His cock was right at her entrance, and her body burned for him. But Silas's first move was to slide downward, breaking away. She nearly protested until his mouth closed around her nipple.

"We were here, you said?"

His warm breath washed over her bare skin, making her nipples ache.

She arched back and moaned something incomprehensible instead of the snappy comeback that got lost in the haze of pleasure that enveloped her. Silas had the hands of a master and the tongue of a pirate. He'd started the night clean-shaven, but now, his cheek scoured her breast as he moved from the right side to the left. She threaded her fingers through his thick black hair and leaned back, greedy for more.

"So good," she moaned.

He squeezed her nipple in and out of his mouth in a popping motion that made her see spots. Then he tiptoed a hand down her belly and between her legs, making her writhe. Using the flat of his palm, he rubbed — teased, damn it — until she was ready to scream.

"Silas..."

Her moan of protest turned into a howl of pleasure when he dragged a single finger through her folds.

"Shh," he whispered.

She bucked up against his hand and squeaked. "You expect me to be quiet while you do that?"

She heard his chuckle, but her chin was tipped too far back for her to see his grin. If Silas thought she was a partner who would silently follow his bidding, he was in for a surprise. Someone had to shake him out of his carefully ordered world. Her new mission in life, as of there and then.

So she called his name, cried out her pleasure, and raked her nails across his back. She did everything but shush, in fact. And it wasn't lost on her that Silas didn't protest. On the contrary, his breath grew faster, his touches less measured. His tongue lashed out at her, probing deeper, and his chin scratched harder. He paused long enough to get a better grip on her hips before dragging her closer and closing his mouth over her again.

"Yes... Yes..." she cried, not sure if she was urging on the man or the beast.

Then he muttered and rose above her again.

Their eyes locked. No *last chance* warning this time. Silas looked serious as ever, and his eyes blazed. And for once, she was speechless, because she felt it too. The feeling of destiny at the door, playing out a hand of cards she couldn't see. The feeling of some momentous event being thrust into motion by what they did next. Something bigger than sex. Bigger than the two of them. Bigger than one night.

She nodded once and spread her legs wider. Whatever her fate was, she'd embrace it, as long as she got this one night.

Silas pushed forward, driving in deep.

To hell with destiny, his determined expression said. *We'll make our own fate.*

Her whole body convulsed, and her arms flew over her head. She gasped at the burning sensation.

He paused until her eyes fluttered back to focus and found his.

"Don't stop," she gasped. "Please, don't stop."

Silas studied her for a heartbeat longer. Then he withdrew an inch and hammered forward again, making her howl.

"So good." If he stopped now, she'd scream. "So good..."

He did it again — a slow retreat, a sudden thrust forward, shoving her body up the bed.

"Yes..."

She pushed against him, begging him to move faster and thrust harder. Silas plunged deeper and deeper, pinning her hands over her head. Claiming her with every sharp punch of his hips, every swallowed growl.

Mine, the glow in his eyes crowed. *You are mine.*

I am yours, she might have said — if she could manage more than moans of delight.

Silas hitched her leg higher and pounded deeper. She bucked against him, crying out each time.

Like the sea over sand, they broke apart then crashed together in intensifying waves. The moon dipped lower, blazing right through the open door and lighting Silas's back. She raised her head and watched the muscles ripple, loosen, and tense again. The bigger slabs on his shoulders, the oblique lines by his ribs, the chiseled line of his ass — all that power helping him piston into her again and again.

"More," she chanted breathlessly. "More."

Urgency built inside her, as if they'd resisted the attraction for years and not days. As if her life only really started now.

When Silas briefly paused to hitch himself higher on his elbows, a drop of sweat dropped from his chest to hers. She watched it roll between her breasts and toward her stomach. Silas watched too, and for a moment, the world was still. The calm before a storm.

Then he pushed her legs wider and hammered forward, making her cry out. His teeth were bared, his body glistening with sweat. Gone was the cool-headed commander, the well-mannered gent. Within his glowing eyes was a beast who hungered for her.

153

I will worship and protect you for all my days, those eyes said, warming, not frightening her.

She locked her eyes on the glow. That beast was part of Silas, and the deeper she looked, the more she saw the interlocking facets of his character. The raging dragon, the fearless leader, the passionate lover. Then she couldn't see anything. Her vision blurred.

"Yes." She panted with each of his wild thrusts. "Yes..."

She clamped down with her inner muscles, making him groan. Inside, the waves of ecstasy swirled, spinning her in a whirlpool of wild pleasure.

"Yes... Yes..."

Was she screaming? Whispering? She couldn't tell. All she knew was no man had ever driven her this far past her threshold to a place of pure ecstasy.

Then Silas jerked inside her, and every nerve in her body exploded.

A roar filled her ears. Heat raged through her body. A tear slipped down her cheek. Her muscles relaxed briefly then spasmed as she came for a second time.

"Yes," she moaned, squeezing Silas's hands as her body shuddered in an absolute high.

Slowly, she let herself unwind, one muscle at a time. Succumbing to an afterglow like none she'd ever experienced before. Silas lowered himself gradually, resting his body on hers. He tucked his cheek beside hers and panted into the sheets. She patted his back, not coordinated enough to say or do much else. Which was good, because what exactly was there to say about an experience that pushed her so far off the charts?

"Are you sure you don't have any dragon in you?" Silas murmured.

She chuckled, tightening her legs around him. "Actually, I think I have a lot of dragon in me."

She wiggled to emphasize the point, and they both collapsed into the sheets laughing. The perfect end, Cassandra decided, to perfect sex.

Not that she was done for the night. Candles flickered all around the room, assuring her they still had plenty of fuel. The moon glittered over the sea, winking at her.

She grinned at the ceiling. No, she was definitely not done for the night.

"Just a quick breather and then..." she murmured.

"And then?" Silas popped his head up and arched an eyebrow, making her melt all over again.

She hadn't actually meant to let the words slip, but now that she had, she might as well run with them.

"Well, now that we're warmed up and all," she teased.

"Warmed up?" he protested.

She laughed and ran a hand slowly down his chest, reaching lower and lower. "You don't think I'm going to sleep away a perfectly good night, do you?"

Chapter Sixteen

Silas tried to remember the last time he'd roared, climaxed, and laughed himself silly all in the same night, and came up blank. And, hell. The night was still young.

Best night ever, his dragon puffed.

Of course, his inner beast had been declaring that every night for the past week. Not the night after the auction, maybe, but every other evening since he'd met Cassandra. Just having her nearby was a treat. Hearing her movements and little mutters in the library, sniffing her scent, and best of all, having her stop by his office to say goodnight. Every time she had, he'd fantasized about a night like this.

Not a fantasy any more. His dragon grinned.

The beast was oversimplifying, and he knew it. One night with Cassandra did not equal happily ever after. But, hell. He'd take it one step at a time.

"That tickles," he laughed as she inched her fingers down his belly.

She snorted and imitated his voice, which had dropped several octaves. "That tickles." Then she laughed and spoke in her normal voice. "Only a dragon could say it that way."

He forced himself to lie still instead of rolling around. "Well, it does tickle."

"Softy." She sighed, pushing a finger against his abs.

He flexed. "Nothing soft down there."

Cassandra's eyes lit up with mischief. "Oh, no? I might have to verify that."

She drew a box around every muscle of his abdomen then circled his navel, going torturously slowly. Her eyes, though, kept wandering to his cock. When she licked her lips and

157

reached lower, his eyes rolled back. The second her delicate fingers touched his cock, he inhaled sharply.

"See? Nothing soft," he said between clenched teeth.

She ran an index finger up his stiff cock, featherlight. The skin all over his body tingled as if she were touching him there too. The woman was magic.

She is part witch, his dragon murmured, pleased as punch.

Which really went to show how far gone his dragon was. Witches were supposed to be the enemy. To be avoided, at best.

His dragon huffed. *See what dragons have been missing for centuries?*

She tapped the tip of his straining cock then circled the head.

"Aha. Soft. I knew it."

"That doesn't count."

She raised an eyebrow, obviously enjoying his indignation. "Soft is soft, mister."

He was about to protest, but she licked her lips and looked at his cock, making his mind go blank. Well, almost blank.

Please, yes. Please, yes. Please. . . his dragon whispered inside.

Cassandra collected her hair in one hand and twisted it behind her neck. Just that move would have been enough to make him rock hard, but what really did him in were her eyes. Intent. Focused. Appraising.

"Velvety soft," she whispered, dipping her head.

With her free hand, she circled his cock, barely applying pressure, making it all seem like a dream. Then she angled him slightly and exhaled over the tip.

Silas hid a groan. Barely.

"Hard," he muttered, keeping up the game. "Definitely hard."

"I'll be the judge of that," Cassandra said, pinning him with a naughty look.

She worked her lips against each other until they were as shiny as her hair in the candlelight. Her eyes held pricks of light, making it all too easy to fantasize about her being a dragon. Her being his.

Then he couldn't imagine anything, because she opened her mouth and drew him in.

His head flopped back on the pillow, and his eyes slid shut as he succumbed to pleasure. Pure, gentle pleasure unlike anything he'd ever felt. Then she sucked, increasing the air pressure, and he groaned out loud.

"See?" he managed a second later. "Hard."

She released him long enough to kiss the glistening tip of his cock. "Velvety. Now, hush."

A good thing she couldn't hear his dragon moaning inside. Roaring like the king of the world, ruler of the seven seas. He threaded his fingers through her hair, following her next moves. The downward bob, the upward slide. The side-to-side wiggle while her tongue circled him. She came up for a breath of air with a tiny gasp, and he peeked just in time to see her glazed eyes. His must have been the same, because everything he saw was out of focus, like those old-fashioned photos where only the center was clear. Then she inhaled and started moving over him more boldly, and his whole body went stiff.

Please don't stop, his dragon murmured inside. *Never stop. Please.*

"Good?" she whispered between licks.

He didn't answer. He couldn't answer. He'd never felt anything so amazing in his life.

Cassandra chuckled and slid over his cock again, pumping faster. His hips jerked up at the same time, and his heels dug into the mattress. His lips moved, mouthing strings of nonsense that would have come out as sounds if he hadn't bitten his lip — hard. He was about to lose it completely.

Finally, his dragon snipped. *See how good it feels to let go sometimes?*

Yes, he was starting to see that now. But damn it, he was not going to come yet. Not before he treated her to her own high.

Just as he was going to nudge her head back, she pulled away and looked at him with smoldering eyes. She'd read him perfectly, and a second later, her mouth was on his, wild and hungry.

"Just one more second," she groaned as if she had the same vision of rolling and letting him pound into her with all his dragon might. "One more second..."

She reared back, straddling him, dragging her core over his cock.

He gripped her hips, guiding her into position. Then she thrust her hips down and cried out as he pushed up, penetrating deep.

"Yes..."

She leaned back, taking him deeper still, and started to dance over him. Her hair danced too, and a strand caught at the edge of her mouth. Her wide-open mouth that moved as she whispered in ecstasy.

"So good..."

He held her hips tight, pinning her in place as he drove upward. Watching her through half-lidded eyes. Her nipples barely moved, but the soft flesh around them swung gently, driving him wild. She threw her head back, showing him the smooth skin of her neck. His dragon immediately started calculating where he'd place his mating bite.

He stretched a thumb wide to press her clit, distracting himself from that idea.

No mating bites, he ordered his dragon.

For once, he was going to enjoy himself and not think too far ahead.

"Oh!" Cassandra cried, sliding against the pressure.

He circled her tight bud with his thumb, then pressed hard.

"So close..." she moaned, jerking over him.

He captured the view for that special place in his memory — the one with the best moments of his life, all of which seemed laughable compared to this. Cassandra, backlit by moonlight and the shadows of dancing palms. The ocean, sweeping up and down the shoreline, egging them on. The scent of her desire, filling the room like a bouquet.

"So good," he croaked, letting her know what she did to him. Did she know how beautiful she was?

She arched backward for one more hot gyration, then hunched forward and kissed him again. "Turn. Please turn."

Her voice was desperate, her eyes wild. They rolled in one perfectly synched move, bringing him to all fours over her body. Her legs hooked around his waist, and a split second later, he was buried deep, deep inside.

Cassandra threw her head back and cried out. Her nails raked his skin. "Harder. Please, harder."

He withdrew, trying to control his rattling breath, and hammered in again.

"Harder," she cried, digging her heels into his ass.

He pumped and thrust like never before. Wildly, blissfully out of control. A corner of the sheet tangled between them, and he ripped it away. The sound of tearing fabric mixed with Cassandra's hungry pants and the creak of the bed, driving him wild. Clenching his teeth, he thrust harder and harder, chasing an invisible high. His blood rushed, and his balls tightened in one of those burning moments between pain and pleasure. Cassandra's voice became a mindless chant as they both edged closer to the line between sheer ecstasy and—

Bliss. Utter bliss.

His vision went white as he emptied into her, powered by every aching muscle. Filling her, planting his seed deep. Vaguely aware that maybe that wasn't the best idea, but not caring one whit.

Cassandra moaned and clamped down over him, milking every last drop from him. Either she didn't care about the consequences, or she was as out of her mind as he was.

"Yes..." She shuddered through her orgasm, squeezing down hard on him. Her hands were tense on his rear, her legs wide, keeping him tight and deep.

Silas dropped to one elbow and stroked her collarbone as she shuddered through another few aftershocks. Watching her eyes begin to focus then glaze over again. Hearing her breath catch as each successive wave of pleasure steamrolled through her body. His cock ached as he held on, keeping her filled, giving her what she needed until, finally, they both went limp.

The sheets were a twisted mess. His breath came in wild pants. Sweat streaked his skin, but damn. He'd never felt as good in his life.

Cassandra smoothed her hand over his shoulder, and he pulled away to watch her. Her nostrils flared. Her chest rose and fell with every rushed breath. "Holy shit."

He broke into a laugh. That pretty much hit the nail on the head.

"You mean that in the good way, right?"

She tried — and failed — to give him a stern look. "No, I'm wildly disappointed. Can't you tell?" A second later, she play-smacked him on the back. "Insanely good, if you must know."

She wrapped her arms around his shoulders and drew him down for a kiss. A fairly messy kiss, but a delicious one that held a whole potpourri of flavors. He tasted himself along with her various essences. The sensual woman, the passionate lover, the thinker slowly going over what had just happened in her mind.

"Oops. No condom," she murmured.

He nodded slowly. "Sorry."

She thought it over for a moment then pulled him closer. "Not going to worry about that tonight."

And just like that, she rolled, spooning up with him and pulling his hand into position over her breast.

He smoothed her hair to the side and kissed her shoulder. Did he really deserve a woman like this?

"Silas?" she murmured a second later.

"Hmm?"

"Stop thinking. Relax." She pressed her fingers over his and guided them over her nipple. It was soft now and nearly flush with her breast. He circled slowly, exploring the tiny bumps.

She nestled closer with a sigh, and he marveled at how she always seemed to know exactly what he needed and when.

Of course, she does. She's our mate, his dragon said, all matter-of-fact.

At that moment, it seemed so clear, so easy. And despite the muffled alarms sounding from the back of his mind, he let himself believe for a time. That the world was as small as the guesthouse and as simple as a man and a woman holding each other tight. He closed his eyes and counted the beats of her heart.

"Thank you," she whispered, kissing his hand.

His mind turned in lazy circles like a bird in the breeze. "For what?"

"For everything. For tonight. For trusting me."

He smiled ever so slightly. "Maybe I'm just hiding my evil side from you. Maybe I have a devious plan."

She laughed. "Maybe I'm the one with a devious plan."

"And what would that involve?"

She lifted her leg and hooked it over his, then slowly guided his hand lower.

"Oh, all kinds of dastardly, evil things." Her voice was low and hoarse, half joke, half earnest. He could sense the lust well up in her all over again, just as it did in him.

The mating instinct, his dragon said. *The urge to bond again and again.*

He pulled her hips back against his, letting his hardening cock press against her back.

"Perfect," he murmured, running his hand along her inner thigh as a second wind revived his weary body.

Third wind, his dragon joked, sounding ridiculously pleased with himself.

"I happen to have some dastardly deeds in mind too," he finished, inching closer and closer to her core.

A second later, he was circling her slick heat and tugging her toward him. Cassandra rolled with a wicked smile. "I like the sound of that. But me first."

He crooked an eyebrow, playing along. "And what exactly does the lady desire?"

She grinned, popped a kiss on his lips, and turned under him, her back to his chest. She rose up on all fours and wiggled her perfect ass under his hips. "This. Think you can oblige?"

The heat in his eyes grew, and the glow reflected on her glistening skin. She wanted it from behind, dragon style?

"Hard, Silas," she murmured as if she'd read his mind. "Hard and deep."

I'll show you hard and deep, his dragon howled.

A little puff of steam escaped from his nostrils. Good thing Cassandra liked a wild ride.

He leaned over her from behind, twisting her hair to one side. He kept his hand fisted in it, tugging slightly. Then he puffed a hot breath into her neck, instinctively thinking of the mating brand. Finally, he kissed her creamy skin and coiled his muscles for a powerful thrust.

"Oh, I can definitely oblige."

Chapter Seventeen

Cassandra woke early, snuggled close to Silas, relishing the warmth of his bare skin against her. His arms were tight around her body. The sun was barely rising, and she was tired. So she closed her eyes again, expecting another hour or two of satisfied sleep.

Instead, she tossed, turned, and dreamed increasingly disturbing scenes. They started with a bloody, sunset sky that spoke of death and destruction. The red color extended toward the ground, where she saw a line of low, bubbling fire. Wait, not fire — lava. She was standing close enough to feel the searing heat, and her feet burned. But somehow, she couldn't back away.

Shadows rushed overhead, and two dueling dragons swooped through the sky, roaring and spitting long plumes of fire at each other. She screamed, trying to stop them, but the fight raged on. A woman's voice cackled from behind her, egging the dragons on. Was that Eloise? Moira?

"Silas!"

Cassandra woke in a sweat and reached for him. Just one night with him and she already felt like half of a whole. As if she'd never have to wake up alone and face the challenges of a day on her own.

But Silas was gone.

She groped around the bed as though he might be hiding under the sheets. Of course, he wasn't, and the open bathroom door showed he wasn't there either. She sat up and looked around, clutching the sheets. Silas's clothes were gone, and the dress she'd discarded the previous night was hung neatly over a chair.

She stared at the seat of the chair, where a single rose lay.

She didn't know whether to yell or sigh. Silas leaving without a word hurt more than it ought to. She had so much to say, so much she wanted to ask. But at the same time, her heart warmed. The rose said so much more than words or a note could. She stood and brought it gingerly to her nose. The scent was sweet, the stalk smooth. When she looked closer, a sad smile played over her lips. Her lover had removed all the thorns.

Good old Silas, keeping the world safe for everyone.

She peeked out the door on the vague hope that he might be lounging on the front porch, watching waves roll over the sand. Which was about as likely as catching him swinging in a hammock, but a girl could dream.

"Silas," she whispered, wishing he were there.

Maybe if she stuck around long enough, she could teach Silas some bad habits, like sleeping in. Slowing down. Enjoying life.

Her mind flashed back to one of the times they'd bonded the previous night, and her cheeks heated. She'd never felt that kind of urgency or burning need in her life. They'd been like a couple of animals, overcome by the instinct to mate.

She froze at the word. Mate.

Dragons are the most passionate, possessive lovers, one of the books in the library had said.

She gulped and looked at the bed — and the floor, and the porch. . .

Passionate. Possessive. That fit Silas, all right. Her body ached inside and out — in the very best way.

While some males prefer harems, most dedicate themselves to a single mate, often waiting years for the right woman to come along.

She shivered a little, considering Silas's stubbornly single status. Could it really be?

Wrapping a sarong around her torso, she made herself a cup of coffee and flopped into the lounge chair, twirling the flower and listening to the sea.

Mate. Could she and Silas really be destined for each other?

166

Part of her wanted to believe it, but another part scoffed. What if that was just goofy dragon lore? Right now, it was more important to make sense of her ominous, insistent dreams.

Volcanoes. Dragons. A raging battle. She shivered though the morning was clear and balmy. The remnant of another dream drifted through her mind, carrying the sly, scheming faces of Drax and Moira.

She closed her eyes. Was that a dream or a hint of trouble afoot?

Everything is a secret, Silas had commented. *Everything is hidden. Every problem is solved alone.*

A sea gull cried, and she squinted upward. For all that she'd learned about Silas, there was still so much to discover in his private world — and the world of dragons.

She stayed there for nearly an hour, telling herself Silas would come along. Imagining how he would walk up behind her, cover her eyes, and whisper *Surprise* in that resonant baritone that turned her on. Or maybe he would bring her another rose and ask her over for brunch. Alternatively, she imagined him hurrying by and saying, *Cassandra, I need your help. Will you come with me?*

As it turned out, those were all fantasies, because Silas never appeared.

"Some mate," she griped, putting that crazy theory to rest.

She showered, growing grumpy, and looked over her choice of clothes. The cocktail dress hung over the chair, goading her. Had the previous night just been her fleeting Cinderella moment? Was none of it as meaningful to Silas as it had been to her?

"Damn it," she muttered out loud.

She decided to dress as if she were going to work on a hot summer's night, which meant a pair of khaki shorts and a comfortable tank top. An outfit that reminded her she could damn well stand on her own two feet.

She stomped over to the meeting house, preparing something cool, calm, and collected to say. But before she even crossed the lawn, she could see Silas wasn't there, so she headed to his house instead. The creek alongside the path bubbled cheerily, welcoming her to explore, but when she reached the lower terrace, the house seemed to loom above her.

"Hello?" she called from the entrance.

The place echoed with emptiness as she slowly ascended the stairs and walked the empty halls.

"Silas?"

She peered into his office with a growing sense of unease, then checked the library. Still no Silas, and her irritation became concern. She checked every level of the eclectic home, then came back to the office and stared at his empty chair.

If only he were there. She would walk up behind him, knead his shoulders, and work the tension out of his soul. She would kiss him on the back of the neck and smooth her hands over all the cords of muscle in his arms. She would get him to stop work long enough to enjoy the view and put everything in perspective again.

Of course, having a ruthless dragon like Drax scheming to steal everything Silas held dear had to make *perspective* a tricky thing.

She made another listless lap through the library and headed back across the estate. Silas's roadster wasn't in the garage, and somehow, she was no longer surprised. He had left the property. She could feel the emptiness, somehow.

Not knowing what else to do, she walked toward the meeting house. Her steps slowed as she drew near, and her cheeks heated. It was already eleven o'clock. Much too late to be waking from anything but a spectacularly late — or active — night. Even if it was nobody's business to speculate on how she'd spent the night — or with whom — she still felt self-conscious. Shifters were incredibly perceptive about such things. Would the others notice?

"Hi!" Tessa called brightly. "Perfect timing. I'm experimenting with a new coconut bread recipe. Can you try some for me?"

Kai and Hunter were there too, and both seemed more interested in the steaming hot loaf Tessa pulled from the oven than how Cassandra had spent her night. And if they did notice — well, no one put her on the spot with flared nostrils or knowing looks. She sat, making sure to choose a place downwind.

"Yes, please," she said, taking a piece.

Kai smeared his bread with jam while Hunter spiraled honey in neat circles across his.

Cassandra glanced around. Had Silas already been through for a meal? His favorite coffee cup stood beside the sink with nary a dark ring in it, suggesting he'd moved on quickly. So where had he gone?

"How was the dinner?" Tessa asked. "Did that Penelope van Whatshername show up?"

Cassandra wasn't quite sure how to answer. *Yes, and Drax and Moira were there too?* That was obviously critical information, but Silas ought to be the one to share that, not her. Or had he missed Tessa and the others altogether?

"It was interesting," Cassandra murmured, gulping a piece of bread.

She was dying to ask where Silas had gone, but she didn't dare. And since everything seemed so quiet, so normal, she'd bet he hadn't told the others about Drax.

I don't want to involve them, he'd said the previous night. *If I can find a way to engage Drax one-on-one…*

She knotted her fingers together under the table. Drat the man. Had he gone out to hunt Drax down?

"Gotta go," Kai said, kissing Tessa on his way out. "Got a few sightseeing flights to run."

Hunter stood next. "Can I take a piece for Dawn?" The bear shifter headed into town nearly every day to meet his mate for lunch.

"Sure. Bye, guys," Tessa called.

"Bye," Cassandra mumbled, wondering what to do.

"Oh. When did Silas say he was coming back from the Big Island?" Kai called from the edge of the lawn.

Cassandra's head snapped up. The Big Island? She looked out toward the ocean. Why would Silas go there?

"He said he might not be back until late," Tessa replied.

169

ANNA LOWE

Cassandra forced a bite of bread down. Drax was on Maui, not the Big Island. So why would Silas go there?

"What's on the Big Island?" she asked, oh so casually.

Tessa shrugged. "Who knows? Silas manages so many business interests for the owner of the estate, I can't keep track. It is an interesting place, though. Not as beautiful as Maui." She winked and pointed to one of the picture books on the coffee table. "But still nice."

The owner of the estate. If only Tessa knew.

Cassandra picked up the book and started leafing through the images while trying to puzzle everything out. She flipped past incredible scenes of black sand beaches and swaying palms. Surfers in aquamarine waves. Turtles. Then she got to the centerfold and stopped abruptly at a nighttime image of a volcano spewing glowing red chunks of molten lava.

Volcanoes. Lava. Flames.

She sat perfectly still. Those volcanoes had formed the backdrop to her dream.

Tessa glanced over from the kitchen. "Have you been to the Big Island?"

Cassandra shook her head numbly and bit back the words on the tip of her tongue. *No, but the Windstone is there. I sent it there to keep it safe. Ironic, huh?*

Her jaw had just about come unhinged when she discovered the private jet's flight path was New York to Maui. She'd mailed the diamond to a relative on the Big Island because it seemed like the end of the world at the time. Was that a crazy coincidence or an act of fate?

"The volcanoes are quite a sight," Tessa went on. "They've been really active lately. Kai and I went over not too long ago to practice spitting fire."

Cassandra's eyes went wide. "You what?"

Tessa grinned. "There's a little place past Kapalana, all the way at the end of the road — and I mean, the end of the road. One lonely cottage and not much else. Hardly anyone goes there now that they've closed the road. But it was perfect for us. If you fly at low altitude at night, no one spots you,

170

and no one thinks anything of bursts of flame. It's a perfect place to practice. I'm finally getting the hang of it, too."

A month ago, Cassandra wouldn't have believed she'd be part of a casual conversation about spitting dragon fire, but now, her mind was too busy to dwell on that. She pretended to look at the book, turning the page to a waterfall in case Tessa glanced her way.

Volcanoes. Spitting fire. Out-of-the-way places.

If I can find a way to take Drax on without involving the others — to lure him into a fair fight...

She clutched the book. Had Silas already put his plan into action?

But none of it made sense if Drax was on Maui. Then she froze. Had Drax tracked down the diamond?

Just you wait and see, she remembered Eloise cackling, back at Cassandra's last visit before the shit hit the fan. *A lure spell. The simplest yet hardest spell to weave. But if you manage it — if you weave all the details into place and mix enough magic in, what you envision shall come to pass.*

You're going to kill a dragon by dreaming about it? Cassandra had asked, not taking her seriously.

Eloise had laughed deviously. *No, I'm going to dream of my enemies killing each other.*

Cassandra pictured Drax and Silas, bristling at each other, first in the alley in New York, then at the gala dinner on Maui. The only thing that had prevented an open fight was the risk of drawing human attention. But way out in a corner of the Big Island...

The trick to a good lure spell is the detail, Eloise had said, tapping her chin in thought. *The where. The how. All that has to be in the spell.*

Cassandra had shrugged at the time and said the first thing that came into her mind. *Cast them into a volcano. At sunset. Make it really dramatic.*

She'd been kidding, but Eloise had taken her seriously. *Volcano. Sunset. Good idea.*

Oh God. She wanted to cry. *Eloise, what have you done?*

171

She trembled where she sat. God, what had *she* done? Had she subconsciously contributed to the spell — or worse, had she added the details over time?

Her chin drooped lower and lower until she jerked her head up before Tessa noticed her alarm.

But Tessa had her back turned as she checked a pot on the stove. Cassandra slapped the book shut and chewed her lips. Was Eloise capable of such a devious act or such a powerful spell?

Yes, she was. Cassandra could picture the old woman, gathering her energy for one last, spiteful act.

Just you wait and see.

"Just another few minutes..." Tessa murmured, tasting her soup.

Cassandra's eyes flew to the clock. She couldn't afford to wait. She had to warn Silas and somehow set things right. But how?

She looked at Tessa. Dare she enlist Tessa's help?

A helicopter whooshed overhead, and Tessa followed it with a smile.

Shit. Kai and Hunter were both leaving the estate. And Silas, she was sure, would be furious if she involved them.

Of course, she might have to risk his wrath. The ends justified the means, right?

Her heart sank. Somehow, she knew Silas wouldn't agree. He'd never forgive her for that.

So, then what?

She mumbled an excuse and headed to the guesthouse, where she fumbled for her phone. She paced, looking at the ocean while she waited for the line to connect. The sweeping view showed two islands — Lanai and Molokai. The Big Island was out of sight, to the southeast.

"Come on. Answer, Silas."

The phone rang and rang while she paced and cursed.

"Answer, damn it. Please."

Chapter Eighteen

Silas stepped out of his rental SUV and slammed the door closed. When he turned in a slow circle, his combat boots crunched over loose chunks of lava. He wrinkled his nose at the pervasive scent of sulfur. Entire sections of coastline were steaming — even glowing — where lava emerged from underground and hit the sea. Fire and water, battling it out.

There was no one in sight, only a cluster of vehicles parked at the edge of the road. They were high-end rental vehicles, and all were well beyond the *Road Closed* sign half engulfed in lava. No tourist would come out this way, and locals didn't either. So what was going on?

He sniffed then frowned.

Drax.

He scanned the ridgeline ahead. He couldn't see his nemesis, but Drax was out there, all right. Silas could sense it.

The breeze shifted slightly, and his step faltered. Moira was there too.

Outwardly, he was perfectly still. His breath measured, his arms relaxed at his sides. But inside. . .

Damn it. He was a mess.

Tearing himself from Cassandra's side had been the hardest thing he had ever forced himself to do. Which was ridiculous. He'd headed into enemy fire against impossible odds in his army days — the kind of artillery fire that could mow down not just humans, but quick-healing shifters too. He'd faced countless deadly shifters in his time. At a young age, he'd dug his father's grave, fighting tears the whole time. He'd even watched Moira — the woman he thought he loved — leave him for his archnemesis.

But none of that was as hard to face as the simple act of slipping out of bed, gathering his clothes, and stepping out the guesthouse door. He might as well have stuck daggers in different corners of his heart as he went.

Mate, his dragon mourned. *Need my mate.*

Yes, he needed Cassandra. He loved her, desperately. But that was exactly why he'd had to leave — to protect her. To finish off Drax or die trying.

But if we die... his dragon started.

He stared into the distance. The only reward in dying would be knowing that Cassandra had a chance of survival. He'd seen the threat in Drax's eyes the previous night. His archenemy had sensed what Cassandra meant to him, and those evil eyes had lit up with glee at the prospect of stealing yet another treasure from Silas. The most precious treasure of all. His mate.

My true mate, his dragon breathed.

He nodded. *My true mate.*

Years ago, he'd believed Moira was his mate, but looking back, it was all so clear. He'd had to talk himself into loving Moira — the woman his parents had betrothed him to. Bit by bit, he'd come to inhabit the fiction he'd created. That Moira loved him and he loved her. That together, they could lead the dragon world into a new era of peace and prosperity.

He kicked the ground, then gazed out over the crashing waves.

Cassandra was the opposite in every way. He'd had to talk himself *out* of loving her. From day one, it had been a battle to resist her. A battle he had no hope of winning, because Cassandra was his destined mate. And as any of his brothers-in-arms would say now that they were happily mated, *You don't fuck with that.*

For a second, he was transported back to Koa Point in the morning. The palms had swayed quietly overhead. Waves whispered over the sand. Cassandra's chest rose and fell within his embrace.

Peace. Goodness. Tranquility. He'd had it all for one night.

Then he opened his eyes, and the image vanished, replaced by this desolate landscape. A deep breath brought him a lungful of rotten-egg smell, and he remembered where he was. The Big Island of Hawaii, where he would face Drax in a final battle to decide it all.

What were his chances? Less than fifty-fifty, at best.

Drax was older, wiser. A tick slower, perhaps, but more experienced, especially when it came to the art of devious warfare. Drax had risen to power by outmaneuvering, outthinking, and outsmarting every dragon who'd dared stand between him and utter domination of the shifter world. Most importantly, Drax had no honor code. That alone tipped the odds from fifty-fifty to...

Silas couldn't come up with a number. How did one quantify courage? Determination? The fury and frustration born of a lifetime of always being one step behind Drax?

If only he'd been born a few decades earlier. Drax had only won the upper hand through crafty maneuvering back when Silas was too young to defy him. Drax had capitalized on each victory, entrenching himself in an ever more secure position while stripping Silas of every advantage he could.

If we had been born earlier, we might have missed Cassandra, his dragon pointed out.

That made him smile, at least briefly. A bittersweet smile, because he'd always hoped to have his mate for more than one night. He wanted a lifetime of slow mornings and languid afternoons. A lifetime of joyous years that ticked by at a *My, where did the time go?* pace. Years filled with love and laughter. Maybe even kids.

He took a deep breath. That might not be his destiny, but at least he'd won a night with his mate. No one could take that from him.

Not even death.

He looked up at the ridgeline. If it was just Drax out there, Silas had a chance of success. But who knew? Drax had to have sensed the inexorable pull that had drawn Silas here, steering him to an exact place and time that was foggy to him until the moment he'd arrived. Drax would have known to be wary of such things. Even if he couldn't resist the mysterious pull, he might have been suspicious enough to bring backup forces with him.

And if he had, Silas's chances were essentially nil.

Not that he'd been foolish enough to leave Koa Point without a backup plan. This was his chance at defeating Drax one-on-one. But if he failed. . .

He flexed his fingers, feeling the push of dragon claws inside.

Failure isn't an option, his dragon growled.

Silas didn't comment. Pep-up slogans like that were all well and good, but in the end, they didn't decide battles. Neither did destiny; all she did was arrange chess pieces on the board and sit back to watch the game unfold. It all came down to preparation, split-second decisions, and sheer firepower.

So, yes. He might fail. Every good commander considered the possibility. That was why he had left detailed instructions for Kai in the form of an urgent message scheduled to ping in his cousin's inbox very soon. Too late for Kai to interfere with the fight on the Big Island, but enough time to prepare the shifters of Koa Point for the worst. Drax was capable of anything — like sending part of his private army on a surprise attack on Koa Point to obliterate the only other thing that Silas cared about.

His gut tightened. Koa Point meant everything to him. The place *and* the people. It was home, and they were family. A family Cassandra could easily be part of, if she agreed. So Drax was likely to strike there, even if it was just to gloat over Silas in the afterlife.

Then he corrected himself. Drax was *sure* to strike Koa Point because he was desperate for the Spirit Stones.

So Kai would be ready. Whether that meant rallying everyone to fight or hastily packing their most treasured belongings and fleeing would be a decision for Kai as the new leader of their band. Kai would find some way to build a new life for everyone.

No one wants a new life or a new place, his dragon complained. *Everyone likes what they have.*

176

They did now that they had found their mates. But they would have no choice if Drax won this fight.

Silas rolled his shoulders and forced himself to focus. The big picture was important in the planning stages, but on the battlefield, everything came down to the there and then.

His eyes roved over the harsh landscape. The *there* was up beyond that ridge. He could feel it as surely as he could feel the mysterious, almost magnetic force that had guided him to this remote place. The *then* was soon — very soon. The sun was sliding toward the western horizon, ready to turn the islands over to night.

So let's go, his dragon huffed. *Let's get this started.*

He shook his head. *Soon* didn't mean *instantly.* The ticking countdown in his head told him that. The strange thing was, he sensed two countdowns. One stemmed from the force that had drawn him to this final confrontation with Drax. The other ticked at a slightly slower pace as if trying to slow the first clock down, whispering, *Just a little longer.*

A little longer to what? he wanted to shout.

That message came from a foggy section of his mind that refused to reveal anything. It just tugged on him, slowing him down.

You need to buy time. Stretch every second out.

Buy time for what? The longer he waited, the more time Drax had to mobilize his army of mercenaries.

Somehow, though, Silas couldn't ignore that call, just as he hadn't been able to ignore the lure of his true mate. So he stood still as a statue for another five minutes, letting the wind whip his clothes as he went through his usual pre-battle routine. Clearing his mind, compartment by compartment. Piquing his senses, concentrating his power. His skin itched as dragon scales fought to emerge.

Just a little longer... Stretch every second out...

His dragon huffed and puffed, growing angrier by the second. Which was good, because an angry dragon was a powerful one. As long as his human mind played commander, his dragon could be his battering ram.

It's time, that first clock hissed. The one he didn't trust. *Get moving.*

That clock was armed with an irresistible force that pushed his legs into action. So he walked up the path to the ridgeline — but slowly. Cooperating yet subtly resisting at the same time.

Good. Just a little longer, said the clock that lay closer to his heart.

He picked his way over the uneven field of lava. *Pahoehoe* lava — the smooth kind that looked like waves frozen in time. Long, black ripples of it that looped this way and that, one section rolling over another. Once upon a time, that had been molten lava, glowing red hot.

Just like my eyes, his dragon hissed, ready to fight.

A steam vent hissed to his right, reminding him that molten lava still crept along underground. The sun inched lower, tinting the sky red and orange. Silas picked his way over a circuitous route, banking fractions of a second for whatever it was that seemed so important.

A raven cawed, and the sound echoed across the empty landscape.

Hurry up already, the pushy timepiece ordered.

He headed for a saddle in the ridgeline where he would have the clearest view of whatever lay ahead. Though, by now, he knew. He covered the remaining distance, stopped, and spoke casually.

"Drax."

Drax stepped into sight and sneered. "My dear young cousin."

Silas glared. Drax was a master of reinforcing their inequalities. They faced each other, nostrils flaring, fingers twitching, barely moving while their dragons readied themselves inside.

Kill him, Silas's dragon roared so loudly, he barely heard the whisper in his mind.

Buy time. You need more time.

"Finally, you're here," Drax continued, baiting him.

Finally, I get my chance to fight you one-on-one, Silas's dragon growled.

178

He looked around, searching for whatever tricks Drax had planned.

Drax snorted. "You didn't think I would come alone, did you?"

Silas had hoped Drax would come alone, but no, he hadn't counted on it. The question was how many bodyguards Drax had brought along.

"Why would I think you would fight honorably?" Silas spat.

Drax laughed. "Your father was always one for honor, tradition, and principle. A pity it killed him in the end."

"You killed him," Silas said, careful to keep his voice even. "Just like you killed Filimore."

Drax shrugged. "They had to go."

Silas's face blazed with heat, but he didn't say a word.

"My time, on the other hand, has come," Drax said. "Or should I say, our time?" He motioned to his left.

Silas followed the gesture then took a deep breath. "Moira."

Of course, she had come. She made her usual grand entrance, stepping out from behind a lava outcrop. Her arms moved slightly, making her red dress seem to float. Silas snorted, remembering how she used to practice that in front of a mirror. God, what had he ever seen in her?

The irony hit him. Everyone had warned him of witches' spells, but it was a dragon who had cast her spell over him back then. A spell that had shattered, leaving his heart in shards. In his mind, he saw a thousand splintered Moiras, all wearing the same crocodile smile.

"Silas. Darling," she cooed.

The first time he had met Moira a long, long time ago, he'd cringed at that nails-over-a-chalkboard voice. But duty was duty, and his parents were convinced Moira was a good match. So he'd trained himself to endure the sound. In fact, he'd even convinced himself he liked it. But now?

He winced.

"So good to see you again," Moira went on.

179

He kept his mouth firmly sealed. Let Moira put on her show. Every second that ticked by was a second in his favor, even if he couldn't put his finger on why that might be.

Moira was smiling, but he knew she would reveal her fangs if push came to shove. She wasn't one to engage in all-out aerial duels the way Tessa was learning to do, but she would shift to dragon form and clip him with carefully aimed bursts of fire to support Drax. Anything to be on the winning side.

Well, he'd be ready for that. He'd fight Drax but keep one eye on Moira.

Bet your ass, I will, his dragon murmured, borrowing a line from Cassandra.

Then something fluttered behind Moira, and his hopes sank. There, on a craggy ridge, stood six hunched shapes. Dragons. A quarter of a mile away, watching closely.

Drax grinned, looking at his mercenaries. His aces, so to speak. They might not join the battle immediately, but if Drax faltered, they would swoop in. Of course, they would back away at the bitter end, allowing Drax to pretend the ultimate victory was all his work.

It turned Silas's stomach, but what could he do? He would fight to the death, and fight honorably.

"You know how it is." Drax grinned. "You plan a nice little getaway for two, but you end up bringing the whole entourage."

No, Silas didn't know how that was.

Silas stood as still as the statue that would probably never be cast for him. Honor went unrewarded sometimes. Principle was a dull companion. Traditions had a way of fading into nothingness.

Not that he wanted a statue. All he wanted was his mate.

A steam vent blasted a plume of heated air to his right. Silas steeled himself, ready to let his inner dragon out. But footsteps hurried up behind him, making him spin.

Mate! My mate! his dragon cried at the sight of Cassandra stomping up with determined strides.

Silas could have cried too — really cried. The only reason he'd torn himself away from his mate that morning was to keep

180

her safe. Instead, he'd managed to draw her straight into the line of fire.

"Cassandra," he whispered.

She was unarmed, except for anger and whatever self-defense moves a New York bartender was bound to know. Which made her virtually defenseless against dragons.

The inner clock that had been urging him to slow down suddenly pinged as if the cavalry had just arrived and everything could proceed. What the hell was that all about? The situation had grown worse, not better.

Cassandra strode right up to him, glaring everyone down. Her brown hair tossed. Her eyes blazed.

She'd make a great dragon, his inner beast sighed.

That, she would, he agreed.

She stomped right up beside him, channeling brassy New York vibes as if someone had stolen the taxi she'd hailed or made her miss her subway or any of those other serious Manhattan crimes.

The next best thing to a real dragon. His dragon smiled.

Silas grinned too, but only briefly. *Next best* wasn't good enough, not when the enemy was Drax.

"Hi," Cassandra murmured a little breathlessly.

Her eyes had a certain gleam, and Silas wondered what the hell she could possibly have up her sleeve.

"Hi," he managed, wishing he had time to say much more.

Chapter Nineteen

Cassandra tried to keep her knees from shaking as she took in the desolate scene. Ash-colored lava covered everything in sight. Wisps of steam rose here and there. The air was stifling, as was the heat. A scene straight out of hell. Her heart swelled the second she'd spotted Silas, but moments later, it sank. She was too late. Drax stood behind him, and an entire squadron of dragons loomed on a rise.

A lure spell. God, it really had come to pass.

Just you wait and see... She could practically hear Eloise cackling in the background.

No, she wanted to scream. *I don't want to see. This can't be happening. Please, Eloise. Undo this mess.*

Nothing but silence greeted her ears, and she gulped. It was up to her now.

"What are you doing here?" Silas said, searching her eyes.

His clothes matched his grim expression. For the first time she'd ever witnessed, Silas wasn't wearing formal, tailored clothes. Instead, it looked as if he'd raided Boone's closet for a pair of camo pants and a plain black T-shirt. The military commander she'd always sensed in him was suddenly front and center. A man who led from the front and sacrificed himself for his men.

A man she could fall in love with all over again.

"Um... I was in the neighborhood?"

Which was only half a lie. Her mind spun over the past few hours. She had rushed to the airport on Maui without telling anyone, booked the last available seat on the next flight to the Big Island, and drove her rental car to Bernadette's address.

Bernadette was her father's stepsister, the only member of that branch of the family Cassandra had stayed in touch with.

If you must, Eloise had warned, *leave the Spirit Stone with a person no one would ever expect.* She'd even joked, *Like that no-good father of yours.*

So, no, Cassandra hadn't sent the diamond to her father. She wouldn't know where to find him anyway. But her father's stepsister, yes. Bernadette was the sweetest, least witchy person she'd ever met, and her address was the only one Cassandra could recall that petrifying evening of the auction, so she'd scribbled the lines quickly and thrown the package into a mailbox as she fled the auction house.

Bernadette Bernow, 17 Sunset Drive, Pahala, Hawaii, 96777.

Easy street address, easy zip code. It had always stuck in her mind, and Bernadette wasn't the type to open a box marked, *Please hold for me.*

"But you just got here!" her shocked aunt had said less than an hour ago.

Cassandra had barely stopped for a quick hug before grabbing the package and rushing off again, promising to explain later.

She gulped, looking at the dragons. Would there be a later or would she die here?

She'd come on the hope of a best-case scenario — that the lure spell hadn't worked and all her fears were unfounded. Drax would be nowhere in sight, and she and Silas could take the diamond back to Koa Point and talk things through.

The more likely scenario, she'd known, was encountering Silas and Drax. But the Windstone was purported to have incredible powers, so ideally, she would be able to use it — somehow — to help Silas. If only the jewel had come with a set of instructions. . .

Worst-case scenario? She'd be delivering the Spirit Stone directly into the hands of the cruelest dragon lord of all.

Drax grinned at her, showing the points of his teeth.

"Cassandra," Silas whispered. "What are you doing here?"

What are you really *doing here?* his tone asked.

When she locked eyes with him, a little bit of courage crept back into her. She could have said any of a dozen things. *I was wrong about all dragons being evil.* Or, *I love you.* Maybe even, *I need you.*

But she settled for, "I'm here to help a stubborn dragon."

One corner of his mouth curved up while the other remained firmly down. "Stubborn? I suppose that makes two of us."

"I suppose it does."

The air between their bodies stirred, coaxing them to step closer and touch.

Mate, she thought to herself. *He really is my mate.*

Silas took a deep breath, and his lips moved a few times. "For the record, I love you."

She stuck her hands on her hips. "For the record? Silas — seriously?"

The right corner of his mouth crooked up. "Seriously. I wish I could follow you to the end of my days."

Her cheeks heated. Hell, her whole body heated. "For the record, I love you too."

"Aren't they adorable," Moira muttered.

Cassandra ignored her and leaned closer, faking bravado. "And about that following to the end of your days part — no one says they're over yet."

"I do," Drax boomed.

Oh, shut up, she wanted to say. But Drax wasn't a loud-mouth customer at her bar. He was a dragon, and this was it.

She looked around and took a deep breath. Silas hadn't protested the *help* part. Clearly, he needed backup — badly. But, shit. What was she going to do against six dragons?

She fingered the diamond in her pocket and steeled her nerves. *Okay, diamond. You'd better have the power they say you do.*

She nearly yelped when the jewel warmed under her hand.

Silas tilted his head at her, but before he could ask, Moira's shrill voice turned every head.

"Isn't that precious? She thinks she can stop us."

185

Actually, Cassandra wanted to snort. *I kind of doubt I can. But I'm here because I love my man. My man, you got that?*

The way Moira's hungry eyes roved over Silas hinted that whatever had once passed between them wasn't entirely extinguished, at least in Moira's heart — if she had one.

"Shut it, Moira," Cassandra barked.

Silas's eyes blazed. Ever the noble warrior, he took one step forward, shielding Cassandra with his body. But she wasn't one to shrink back, so she stepped firmly to his side. If they were going to survive this, they'd do so together.

Drax let loose a peal of laughter. "Now don't you wish you had let me buy that diamond at the auction?"

"You're the one wishing," she snapped.

In truth, her first reaction was *yes, that would have been nice.* She would have been three million dollars richer and ignorant of the archaic world of dragon shifters. But, no. She wouldn't go back in time if she could. She never would have gotten close to Silas if she had let the diamond go, and she would have failed in the mission assigned to her.

You must keep the Windstone out of the hands of dragons. Kill if need be.

Eloise had been wrong about a lot of things, but Cassandra agreed with the core message. Keep the Windstone away from Drax, and kill evil dragons if need be. The question was, how?

Her thigh heated, and she placed her hand over her pocket, keeping the motion slow and subtle. If the dragons realized she had the diamond with her...

"You will never have it," Silas declared.

"Oh, but I will. It's here on the Big Island, isn't it?" Drax crowed. "It's only a matter of time before I track it down and claim what is mine." His eyes glowed an eerie pinkish-orange.

Mine. Moira's lips formed the word, though she didn't speak aloud.

Cassandra looked between Moira and Drax. Something told her it was only a matter of time before Moira claimed the diamond for herself. And maybe more than the diamond. Was she after Drax's empire?

Another steam vent huffed loudly, reminding Cassandra she had more immediate problems than that.

"You won't be tracking anything, Drax. It all ends here," Silas said, looking every inch the warrior. He held his arms out from his sides, ready for action, and his feet braced wide. Uncompromising. Determined.

"No, it starts here," Drax shot back. "A new phase in my illustrious career. New properties. New powers. New horizons."

Cassandra shuddered to imagine what that meant — not only for the shifters of Koa Point, but everywhere.

"Yes, I think I can make myself quite comfortable on that estate you've been taking care of for me," Drax said. Then he looked right at Cassandra and licked his lips. "To the winner go the spoils."

Cassandra's stomach turned. What did Drax mean by that?

Silas growled, and his fingers flexed. He pushed Cassandra gently from his side — a subtle cue that he was preparing to shift into dragon form?

"To the winner go the spoils," Silas echoed.

Drax hunched his shoulders and bared his teeth. Moira looked on, practically rubbing her hands.

"The winner? That would be me," Drax grunted in a voice that grew deeper with every word. His eyes started to glow a greedy green.

Cassandra looked on dumbly, then stumbled when Silas nudged her back.

Run, his expression said. *Run while you can. Hide.*

Like hell, she'd run or hide. She slipped her hand into her pocket and closed it around the diamond.

A sea breeze had been blowing steadily, pushing wisps of hair over her face. But the second she touched the diamond, the wind direction reversed. She lifted her face, and the wind pushed her hair back behind her ears.

So the Windstone did have some power. The question was, how to harness it?

A powerful witch can control almost anything, Eloise had once declared.

Great. Cassandra couldn't summon a single spell. She was totally out of her league.

Just fake it, her first bartending mentor, Louanne, had always said. *Whatever you do, never show weakness.*

Of course, Louanne had meant customers in a bar, not diamonds with magical powers.

She ran her fingers over the diamond's hard edges and reached out with her mind. *Are you really as powerful as they say?*

The wind shifted again, and even Drax looked around, furrowing his brow.

She turned the jewel over in her pocket.

Okay, then. Here's the plan. You help me, I help you.

The wind flickered, tossing her hair. Was that a yes or a no?

You have to keep your inner beast on a tight leash, she'd overheard Kai coaching Tessa. *Make sure it knows you're in charge.*

Cassandra gulped. Did that apply to Spirit Stones, or was she playing with fire?

She made a split-second decision and gripped the Windstone harder, eying the nearest steam vent. *But if you fuck with me...*

The jewel burned in her hand, but she clutched it harder. *I am in charge here, you got that?*

She nearly yelped from the burst of heat, but hung on as she sidestepped to a crack in the earth where flowing lava glowed a menacing red.

Witches gave you power. Witches can destroy you, she grunted in her mind. *So play along, all right?*

The wind whispered in her ear, carrying the echo of an earthy voice. *Oh, I'll play, all right.*

Cassandra wasn't sure how to interpret that, but she was out of time. Silas was stepping toward Drax, growing taller by the second and yelling something that came out half roar.

"It ends here," Silas boomed, raising his arms wide.

Cassandra stared then ducked as all hell broke loose.

Chapter Twenty

One second, Cassandra was standing still, holding her breath. The next, she was tumbling head over heels, shoved by a mighty force. A roar broke out in front of her, and she stared at a long line of scorched earth.

"Watch out!" Silas shouted.

She rolled aside, barely avoiding Drax's second plume of fire. Lava bit into her palms and knees, and another roar thundered out. She looked up just in time to see Silas's shirt split down the back. The air around him shimmered, and then—

Her jaw hung open. "Silas?"

It was one thing to know that he could shift into a dragon, but another thing to witness him transform. Back in New York, she'd only caught a glimpse of his dragon body. But now that she had come to know Silas – to spend time with him, and even to make love to him – she couldn't quite believe the creature that rose before her eyes. A huge black dragon — black with a subtle undertone of red — who spread his wings wide and roared.

She dashed aside as Silas and Drax rose from the ground with mighty beats of their massive wings. The force was so great, she nearly fell again. In the distance, an excited, keening cry went out. The other dragons were cheering Drax on.

"Wow. Silas," she breathed, marveling at Silas's new size and shape. His hide had a soft, leathery sheen, and the last bit of daylight glittered off his belly scales.

She blinked. Scales. Holy shit. The hard abs she'd run a finger across last night were covered in dragon scales.

Silas chased Drax higher and higher. The streams of fire they spat at each other during the rushed ascent were terrifying enough, but the firepower increased when they leveled out and flew at each other.

Cassandra ducked, covering her head. The flames Drax aimed at Silas were thirty feet long, and they took on a life of their own, chasing their enemy through the sky in angry bursts of orange, yellow, and red. Silas barely avoided Drax's first volley by darting right with a flick of his long tail.

Cassandra stared, taking in that tail.

"Get him, Drax," Moira shouted from somewhere to the right.

Cassandra glared, reminding herself there was more to this fight than just two dragons. She had Moira to contend with, not to mention the six beasts lined up on the ridge. One after another took flight, hurtling through the air toward the two dueling dragons. How would Silas ever overcome those odds?

Her thigh heated, and she dug deep into her pocket and drew out the Spirit Stone, letting her eyes dart between the dragons and the gem. The flames overhead reflected in each of the diamond's facets, mirroring the lethal forces overhead.

"Okay. Okay..." she muttered, trying to get herself together.

She forced in a couple of deep, slow breaths. This had been her plan all along, right? Or at least as much of a plan as she'd thrown together in the past few hours.

Get the Windstone. Use it to stop the dragon fight. Defeat Drax.

She grimaced. That was all much easier said than done. She'd also been secretly hoping to have learned enough magic to apply, but, hell. That hadn't proven to be the case.

She looked into the heart of the gem, where tiny flames flickered and tossed. Then she hunched over the diamond, drawn in by what she saw. Those flames weren't just reflections. The diamond heated in her hand, fueled by its own inner force.

I have power, the stone whispered. Faintly, then louder. *I have incredible power, and you shall christen the victor of your choice.*

She raised the diamond toward the sky, waiting for it to explain what to do. Which it would, right? The bits of Spirit

Stone lore she'd picked up suggested the jewels had a way of communicating with their bearers.

She bit her lip. Those bearers always seemed to be amazing, courageous women selected by fate. She was just her.

For a split second, her knees wobbled, and she felt sick. But then she stuck up her chin, resolute. Okay, so witchcraft was not going to help her. So what did that leave her with, other than a powerful gem she was afraid to unleash?

She took stock. She had stubbornness. A firm voice that could cut across a noisy bar. A killer stare that could quiet the most unruly customer on a Friday night. Surely she could do this.

You just have to believe.

Eloise had meant magic, but oh well. That also applied to believing in yourself, right?

"Help me," she muttered at the stone. "Damn it. Help me."

Overhead, Drax aimed another burst of flame at Silas, who spun in midair and returned the volley.

Cassandra could feel energy coursing through her body the same way the sea breeze built to a steady wind that tossed and tangled her hair. The diamond glowed white, and she felt alive with power. Almost giddy with it. Her mouth broke open, and she let out a spiteful laugh, very much like Eloise used to do.

Drax would never know what hit him. Moira wouldn't either.

Yes, the Windstone whispered, glowing brighter. *Unleash my power.*

Cassandra drew her arm back, ready to thrust it forward and release the power. But an echo of her own laugh sounded in her mind, and she stopped cold.

Whoa. Who was the vengeful bitch now?

She considered a moment longer. Unleashing the Spirit Stone's power was one thing. Hauling it back under control might be another. Was she opening a Pandora's box?

Her hopes sank. Using the Windstone would also defy everything Silas stood for. It was an ace up her sleeve, a punch below the belt. An unfair advantage.

She lowered her arm, trembling. If she used the Windstone, she would be no better than Drax. If she didn't use it, Silas had no chance of surviving the raging dragon fight.

"Silas," she whispered as a tear rolled down her cheek. What should she do?

Drax's backup troops flew in a wide arc, circling the dueling dragons. Cassandra circled too, turning slowly, watching the fight unfold. She might as well have witnessed two gladiators in an arena — but this arena was high in the sky, and the spectators were a ring of dragons who cheered at each burst of fire.

Silas opened his wings wide and bellowed, releasing a huge flame. Drax twisted and returned fire. Silas immediately rolled, plunged twenty feet, then rocketed upward again, shooting a continuous line of fire at Drax's belly. When Drax beat a hasty retreat, bellowing in pain, Silas pressed on, driving him back.

The other dragons watched too, and Cassandra's hopes began to rise. Maybe they wouldn't interfere. Maybe, like Silas, they knew that honor lay in a fair fight.

But just when Silas was at his maximum advantage and Drax in full retreat, two of the surrounding dragons came screaming down at Silas, one from each side. They each spat fire, and the flames overlapped in a flaming X, forcing Silas to dive. He spun as he plunged toward the ground like a biplane with its engine out.

Cassandra's heart jumped into her throat. "Silas!"

At the last possible second, he flicked his wings open and rocketed upward, more furious than ever.

Cassandra stared, caught between wanting to hug Silas and to yell at him for scaring her to death. Fascinated too. His anger was a raging river that had burst every dam, and her caring lover had become a fighting machine.

Silas zoomed after one of the two dragons, roaring in disgust. Orange flames engulfed the fleeing beast, and a scream pierced the air. The dragon flapped in panic then hurtled to the ground. When he hit, the earth shuddered, and Cassandra did too.

"Cassandra!"

Silas's roar had just enough of a human edge to it for her to understand, and she jerked her head up — then dove just in time to avoid the grappling claws of an oncoming dragon. Huge talons scratched at the air, barely missing her. Her ears popped from the sudden change in air pressure. She'd only barely scrambled to her feet when another dragon whooshed overhead, and she hit the deck again.

"Silas," she murmured in relief. That was him, chasing her attacker away.

She jumped to her feet and ran, jumping over a glowing crevasse.

Don't look down. Don't look down, she ordered herself.

Of course, she did look, and her heart nearly stopped. The gap was only three feet across, but under her was free-flowing, molten lava. When she landed, the earth shuddered, and she yelped. Holy crap. She wasn't standing on firm ground. She was standing — no, leaping — over a thin crust. Beneath that was red-hot lava that peeked out between slabs of cooled rock.

She sprinted onward, trying not to tread heavily. In the life she was used to, a place like this would be cordoned off and signposted with a dozen signs that said, *Danger! Keep away!*

But, hell. She'd long since entered the realm of shifters, who operated by a different set of rules. Rules that mirrored the harsh laws of nature: dog eat dog. Eat or be eaten. Survival of the fittest.

"Get him!" Moira shouted from Cassandra's right.

Cassandra looked over, alarmed to see Moira closer than before. Her red dress billowed in the wind, and her face glowed with excitement. *Excitement,* as if the scene above were a game and not a battle for life or death.

Silas climbed back to high altitude, immediately reengaging Drax. The other dragons backed away, letting the fight proceed. Their eyes glinted, and each wore a knowing smirk as they observed the fight. Every time Drax faltered, a pair of his henchmen would sweep in, attacking Silas until he had no choice but to break away and engage them instead. Cassandra's cheeks burned as anger built inside her. She had to use the diamond. If Drax could fight dirty, so could she. What choice did she have?

Silas will hate me for this, part of her mind screamed. *I'll betray his trust.*

There's no other way, another part yelled.

She turned in a slow circle, watching the fight rage on overhead. Slowly, she lifted the diamond and looked upward through it.

Release my power, the Windstone urged. *Release it now.*

"Silas..." she cried, holding on to the last S, drawing out his name in a plea. What should she do?

The air around her stirred as if she'd blown hard, and an image formed in her mind. An image of the candle by her bedside the previous night, flickering then extinguishing when she blew at it. Little tendrils of smoke had swirled in the breeze for a while, revealing the motion of the air.

The cigar smoke Drax had puffed at her at the gala was similar. She'd blown it right back at Moira, and man, had it been satisfying to watch the smoke churn near their faces.

She blinked. If one little puff could stir the air around her, then a big puff...

She looked up, wondering if she were crazy even to consider such a thing.

Yes, the Windstone whispered. *Release me.*

Cassandra sucked in a long breath the way she would for a deep dive. Then she exhaled, pushing all that air back out. A whoosh of wind blew out of nowhere, sending a dust cloud across the barren landscape.

The ends of her hair were dragged forward, and the diamond glittered in her hand.

She stared then tried it again. One little puff, then another, growing bolder each time. Each of her breaths unleashed a burst of wind that took on its own life, eager to attack anything in its path.

"That way. I want you to go that way," she said as bushes bent and ashes scattered.

I'll go anywhere I want, a contralto growled in her head.

She shook her head furiously. "You go where I want, or I don't lend you my breath. Got it?"

An angry hum sounded in her head, and she wondered what that meant. Was she nuts to defy that mysterious power, or could she truly harness it? Apparently, the Spirit Stone depended on her to initiate each blast of air, so if she played her cards right...

A yellowish-brown dragon shot through the periphery of her vision, and without thinking, Cassandra brought the diamond to her lips and blew. Hard.

The wind howled, and a split second later, the yellow-brown dragon lurched as if hit by an invisible arrow. He tumbled head over heels before pitching to one side and flying off like a drunk.

Kill them. Kill them all, the voice in her head snarled.

The diamond glowed a terrifying white in her hand. The gem seemed just as greedy as Drax, ready to blast anything in its path, and she struggled to rein it in.

"Just the bad guys, damn it."

The stone flared. *I choose who and what I destroy.*

She squeezed her hand in a choking motion. "I choose who and what you destroy. And if you don't cooperate..." She motioned toward a steam vent.

It was terrifying and exhilarating at the same time — grappling with a force far more powerful than herself. A force that pushed at her like an internal wind, threatening to blow her soul away.

Cassandra gritted her teeth and shook her head, using every ounce of determination she had. "You will not interfere with those two, got it? Just the other dragons."

The diamond growled its displeasure, but she refused to relent. It was Silas's right to battle one-on-one, fair and square. All she would do was assure a fair fight.

She focused on the five remaining dragons that circled Silas and Drax. One extended its long neck and dive-bombed at her.

"There. That's the enemy. You got it?" she screamed at the stone.

The gem warmed in her hand and yelled, *Now!*

She fought the urge off until the dragon was even closer. Closer...

Release my power before we are both destroyed! the Spirit Stone screamed.

"I decide. You wait," she boomed.

The light coming from the diamond dimmed as if in surprise.

She gritted her teeth and waited until the dragon opened his mouth.

"Watch out, asshole," she murmured, releasing another heavy puff of air.

Now, she barked in her mind.

The diamond flared as another windstorm erupted from her hand, knocking the dragon sideways. The beast rose, seeking escape, but she followed it with the diamond, keeping up the pressure until the dragon careened downward, flapping wildly.

Boom! The creature crashed into the ground.

Cassandra scurried backward as the dragon plowed along the landscape, barely keeping out of its way. When it stopped at last, the beast's eyes glowed brighter, then dimmed. She let out a breath. Jesus, she'd have to be more careful next time.

More, the Spirit Stone cried. *Give me more.*

It was terrifying to feel that thirst for power, that desire for destruction. And even more terrifying was imagining it in Drax's hands.

So do as I say, silly human, the voice scoffed.

Cassandra bared her teeth and snarled a reply. "No, you do as I say. Now be quiet and let me think."

A ponderous silence filled her ears, and she gave herself a satisfied — if wary — nod. "Two down, four to go."

She turned in place, watching Drax's dragons wheel overhead. Two had huddled closer and were spitting daggers at her. Would they attack next? She frowned. Picking them off with hurricane-force winds might work when they didn't expect it. But if the next attacker dodged her, she was toast — literally.

The ground underfoot crunched as she turned in a slow circle, desperate for a new tactic.

Turn. Keep turning, the Windstone whispered.

She did, keeping the gem raised, exaggerating the motion with every turn. Every time she exhaled, the wind howled. She traced an arc across the sky, building a circular shape, and kept blowing with brief gasps for fresh air.

Yes. Like that, the Windstone said.

Her eyes went wide as its tactic became clear. She was setting up a wall of wind, a perimeter the lesser dragons couldn't cross. But, yikes. Did she have it in her to maintain that barrier?

Just keep blowing, the Windstone urged her.

She'd heard somewhere that dolphins used a similar tactic to trap schools of fish. They would circle beneath the fish, sending up a wall of bubbles the fish wouldn't cross.

With one important difference, of course. Instead of trapping the dragons inside her circle of wind, she would trap them outside, leaving Silas a clear area for his fight with Drax.

She turned and turned, keeping up the wind. Letting it build and take on a life of its own. The air churned as a whirling storm cloud formed overhead.

Perfect, the Windstone hummed.

Silas darted toward Drax, launching a fresh attack, and one of the outlying dragons flew to his master's defense. But the moment it entered the swirling wall of wind, the beast jerked from side to side like a plane in turbulent air. With a frustrated roar, the dragon twisted away and shot a frustrated flame into the deepening night sky.

The remaining dragons each took a turn at trying to sneak through the wall of wind, but it was a boundary that wouldn't be breached. It was exhausting, but she steeled herself to keep it up as long as necessary. Silas was fighting just as fiercely, and it was up to her to cover his back.

Every time Cassandra turned, she glanced toward the outcrop where Moira was perched, yelling at the top of her lungs. But Moira's cries were drowned out by the boom of the dragon fight and the crackle of thirty-foot flames.

Cassandra kept turning. One of Drax's henchmen crossed her line of sight, and she pushed her upper body forward in a sudden spurt of breath. That translated to a punch of air that sent the dragon careening into the flight path of his comrade. Their wings clipped, and they broke apart. One flapped wildly, drawing clear, but the other swirled in the windstorm then dashed to the ground.

Boom! Another deadly impact vibrated through the ground. Another enemy down. And, shit — another fissure opened in the raw ground, exposing the glowing lava beneath.

Cassandra flailed her arms as the brittle lava gave way. She had no choice but to leap backward, hoping to get clear. She landed, first on her feet, then on her butt, blinking at the river of molten lava that had appeared where she had been standing a moment before. She scuttled backward, cutting her palms as more and more of the slope gave way. Finally, she reached what felt like firmer ground, and she looked around uncertainly.

Clumsy thing, the Spirit Stone sniffed.

"I'll show you clumsy," she muttered, jerking her hand toward the glowing lava.

That shut the gem up, all right. Cassandra scowled. If she survived this experience, she would write her own manual of handling Spirit Stones — or at least, this finicky one.

Rule number one, she mentally dictated. *Show it who's boss.*

But it was hard to feel like the boss when the ground crumbled around her feet and her knees shook.

"Over there!" a deep dragon voice cried.

Wait. Had she heard that, or was the voice in her mind?

She spun and exhaled fast, countering a smaller green dragon that hurtled toward her with his mouth wide, about to exhale. And, shit. Those bastards spat fire, not wind.

She barely got her own huff out in time, stoking the Windstone. The dragon was blasted backward, dragging along the earth. A hissing sound exploded, and an entire section of earth gave way.

"Oh!" She threw her hands out for balance and backed up.

The dragon flapped his wings wildly, but it was too late. He fell into the magma, and after one last, tortured bellow, went still.

Cassandra looked away with a mortified gulp. Four down, two to go.

"Cassandra!" The sound was a garbled roar, but somehow, she understood it perfectly. Silas was warning her.

She stood quickly, rebuilding the wall of wind that had petered out. The other dragons screamed, shut out from the fight again.

And for a while, it worked. Cassandra kept up the exhausting task of maintaining that wall of wind, glancing down at her footing, then looking up again, guiding the wind around and around. But it was only a matter of time before she collapsed from the effort, and what then?

"Look out!" Silas roared.

She whirled just in time to see Moira rush at her from behind.

Cassandra thrust up her hands in defense, but she was too late to react other than with a scream.

"No!"

Chapter Twenty-One

Moira wasn't a big woman, but she sure as hell could body slam. Cassandra crashed sideways, smashing her shoulder into the ground.

"It's mine!" Moira screamed, reaching out with one hand.

Cassandra reached too, because the diamond had flown out of her grip. The instant it did, the wind died away. She watched in horror as the gem arced through the air. White light blazed in the darkening sky, heading directly for a crack in the earth — a crack that grew wider by the second.

"You fool!" Moira screamed.

Cassandra rolled clear of Moira as the earth rumbled and shook. The rock underfoot gave way, and she plummeted toward a freshly exposed river of lava. Heat rushed up at her as yet another section of rock gave out, and her skin scraped along the sawtooth edge.

"No!" Cassandra cried, clawing for a grip.

More rock crumbled, and she screamed as the outer crust gave way like too-thin ice. Then she was hanging by her fingertips, kicking in thin air. Her feet swung over a glowing river of fire.

Oh God. This was it. She was going to die.

As she flailed and held on for dear life, a flash of white light led her eyes to the diamond. It had bounced off a rock and balanced – barely – on an outcrop of smooth lava tipped perilously toward the river of fire.

"It's mine!" Moira screamed.

Cassandra hung on, praying the ledge wouldn't give. Moira was across the chasm of lava that had opened up. Any minute now, she expected the she-dragon to shift, take flight, and whisk the diamond away.

But Moira, it seemed, preferred to let Drax do her dirty work, because she just hollered. "Get it! Get it!"

Cassandra looked up, wondering if she could possibly haul herself up. A whistling sound rushed at her from above, and she yelped.

"Hang on!" Silas roared, plunging toward her with wide, alarmed eyes.

If she could have hung by one hand and gestured with the other, she would have. "Get the diamond, not me."

Whatever possessed her to say that, she wasn't sure. Because she *really* wanted to live. But Drax was hurtling toward the diamond, and if he got to it first. . .

Her finger slipped, and she gasped, throwing her left hand forward in a desperate attempt to hang on. A screeching sound filled her ears.

"Cassandra!"

A black dragon with glowing red eyes dove toward her with outstretched claws. Claws shaped like scimitars that could tear through her shoulder in one effortless snip. She squeezed her eyes shut.

The claws didn't pierce her skin, though. One closed over her right arm without injuring her at all. Her eyes flew open, and for a second, she felt relief. That was Silas holding her tight.

Then she was jerked into the air, and she screamed. Her arm felt as though it had been torn from its socket. For a minute, she couldn't tell up from down. Only that she was flying, flying. . .

Hold on, Silas's voice boomed in her mind. *I've got you.*

Her heart pounded in triple time. Silas had her. A plus and a minus, because holy shit, she was suspended high above the ground, airborne.

Then she did a double take. Wait a second. Had she really heard Silas's voice in her mind?

A dark shadow raced under her — a dragon barreling toward the ground.

"Silas! Look!" she screamed.

That was Drax, extending his claws to grab at the diamond like an eagle plucking a fish from a stream.

But Silas didn't care about the diamond, it seemed. He glided onward, ducking his head to look at her. And though it was terrifying, her heart warmed. If she had any doubts about Silas's priorities, they were all dispelled now.

"Get ready," he murmured in a soft undertone.

An image formed in her mind, and her feet moved in the air just in time for Silas to set her down. She ran a few steps and tripped over to all fours but, whew. She was safe, back on firm ground.

Silas landed beside her and clawed at the rough ground, looking at her. Desperate to check that she was all right. She stared.

"Wait. You chose me over the Spirit Stone?"

His eyes swirled. *Of course I did.*

"Are you crazy?"

He smiled a huge, toothy, dragon smile that ought to have been terrifying. Instead, it melted her heart.

She stood motionless for a second, then gestured upward. "Well, get going already."

Silas's eyes turned back to a murderous hue as he took off with a mighty leap.

Cassandra ducked, covering her head from the powerful backwash. Silas beat his wings, taking up the chase. When she straightened again, she spotted Drax's henchmen spiraling overhead. Anger overtook her, and she gestured at them in a frustrated motion.

And, whoa. They cringed and backed away.

Cassandra stared, then gestured again — and again, the dragons skittered away.

She broke into a grin, then promptly hid it. Apparently, the dragons thought she still had the Windstone. And as long as they did. . .

She kept her fist closed, hiding the fact that her hand was empty. The wind was no longer forming a blockade against

205

the dragons, but their wary looks told her they expected the worst.

She glared at them, bluffing wildly.

Drax, meanwhile, rose higher and higher, heading for the center of the island. Silas rushed after him, shooting a long plume of fire until Drax had no choice but to circle back. Silas soared right on his heels, punishing Drax with blast after blast of unrelenting fire.

Cassandra spun around. Where had Moira gone? She couldn't spot the silk dress anywhere in the black landscape.

Then a thunderous explosion sounded overhead, making her look up. Silas emitted one last determined blast of fire that caught a startled Drax full on. Drax screamed and dropped the diamond.

"No!" she screamed, watching it go.

Both dragons plummeted toward the earth — Silas racing after the diamond, and Drax with his wings on fire. Drax plunged toward the river of the magma, screaming. Silas pulled up at the last possible second, but Drax...

A hiss filled the air, along with a sickening singeing odor. Drax's tortured scream echoed over the lunar landscape as the magma swallowed him up. The diamond pinged against rock, as clear a sound as that of a spoon against a champagne glass, then came to rest on a smooth, rocky outcrop.

Cassandra sprinted toward the gem because Moira was sprinting too. Not quite as fast, maybe, in that fancy red gown of hers, but she had less distance to cover. Moira's eyes shone as she ran, screaming like a banshee.

"It's mine!"

Cassandra launched herself at the diamond like a linebacker making a tackle — the kind she'd seen so often in Tony's Bar, captured in slow motion and replayed dozens of times.

She skidded, scraping every inch of exposed skin. Lucky, it was *pahoehoe* lava and not the razor-sharp, *aa* kind. She strained for the diamond, stretching as far as she could. Her fingers closed around the hard edges, and she mentally cheered. She had it!

A heartbeat later, Moira's foot slammed over her hand, and she screamed. A whoosh of air followed, drowning that sound out. Through her tears of pain, Cassandra saw Silas land not twenty feet away. His mouth opened, and his eyes flashed.

"Moira," he said in a deep, menacing tone. "Release it. Now."

Cassandra lay still, grimacing as Moira crushed her hand. All Moira had to do was shift into dragon form, and the foot holding down Cassandra's hand would turn into a claw that would scissor her flesh to bits.

"Silas," Moira cooed as if they were on the red carpet of the gala dinner and not at the edge of a volcano at night. "We have it. We've succeeded. It's ours!"

Cassandra gaped. What the hell?

Silas appeared equally taken aback. He took a step forward, folding his wings slowly, and assumed a less ferocious impression. The air around him wavered, and he stooped. The scales of his chest shimmered, then blurred as he transformed into human form.

"Moira. . . " he murmured the way a person might address someone about to jump from the top of a building.

"Silas, you haven't changed a bit," Moira hummed, checking out every inch of his naked flesh.

Cassandra seethed.

"The Windstone," Silas said.

"Yes — it's ours!" Moira made a grand gesture with one arm. "Can't you see?"

See what? Cassandra wanted to scream.

"You and me," Moira went on, speaking as if Cassandra weren't pinned awkwardly under her foot. "Everything that was Drax's can be yours. It can be ours. And together—"

"Together?" Silas thundered. "What are you talking about?"

"You and I are meant for each other." Moira smiled. "Together, we will build a great future. You and I as king and queen, the most powerful dragons of all time."

207

Cassandra tensed. What if Silas wasn't over Moira? What if he cast her — a third-rate witch — aside at the prospect of a reunion with his old flame?

He still loves me, Moira had taunted in New York. *You'll see.*

Cassandra's stomach turned over. Could it really be true?

"You left me," Silas sputtered.

"I was confused," Moira sniffed, pushing down with her foot.

Cassandra bit her lip, determined not to squeal in pain.

"You weren't confused." Silas growled. "You were perfectly clear when you left me for Drax." His tone rose, mimicking her voice. "You said, 'Why do I need you when Drax is where the future lies?'"

"But, Silas," Moira pleaded. "We were young. I didn't know how good we had it. But I know now. It's about you and me."

Silas snorted. "It's about you and power. It always was, Moira. It always will be."

Moira rocked back slightly, giving Cassandra just enough space to flex her aching fingers. She extended her index finger, rolling the diamond closer. If she could get her hand around it...

"Of course, it's about power." Moira laughed. "What did you think? That it's about love? Love is power. Power is love. And I have it."

It was terrifying, listening to the crazed woman's words. And terrifying because as much as Cassandra believed in Silas, she still couldn't be sure. Moira had entranced him once, a long time ago. There was no denying her beauty, her allure. What if Silas fell for her again?

"Moira. . . " He held out his arm, palm up, and spoke gently. So gently, another tear slipped from Cassandra's eyes. Oh God. He was falling for Moira.

Moira stretched her arm and smiled. "I always knew we were meant for each other."

Cassandra felt sick, but she had just enough presence of mind to register the shift of Moira's weight. The instant

Moira stepped toward Silas, Cassandra gasped and rolled clear, clutching the diamond.

"You and me. We'll have it all," Moira said, reaching for Silas's hand.

Cassandra felt nauseous. She had the Windstone, but so what? She didn't want a diamond. She wanted love. Life. A new start.

Silas's eyes were locked on Moira's, and they glowed. For a brief instant, they flicked to Cassandra's. The light and the color changed to an intense red, making her hopes rise. Then they flicked back to Moira and dulled again.

Cassandra's heart leapt to her throat. Wait. Was Silas still on her side?

Cassandra took a step back, a safe distance from Moira. The next time Silas's eyes darted her way, he gave a small, satisfied nod. The hand he'd extended toward Moira dropped to his side, and his deep voice grew bitter.

"There is no *us*, Moira. There never will be."

And with that, he brushed right by her, stepping toward Cassandra with open arms.

The battle had been won. His battle. Her battle. Her heart pounded in her chest as Silas came closer.

Moira's eyes glowed as she glared at Silas's back. She raised her hand, and—

"Watch out," Silas yelled, darting for Cassandra.

Moira was shifting into dragon form — fast. Her neck extended, and her arms stretched into wings. Her dress shredded, and the scraps danced away, splashes of red in an otherwise black landscape. An instant later, Moira boomed in a deep, smoky contralto.

"I said, it is mine. You are mine."

Silas threw his hand up, but Cassandra could see he would be too late. Moira was already winding up for a huge blast of fire.

But Cassandra was quicker. She thrust her arm up and blew hard, letting her breath wash over the Windstone.

Yes! Kill! the stone cried.

209

Storm-force winds howled out of nowhere. The power thrust Cassandra forward, nearly pulling her off her feet. The wind caught in Moira's open wings and shoved her toward the gaping river of magma.

"No," Cassandra found herself whispering. The hate driving the Windstone stemmed from her soul, and she struggled to control it. No matter how she despised Moira, she wasn't ready to take another life. Neither was Silas, it seemed.

"Moira!" Silas yelled, darting after her.

Not that it was in Silas's power to stop the wind now. Even Cassandra struggled to control it. Moira tumbled backward toward the magma, screaming.

"Stop!" Cassandra ordered the gem lighting up her hand.

The wind continued to howl, holding on to the last bit of her rage as if the Windstone had read her mind too literally and concluded Moira had to be stopped forever, no matter how horribly. The force of the blow pushed Moira to the very brink of the open chasm where she teetered.

"I said, stop," Cassandra yelled, closing her hand over the diamond.

The wind wavered before aiming one last blast at Moira. But that brief flicker was enough. Moira caught the wind with one wing and rose clear of the chasm. She turned in midair and darted north, chased by the Windstone's power. For a moment, the barren cliffside was alive with the roar of a bitter wind and the crash of powerful waves. The remaining dragons took up formation along Moira's sides and flew off with her, disappearing over the lip of the caldera. Cassandra held her breath.

A second ticked by. A minute. And slowly, she exhaled. The wind dwindled back to a whisper, and the light in the diamond dimmed.

"Enough," she whispered. Enough anger. Enough pain. Enough revenge.

Silas's arms closed around her, and she drooped, cradling her injured hand. Her body ached from a dozen cuts and bruises, and her skin was coated with dust. An eerie silence had fallen over the lava fields, but the sea breeze wafting in from the Pacific carried a breath of clean, salty air.

Then another dragon roar split the air, and she cringed.

"Kai. Tessa," Silas murmured in relief.

Two shadows shot overhead, rushing after Moira. They both spat long plumes of fire, making it clear the shifters of Koa Point ruled this territory. Then they, too, rushed out of sight, following the enemy, and the landscape hushed again.

"Are you all right?" she whispered.

Silas nodded, hugging her close to his chest. "I'm okay. Are you?"

She closed her eyes, pushing away her pain. "I'm okay."

The sun had set, and the sky was awash with streaks of pink light. Cassandra opened her hand, relieved to find the diamond dull and dim. But two things still gnawed at her.

"You know I would never bewitch you, right?" She hurried to tell him. "I mean, even if I actually could, which I can't. I would never, ever—"

He stopped her with a finger to her lips. "I know."

She clutched his hands. "Eloise cast a spell. She lured you and Drax here to kill each other. And it scares me to death to think I might have inadvertently..."

Silas raised an eyebrow. "Inadvertently what? Turned up in the nick of time to blow those dragons away?"

Well, now that he put it that way...

She relaxed a tiny bit, then tensed again, looking at the Windstone. Then her eyes drifted to the chasm Drax had fallen into, and her jaw clenched. She stood slowly, every joint aching, and took one cautious step toward the abyss.

Eloise's words echoed through her mind. *Hide it. Conceal it. Better yet, destroy it. We witches created the Spirit Stones generations ago. We can destroy them too.*

Silas stepped to her side, and Cassandra took a deep breath, waiting for him to protest. He'd nearly laid down his life for the Spirit Stone. Wouldn't he want to keep it?

"Do it," he said, surprising her with his conviction. "Destroy it."

Cassandra could practically hear Eloise's spirit, saying the same thing.

"Are you sure?" she asked in a raspy whisper. The Spirit Stone's power had terrified her. But without it, she and Silas would not have survived the attack.

Silas cupped her hands with his. "Honestly? I'm not sure. You're the one who can control it."

"I could *barely* control it," she protested.

"You did better than I could. The Spirit Stones were created by witches, and the Windstone is the most powerful of them all. It takes a witch to control it."

Cassandra made a face. "I'm only one-eighths witch. One measly eighth."

"Enough to bring forth the stone's power and direct it. In any case, the Stone is yours. The choice is yours."

The man was a prince. A naked, buff prince, totally at home in his own skin.

"Mine, huh?" She looked dubiously at the gem. "Are you sure you don't want it?"

A smile spread over his lips. "There's only one thing I want. Well, two." His voice was hopeful, teasing, and uncertain, all at the same time.

"And what would those be?"

Silas's eyes heated as he squeezed her hands. "You. I want you. As my mate." He studied her for a moment, then added, "My friend. Partner. Lover."

Up to that point, her body had throbbed with aches and complaints. But the moment Silas spoke, a warm, comforting goodness spread through her veins, and her cheeks stretched with a smile.

"And what would the second thing be?"

Yes, it was a little unfair, making Silas work so hard when she already knew her answer was an enthusiastic *yes*. But it was kind of fun, and just in case, she'd better check what his second wish was. If it was domination of the shifter world, she was out of there.

"Peace," he said without hesitation.

And Eloise had claimed all dragons were evil. Ha.

Cassandra shrugged. "I'm not sure I can arrange for peace. But maybe this can." She looked at the diamond. "There was something about uniting the Spirit Stones, right?"

Silas looked as reluctant as she was. "So the legends say. But you know what they say about legends..."

She nodded. "Yep. You can't believe everything you read." Then she aimed her meanest glare at the diamond. "Listen, and listen good. Unless you want me to throw you into the volcano..."

The diamond blinked with a weak light.

"...you will do as you're told. No more hurricanes. No more whirlwinds."

"No more revenge," Silas added firmly.

Cassandra nodded. "No *nothing* unless you're asked to. You got that?"

The diamond shone brighter than ever then went dim again.

Cassandra made a face. "Hmpf. I still don't trust it. But it might be worth keeping. Do you have a safe place?"

Silas nodded. "My lair."

"Your what?" she blurted, picturing a dripping cave littered with bones.

"Just a small one," he explained quickly. "An old lava tube behind the house. I'll show you."

Slowly, her blood pressure went back down.

"Still," he added. "Destroying it might still be safer."

Cassandra held his hands, wondering what to do. Then she pictured Koa Point. All the kindness, the camaraderie, the sense of hope. The Windstone had secured all that — and with Moira on the loose, who knew? Nina and Boone's twins would be coming into the world soon, and the others had hinted at family plans as well.

"Peace would be nice," she said, giving the diamond a last shake of warning. Then she slipped it into her pocket and smiled at Silas. "Now, back to that first thing."

"First thing?" Now he was the tease.

"Yes, Mr. Llewellyn. The part about wanting me."

He smiled so wide, his teeth showed. "Want me to say it again?"

She tried to shrug nonchalantly, but Silas's smile told her what an utter failure that was. "I wouldn't mind."

"All right, then, Miss Nichols. I want you as my mate. My friend, partner, and lover. Forever."

"Greedy dragon, aren't you?" she teased.

He nodded firmly. "Yes, when it comes to you."

"Well, it's a good thing I happen to want you too. As all of those things."

They grinned at each other for another few seconds, then fell into each other's arms for a deep, needy kiss. A vow of a kiss that went on and on until Cassandra wobbled on her knees.

"Whoops. I'm not sure if that's the kiss or exhaustion knocking me out."

Silas smiled and took her hand. "Let's say it was the kiss. And exhaustion." He brushed his cracked lips over her knuckles and led her slowly back toward the vehicles. "Ready to get out of here?"

She nodded. God, was she ready.

Then he stopped and studied her earnestly. "Ready for a new start? At Koa Point, I mean."

She smiled and trapped him in another hug. "You sure you can handle keeping me around?"

"I know I couldn't handle *not* having you around."

She patted his bare ass and grinned. "Good. Then I'm ready. Ready for anything — as long as it's with you."

Chapter Twenty-Two

Silas opened his eyes slowly, not quite sure if he was ready to face the truth. Had the triumph over Drax just been a dream, or was it really true?

As his eyes focused, he let out a breath of relief. He really was in his bedroom at Koa Point the morning after the fight, and Cassandra was at his side. The bare skin of her shoulder was scraped raw from the fight, but she was all right.

Safe. She's safe, his dragon murmured again and again.

His gaze wandered slowly over the bamboo walls and arched ceiling above. Was it really over?

It's just beginning, his dragon cooed as Cassandra snuggled closer.

He tightened his arms around her as she slept, thinking over the past few hours. The fight was barely more than a blur — and frankly, he was happy to keep it that way. The end was the only part he didn't mind replaying in his mind. Holding Cassandra on the lava field as they reassured each other Drax was gone forever. Moira had fled along with the remaining dragons, and they wouldn't be coming back anytime soon.

Not with my mate wielding the power of the Windstone. His dragon glowed with pride.

He stroked her arm gently, just as she had stroked his back in the hours after the fight. The two of them had limped to the parking area and collapsed in the back seat of her rental Jeep until Kai could fly back to Maui and return hours later with the helicopter. Silas was too exhausted to fly all the way back to Maui in dragon form, and there was no way he was leaving Cassandra's side. So they had fallen into a restless sleep right there in the Jeep. Not quite heaven, not quite hell, because

215

part of his subconscious remained alert for danger. Tessa had remained in the area to guard over the car, but Silas only felt a wave of relief when the sound of rotor blades buzzed overhead.

He barely remembered getting into the helicopter or Kai arranging for a friend to return the rental cars, but he would never forget the sight of the ocean blurring below on the trip back. And he would never forget Cassandra's tight hug. The *forever* kind of hug, and the way she whispered to him.

"It's over. We did it."

The second they got home – really home, to the master bedroom in his house high on the rise of Koa Point — they had both fallen into a deep, peaceful sleep he could have basked in for hours.

But the sun was shining, the birds singing. Just another morning at Koa Point, yet it felt like a new era. Drax had been eliminated. The Spirit Stone had been secured. And best of all, Silas had won his mate.

"Love you," she murmured, half in sleep.

"Love you, my mate," he whispered back.

He looked around in the pale dawn light, not quite sure what to do.

So don't do anything, his dragon said.

What a novel idea it was *not* to leap out of bed to resume the never-ending battle with problems that had plagued him as alpha of Koa Point. But somehow, they all seemed far away.

They're not just far away, his dragon assured him. *They're gone.*

He closed his eyes again. Okay, maybe all his problems hadn't entirely disappeared, but they were nowhere near as severe as before. With Drax out of the picture...

We can relax. Finally, we can relax, his dragon sighed.

His cheek twitched. Moira was still out there, and who knew what she might get up to. He had learned not to underestimate her, but for the time being, he could relax. Moira might return someday, but he and the shifters of Koa Point would be prepared.

He kissed Cassandra's shoulder and stroked her hair, relishing the warm glow in his soul.

"Mmm," she murmured, turning in his arms. Slowly, her eyes opened and focused on his. The warm brown brightened, and her lips curved into a smile.

He really ought to have come up with some polite line. A *good morning*, or a *How are you?* But instead of speaking, his lips moved over hers, never intending to let go.

She shifted on the mattress, cooing with delight.

When they broke apart for a breath of air, she bit her lip. "Silas, there's so much I want to say..."

He nodded. "Me too. But there will be time for that. Right now..."

Her smile stretched as they kissed again. He wove his fingers through her hair, marveling at the silky feel. Her body began to move under his, and his blood heated.

Mate, his dragon growled. *Need my mate.*

Cassandra ran her heel along his calf, inviting him closer. Her head tipped back, giving him access to her neck. His senses grew misty as he kissed her again and again, succumbing to the burning need to claim his mate and put an end to the dark era he had just survived.

When Cassandra arched under him, he slid an arm under the small of her back, pressing his hips against hers. They were both naked under the sheets, and his cock was already growing hard.

His dragon hummed at her neck as instinct pointed to the perfect spot for the mating bite. *Right there.*

Silas forced himself to continue down to her collarbone, past that spot. It was too soon to think about claiming her, and they hadn't had a chance to discuss it. But Cassandra drew him back to her neck as if she felt the urge too.

"I want this," she said, running her hands toward his ass. "I need this." Her knees split open, inviting him to nestle closer still.

With a supreme effort, Silas broke away and touched her neck. "I want this too." God, did he want it. "But there's so much you don't know about shifters—"

Her laugh was husky. "Do you really think I was just reading about history in those books of yours?"

217

He came to his elbows and tilted his head.

She ran her hand along his side, stoking the fire inside him. "I might have stumbled across a few passages about mating bites. Destined mates. All the juicy details."

Silas's mouth swung open. "You did?"

She nibbled at the edge of his chin. "Right now, I'm exhausted, and I need a shower. Every inch of my body aches. But I need this more than anything else, Silas. I need you. I don't want to wait." She shook her head. "I think of everything Eloise was wrong about. Everything I might have missed if you hadn't brought me here. So, yes. I'm ready to put all that behind me. I want a life with you."

He ran a hand along the fine line of her cheekbone. "But a mating bite means..."

She nodded. "I'll become a shifter."

He stared. "And you're okay with that?"

She laughed then grew serious. "If I can be your kind of dragon, I'm more than okay with that."

"My kind of dragon?"

She nodded firmly. "The loyal, generous kind. The kind that protects others."

I will protect you forever, his dragon vowed in a quiet aside.

"And you know what else?" she asked, cupping his cheek.

"What?"

"I think Filimore wasn't the last of the great dragons. I think there's at least one more." She ran a finger over his chest.

His heart pounded. His blood felt too thick for his veins. As commander of his Special Forces unit and as alpha of Koa Point, he was more used to giving praise than receiving it. He'd always enjoyed watching his men try to hide their pride at his words. Now, he was the one pulling in his lips, wondering how the hell he'd gotten so lucky.

Cassandra lifted her head and tackled his mouth in a heated kiss. "I want this, Silas. I'm sure."

And then there was nothing he could say, because his lips were too busy consuming her. Tasting her incredible skin, inhaling her clean, flowery scent.

218

She arched again, and he slid down to her breast, capturing a nipple with his lips. Cassandra rocked beneath him, embracing him with her legs. Sparks rushed through his veins, and for once, he decided to act on instinct rather than thinking things through.

Good idea, his dragon hummed. *No need to overthink this.*

He nudged her body sideways until they were perfectly lined up. Then he rolled his hips, groaning at the sweet burn in his cock as it dragged along her folds.

"Yes... Please..." she cried, lifting one leg then the other until her heels were pressed firmly against his ass.

Silas turned his head and scraped his stubbly chin along her chest. Then he suckled the other nipple briefly, getting high on her scent. But it was impossible not to rush — not with Cassandra gasping and clawing for more.

He rocked forward, plunging deep. Cassandra cried out and tipped her head back. Her inner muscles clenched, squeezing his cock.

So good, his dragon groaned, relishing the tight, hot slide into his mate.

Cassandra raised her arms over her head, making her breasts lift. He pinned her hands down, anchoring her in place. Levering her hips upward, Cassandra slammed against him, panting.

"Yes..."

His nostrils flared, and his sight dimmed. His hips rocked. And though his shoulders still ached from the fight, his body felt so, so good. On fire. Alive like he'd never felt before.

He thrust into her warm heat time and again, losing control. Muttering his pleasure and nipping her neck between jerky breaths.

There, his dragon roared. *Right there.*

He scraped his teeth along the notch of her throat, homing in on the right spot.

Now! his dragon roared.

Silas held back. The location of the mating bite was one thing, but the timing was just as critical. His canines extended, and his whole body pulsed in anticipation. Any second now, he would explode inside his mate. He thrust furiously, listening to Cassandra's cries of pleasure.

Soon. Soon...

Cassandra met every slam with a buck of her own. She turned her head to the side, tempting him.

Now! his dragon demanded. *Now!*

Every muscle in his body coiled, and he thrust deeper than ever.

Right now! his dragon roared.

He buried his teeth deep, making sure to close the surrounding area with his lips. His groan was a mumble, his body stiff. His teeth strained, plunging deeper.

"Yes..." Cassandra clutched his head, keeping him near.

Her pulse beat a hairsbreadth from his teeth — danger lurking so close.

I will always keep my mate safe, his dragon murmured. *Now finish it. Make her mine!*

Finishing meant the mating brand — a unique part of the dragon mating rite. Silas held his breath for a moment, praying he'd get it right.

Of course, we'll get it right. She's our destined mate!

He pounded into her one more time, pouring his desire into his mate. At the same time, he exhaled, sending a puff of fire through her veins.

Cassandra let out a low, throaty groan and clawed the sheets. Her entire body shuddered. It would have been terrifying if Silas hadn't felt the pleasure running through her nerves, mirroring his own ecstasy. He sensed her joy, her relief. And above all, he sensed Cassandra's utter confidence in him.

Mate, his dragon growled, biting even deeper.

He never wanted to let go. But at some point, his canines receded, leaving just his lips sealed over her skin. He kept his tongue over the wound, helping her heal. The bite marks would become faint scars, a reminder of this incredible night.

Cassandra's legs loosened around his waist, and he caught a glimpse of her thoughts — deep satisfaction and a naughty chuckle as she thought about returning the favor someday.

True mating meant each partner sharing a bite with the other, binding their souls for eternity.

Silas lay still, panting into her neck, inhaling their intermingled scents.

"So good," Cassandra murmured, tensing with an aftershock.

He held on to her, glowing inside. *He* was doing that to her. He was making her feel that good.

Just like she makes us feel, his dragon agreed.

Cassandra drew her hands down his back in a slow, sensual line until they came to rest on his rear. She tapped him lightly, playfully.

"Wow."

He moved away slowly, resting on one elbow to look at his mate. Gently, he pushed a strand of hair away from her face. God, was she beautiful.

Beautiful and mine, his dragon hummed.

Cassandra laughed. "I don't think I've ever felt this tired, this confused, or this sure, all at the same time." She locked him in a full-body hug with her arms and legs. "But damn, I would be happy to do that again."

"Again and again," he whispered, kissing his way back to her lips. A quieter, gentler kiss that signaled the new beginning he could feel in his heart. "We can repeat it, you know."

"Watch out. I'll take you up on that." She smiled, touching his neck.

"You're not worried about being bound to a dragon forever?" he asked, only half in jest.

She twisted her head left and right, making a mess of her hair but still managing to look like the most stunning woman on earth. "If you're not worried about being bound to a third-rate witch." Then her eyes searched the ceiling, and she chuckled. "I guess now I'll be part witch, part dragon."

All dragon, his inner beast declared, picturing her swooping and soaring beside him.

No more lonely flights in the middle of the night. No more solitary hours at home. No more turning to emptiness, wishing he had someone to ask for advice. His dragon grinned from ear to ear as Cassandra held him.

A moment later, he buried his face in her neck, overcome by emotion and not quite man enough to let her see.

Cassandra's steady strokes told him it was too late. She saw him. All of him. All his secrets and his shortcomings. All that, and she still wanted him.

"I love you," she whispered. "You know that, right?"

He threaded his fingers through hers and nodded silently. Yes, he knew. He just couldn't speak yet.

∞∞∞∞

Silas was just drifting into sleep when something tapped at the corner of his mind. He opened his eyes with a bitter groan. Now what?

What is it? He growled at Kai through his mind.

I hate to bother you. . . Kai started.

Not as much as he'd hate to kill his cousin for disturbing him now.

"What is it?" Cassandra asked, touching his ribs in alarm.

He reassured her with a kiss and sighed before reaching out to his cousin. *What is it, already?*

That lawyer is on the phone. Something about resolving Filimore's estate. I told him it had to wait, but he's demanding to speak to you right away.

Silas rested his forehead against Cassandra's shoulder, ready to punch the wall. Still, as long as he had his mate. . .

Mine forever, his dragon crowed.

He rolled slowly, pressing a kiss to her lips. "I'll be right back." Then he aimed his thoughts at Kai. *Put the call through to my office.*

He shifted to the edge of the bed and stood slowly, reluctant to leave his mate. But he loved the sight of Cassandra, spread out in his bed too. Looking absolutely ravished and ravishing.

His dragon hummed with pride. *I made my mate feel good.*

She wiggled a little, arching her back. Had she heard that?

"Don't be long," she said with a naughty sparkle in her eyes.

He walked down the hall to his office, feeling his joints creak more loudly with every step. It seemed the farther he moved from Cassandra, the more he felt the effects of the fight. Still, it was a satisfying kind of weary. The kind you get after a job well done. He grabbed a towel on the way and threw it on his leather chair before sitting down and hitting the speaker on the phone.

"What is it?"

He winced a little at the bark in his own voice. But hell, he had been pulled away from his mate.

"Mr. Llewellyn, I have a few critical details to go over about your great-uncle's will," the lawyer said.

Silas was about to protest, but Cassandra came up behind him and slid her arms over his shoulders, nestling her cheek next to his.

He closed his eyes, keeping his hands clasped over hers.

"I'm not going anywhere," she whispered.

He swiveled around. Maybe she really could read his mind. Maybe the mating bite worked that quickly.

Cassandra's smile was demure. When he swiveled back to jot down the lawyer's key points, his gaze caught on the view. All that water, shimmering in the glorious sunlight. All the lush greenery, forming a frame to the view. All the exotic scents and sounds of a gorgeous Maui morning, filling his senses. How had he failed to notice them before?

The lawyer droned on with the outstanding details of Filimore's estate, but the call didn't take as long as he feared, and it ended as he had hoped: the estate — and all Filimore's holdings — were his, and his alone.

"I'll look out for the documents," he said, terminating the call with a firm click. He closed his eyes and thought of all the kindnesses his uncle had ever shown him — everything that had brought him to this moment in his life. Then he swiveled his chair around to face Cassandra.

She looked more beautiful than ever — and more content. She looped her arms over his shoulders and straddled him in

223

the chair.

"We're going to have to set some limits on how much work you do," she said, nuzzling him.

Oh, he knew. And he was all on board with that plan.

But now that she was close again, all he could think of was bonding with her again.

And again and again, his dragon cheered.

Chapter Twenty-Three

Cassandra stirred slowly, touching Silas. Sex in the office had led to sex in the bedroom, where she could have stayed with him forever — or on the floor, or in the shower, where her dirty mind had already fast-forwarded to. She'd been on fire for Silas for days, but the mating bite had intensified the primal, desperate need for more.

More. I like that idea, a voice registered faintly in her mind.

Her eyes flew open. Yikes. Was she already sensing her inner dragon? It felt a lot like the instincts she'd always sensed, telling her where to go, what to do, and when her body needed release — but all that came with a voice now. A voice attached to a dragon that would reshape her body someday. She gulped.

Want my mate. Now.

She took a deep breath, telling herself she could handle her dragon the way she'd handled the Spirit Stone.

Patience, she said. *My mate has responsibilities, which means we do too.*

That seemed to shush the beast — for now. But, gosh. She had a lot of reading to do.

Better yet, private lessons from my mate, the voice purred, low and sultry.

Without thinking, she wound her arm around Silas's body, sneaking closer to his groin. A second later, her cheeks heated and she detoured that hand to his chest. They couldn't stay in bed all day, no matter how much she wanted to. The others would be waiting, unable to relax until they had been assured that the danger had passed.

So she curled into a sitting position and looked down at Silas. He lay on his back, gazing up at her as if she were some kind of goddess.

She chuckled. "What are you looking at?"

His eyes glowed a warm brick color, the color she'd come to associate with love.

"My mate. I'm looking at my mate." He shook his head as if he still couldn't believe it.

She couldn't believe it either. But in one sense, she felt as though she'd known all along that her destined mate had been waiting for her somewhere. And now that they were together, nothing could drive them apart.

"Well, my mate, I think this bed isn't going anywhere, and we could both use some breakfast." She turned her eyes to the clock. "Oops. Make that brunch."

Her clothes were still at the guesthouse, which was fine because she got to pull on one of Silas's dress shirts and a pair of boxer shorts. She hugged them to her body, and her nostrils flared. Every scent seemed a little more intense. Fresher, newer. Were her dragon senses awakening already?

"How is it that you make those look so much better than they look on me?" Silas asked, watching her every move.

She laughed. "I beg to differ, but if you want to keep dreaming, dream on."

He shook his head slowly and kissed her. "Not dreaming. Not any more."

Which nearly had her detouring back to bed, but she broke off the kiss, remembering the others.

"Come along, mister. Like I said, I'm not going anywhere."

Silas pulled on his usual slacks and button-down shirt, and she made a mental note to get him some jeans. Something more casual to help him relax.

My mate is relaxed, the inner voice hummed.

She peeked sideways and grinned. Silas's version of relaxed may not match Boone's barefoot-in-the-grass style, but he did look different. His shoulders weren't quite as stiff, his jaw not clenched quite as tight.

She'd have to keep working on him. Every day...

... and every night, the inner voice added in a lusty whisper.

She swatted a nonexistent mosquito, keeping herself on track. Silas wrapped his hand around hers and rocked it as they made their way down toward the meeting house. The brook that ran alongside the path had never sounded so cheery, and the sky seemed bluer than ever before. Silas's skin had a radiant tone despite all they'd been through, and her cheeks were probably no different.

Okay, so it would be obvious to everyone that they'd screwed for most of the night. But this was no walk of shame. Silas was her mate. The other shifters of Koa Point would understand that feeling of pride, of completion. So she strode into the meeting house, more conscious of the man at her side than of the knowing looks from the others.

"Hi," Tessa said, casual as can be.

"Hi." Cassandra grinned.

"Cassandra, meet Jody and Cruz," Tessa said as two people rose.

Jody was a freckled blonde, part tomboy, part cover girl. Cruz had dark, flashing eyes and an edge that only eased when his mate slid her hand over his arm.

"So nice to meet you," Jody said, doing the talking for both of them. "I'm so sorry we couldn't get here sooner."

"So come on already," Kai urged. "Have a seat. Eat. Tell us what happened."

Cassandra looked around the table. The rich scent of coffee tickled her nose, as did the aroma of hibiscus tea, and her mouth watered at the sight of freshly baked muffins, still steaming on a rack. Yum.

But there was one problem. Silas always sat at the head of the table, and so far, she'd taken a seat several places down one side, beside Dawn. But even that seemed too far from her mate.

Hunter, the bear, was the first to act. He rose quickly and switched to the chair on his mate's left side, leaving the chair next to Silas free for Cassandra. She closed her eyes as emotions welled up in her. It wasn't just Silas she had won over. It was this family. This community that had embraced her so graciously from the start. A tear slipped from her eye – a happy tear – and she didn't bother whisking it away.

She took a seat and croaked out a grateful, "Thank you." Not just to Hunter, but to everyone.

Nina smiled in a way that said she knew just what Cassandra meant, and the other women did too. The men all leaned closer to their mates as if reliving their first days together, and a thoughtful silence filled the room — until Keiki bounced onto the table with a loud purr.

Cruz chuckled. "Hey, Keiki. Want some milk?"

The kitten purred under his hand then tiptoed to Hunter and looked up expectantly. From what Cassandra had gathered, Hunter and Cruz were the ones who had initially adopted the kitten, and it showed.

When Hunter petted Keiki, the kitten disappeared under his massive hand. Cruz poured some milk into a saucer and smacked his lips, but Keiki detoured around it and walked straight to Silas, staring up into his eyes.

"Hey, little one," he murmured, gently stroking her fur. His eyes shone with love and gratitude.

Cassandra hid a smile. Had Keiki been taking care of Silas when he needed it most?

Keiki flicked her tail, obviously satisfied with what she saw, and meandered back down the table to lap her milk.

"Spoiled little thing." Kai chuckled.

"No manners." Hunter sighed, though no one made a move to set the kitten on the floor.

Tessa pushed a muffin toward Cassandra, who gratefully accepted. She couldn't find any words to express what she felt anyway. The sweet taste of papaya filled her mouth, along with a hint of vanilla, and she closed her eyes.

"Oh my gosh. These are so good," she murmured between bites.

"Everything Tessa makes is good," Kai agreed.

Nina poured her a coffee while a gleeful Boone held up a newspaper. "I think this even beats the helicopter on Molokini."

Cassandra's eyes went wide. What was that about?

Boone straightened the paper and read from it. *"Spectacular nighttime eruptions reported on Big Island. Volcanoes National Park rangers unable to pinpoint exact source of lava outbreak...*" He looked up, grinning from ear to ear. "I wonder why."

Silas stirred his coffee but didn't say a word.

Boone read on. *"Storm-force winds prevent rangers from investigating."* He pushed the newspaper across the table to Cassandra with a wink.

"Damn good thing," Silas muttered, taking a sip from his mug.

Cassandra nodded. Now more than ever, she understood why shifters guarded their privacy so fiercely. And really, locals were better off not knowing what had truly transpired.

"I doubt they'll find much evidence this morning," Tessa said with a proud smile.

Cassandra grinned, remembering how Tessa had swooped overhead to chase away Drax's henchmen. Tessa had mentioned that she'd been practicing the art of breathing fire, so maybe it was a watershed moment for her as well.

Cassandra glanced at the article which featured a photo of a startled local pointing over the ridge and an interview in which words like *amazing, incredible,* and *inexplicable* were repeated again and again.

She folded the paper and pushed it away. Yes, it had been incredible, all right. But she was glad it was over.

"You did it," Kai said to Silas. "You defeated Drax."

"We did it," Silas said, locking eyes with Cassandra.

Cassandra shook her head. "You did it." All she had done was allowed Silas to fight a fair fight.

"And the Windstone?" Dawn asked, leaning forward. "Is it safe?"

Silas looked at Cassandra and squeezed her hand. She took a deep breath, pulled the diamond out of her shirt pocket, and held the stone out on her scratched, open palm. As she did, the sea breeze drifting through the meeting house shifted, stirring the edges of the tablecloth. Everyone stopped, and even little Keiki looked around.

Cassandra pushed the diamond toward the middle of the table and drew her hand back. Yes, she had been able to harness its powers, but that didn't mean she enjoyed handling the diamond any more than she absolutely had to.

"It's safe," Silas said.

For a moment, everyone was silent, and she wondered why. But then she realized that they were waiting for her to explain what she was planning to do with it. Everyone seemed to accept that the diamond was hers and that she had the right to determine its fate.

Her heart thumped harder. How could she ever have doubted these good folks?

"We'll keep it safe here," she said firmly, looking at Silas.

He nodded, and everyone exhaled a tiny bit. "We'll keep it safe, together with the other Spirit Stones."

Cassandra half expected the conversation to conclude there, but one by one, the other women each drew out a jewel and laid it on the table beside the Windstone.

"The Lifestone," Tessa said, setting out a huge emerald the color of her eyes.

"The Firestone," Nina whispered, gently positioning a ruby beside it.

Dawn slid out a gorgeous amethyst. "The Earthstone."

"The Waterstone," Jody said in a hushed voice, pulling out a sapphire.

Each gem was bright and beautiful, but the radiance increased when they were placed together. They all pulsed with colored light that reflected on the white tablecloth. The collection seemed to radiate heat — stirring up energy, a force of its own.

Dawn motioned toward the jewels, whispering, "Can you feel it?"

One by one, the others nodded, and Silas scrubbed his chin.

"We did it," Boone breathed, uncharacteristically quiet. "We united the Spirit Stones."

Nina stared at the gems. "Wow."

Wow was right, Cassandra thought. Still, that energy frightened her. She imagined the power of the Windstone multiplied times five.

"All five," Tessa marveled.

Something niggled at Cassandra's mind. A dim memory, a blur of a picture she'd seen somewhere. She frowned, trying to recall what that was.

Boone leaned forward, watching the jewels glow. "Wow is right. But, man. What now?"

"If they fall into the wrong hands..." Dawn warned.

No evil force can be allowed to command the powers contained in that gem, Eloise had warned.

Cassandra shivered, but the feeling passed when Silas touched her hand.

"They'll be safe here," Kai said firmly. "We'll keep them safe. All of us will."

Everyone looked to their leader expectantly, and Cassandra sensed the weight of responsibility settle over Silas's shoulders again. Maybe not quite as crushing as before, but still. She grasped his hand and held it tightly. He locked eyes with her, grateful for the support, then took a deep breath.

"We'll keep them locked safely away. We'll make sure no one ever abuses their power." His voice was resolute, just like the expression on every person's face.

"What about Moira?" Cruz growled, posing the question no one dared ask.

Cassandra could tell the tiger shifter would be downright terrifying if caught in the wrong mood. But his mate, Jody, slid her arm across his shoulders, and the murderous look in his eyes dimmed.

Moira. Cassandra found herself wondering the same thing.

She glanced at Silas and saw crushed hopes, bitter betrayal, and anger in his eyes. But all of that was covered with a soft mist, as if he had pushed those emotions to a distant corner of his mind and locked them away.

His lips crooked at her, and he kissed her knuckles. He kept his lips pressed to her hand for a good ten seconds, bending his head, and she smoothed a hand over his shoulder. That

231

part of his life was over, and it didn't have to haunt him ever again.

Slowly, Silas straightened and looked at the others. "Moira escaped. And I suspect Drax had Moira to thank for his increasing powers."

Cassandra had the same feeling — that Moira had been using Drax to obtain the stone.

Kai frowned. "What do you think Moira will do next?"

Silas studied the swirling lines of his coffee. "There's no telling. Will she try to take over what she can salvage of Drax's empire? I don't know."

When he paused, Cassandra held her breath. *Drax's empire* made her mind skip to *Filimore's estate*. The others still didn't know about that.

Silas stared into her eyes for another few seconds then smiled. "Speaking of which. . . "

The others all leaned closer, and even Keiki tilted her head.

"Moira will probably try to take over Drax's empire, but she'll have to battle the lieutenants who want to carve a piece of that empire for themselves. However, one part of Drax's holdings, she will never have."

"What do you mean?" Boone asked.

Silas flattened his hands on the table. "I'm sure Drax is responsible for poisoning my uncle Filimore, the senior member of our extended clan, in an attempt to accelerate the inevitable."

"What do you mean, the inevitable?" Kai demanded.

"Filimore never revealed the details of his will while he was alive, but Drax gambled — correctly, as it turned out — that Filimore would follow tradition and leave all his holdings to the senior members of each branch of the family."

Kai's narrowed. "That would be Drax — and you."

Boone's eyes went wide. "Whoa. Does that mean you get that penthouse in New York?"

A tiny smile played over Silas's lips. "I get a lot more than that. Filimore owned property and businesses around the world. But I won't be going anywhere soon."

"Well, I hope not," Nina said. "It's been great meeting Cassandra, and now that we're all home..."

Everyone bobbed their heads in agreement, and another wave of gratitude washed over Cassandra. She was part of that *we*. This was her home.

"I'm not particularly interested in the properties," Silas explained. "But there is one estate..."

He was teasing, Cassandra sensed, and a grin grew on her lips as everyone went still.

"You mean...?" Nina whispered.

Silas nodded. "A very comfortable seaside estate with exceptionally good views."

Kai, she saw, was breathless. Hunter raised one bushy eyebrow. Boone looked at Nina, confused.

Tessa gestured impatiently. "Come on, Silas. Tell us already."

But Silas took his time, extending the tease. "I'd have to share the place with a few others, but I hear they pull their own weight."

Tessa broke into a huge smile. "That we do."

"I don't get it," Boone muttered, still not catching on.

Silas pointed around. "The owner of this estate – that reclusive, private man — was Filimore. My great-uncle. Koa Point belonged to him."

"What?" Boone gaped.

"All this time..." Kai murmured.

Silas nodded. "All this time, I respected Filimore's wish for privacy. He hired me as chief caretaker and each of you in turn, exactly as I've always said."

"And now that Filimore is dead? And Drax too?" Kai asked.

Boone's eyebrows shot up. "Holy crap!"

Silas grinned. "My feelings precisely when I found out about the will."

Everyone was silent for a moment before breaking into a hubbub that made Keiki scramble to Hunter's shoulder and peer around.

"Oh my God."

"I can't believe it."

"Wait, does that mean this place is yours?"

"Ours," Silas corrected. "Koa Point is ours."

Silas was a man of few emotions, and Cassandra watched him, savoring one of the rare times when he let them shine through. Of all the joys she'd shared with him recently, this was the icing on the cake. That *Wow, we really did it* sense of completion.

Tessa raised her coffee mug. "Well, then. I think we need a toast."

Kai nodded, looking Silas in the eye. "You know what this means, don't you? You could be the greatest dragon lord of all."

Silas held up his hand quickly. "That's not what I want. I never did."

Tessa raised her mug higher. "How about being the one to bring peace and stability to the dragon world?"

Cassandra watched, falling in love with Silas all over again as he hemmed and hawed modestly. The man wasn't about power. He was all about duty and honor.

He allowed himself a tiny smile. "That, I wouldn't mind." Then he gazed into the distance. "But, honestly? That's a big idea to get my head around, and I'm too tired to think straight." He looked up at Cassandra and grinned. "Too lost in love."

"My sentiments exactly," she whispered, imitating his voice.

Tessa clinked her mug against Nina's and gave an exaggerated sigh. "Finally."

"No kidding." Kai grinned.

"Finally, what?" Silas asked.

"Oh, nothing." Tessa winked and gave Cassandra a half-hidden thumbs-up.

"Oh! Tell Cassandra our idea!" Nina clapped and beamed at Tessa.

The redhead's eyes shone brighter. "Well, I just finished my first book of grill recipes, and the publisher I'm hoping to sign with says it has to have something totally new for it to compete in a tight market."

Nina flapped her hands in excitement. "So I was thinking you could help Tessa pair each recipe with a cocktail. Wouldn't that be cool?"

Cassandra broke into a broad smile. "That would be fantastic. Although I am too tired to think straight right now. Can I tell you for sure tomorrow?"

Tessa nodded eagerly as Kai brushed a hand over her back and spoke. "I think we're all exhausted — and frankly, a little distracted by our mates. It might not be a bad idea to bring in someone to help keep an eye on things over the next few months."

Boone nodded immediately. "It is kind of hard to run a good night patrol when you keep thinking about your mate."

Hunter scratched his beard. "How about the Hoving brothers? Weren't they retiring from the Marines soon?"

Cruz shook his head. "They've got two more months, at least."

"What about McElroy and those buddies of his? Weren't they looking for work?"

Kai frowned. "They reenlisted from what I know."

Boone smacked his hand on the table. "Wait. I know just the man we need. Make that, just the woman."

Everyone looked over. "Who?"

"Ella. The desert fox. I think a working vacation in Hawaii is just what she needs. And hell, maybe she can bring one of the wolves from Twin Moon Ranch with her — or one of those bears that runs the Blue Moon Saloon. Those guys don't mess around."

Silas nodded. "Great idea. I'll get in touch with Ella."

Kai grinned. "I'll do it. I think you might have pressing business with your mate."

The bite marks on Cassandra's neck itched, and her body heated up. Now that Kai mentioned it, yes. She would love to get Silas somewhere private again.

"His mate," Tessa chuckled. "Music to my ears."

Silas raised one chiseled eyebrow at her.

235

Tessa raised her mug again. "So here's my toast. Everyone ready?"

Everyone raised their mugs, unconcerned they weren't the finest crystal containing expensive champagne.

"To Silas, our fearless leader," Tessa started.

"Hear, hear," everyone cheered.

"To Cassandra," Tessa added with a genuine smile. "You might be crazy for loving Silas—"

Everyone laughed.

"—but you're perfect for each other. May the two of you discover the joy of being mated like the rest of us have." Tessa winked, and everyone chuckled.

Cassandra felt the blood rush to her cheeks. She had to be blushing bright red by now. Silas kissed her knuckles again, unabashed.

"And to Koa Point," Tessa concluded. "Our beautiful, cozy home."

A sprawling estate shouldn't seem cozy but Cassandra agreed it was in every possible way.

"To Koa Point," each person echoed, looking at his or her mate. "Home."

Chapter Twenty-Four

Glasses clinked, and everyone sipped. Then they broke into conversation that ebbed and flowed.

"Who would have thought..."

"I still can't believe it..."

"Start from the beginning..." Cruz demanded of Kai.

Boone cocked his head at the collection of stones. "It's funny. I thought that when we had all five, something big would happen. I mean, something *really* big."

"Like what?" Nina laughed. "Fireworks?"

Boone gestured vaguely. "I don't know. A burst of light, maybe? A heat wave?" He laughed. "I guess we should be happy that's not the case."

"Exactly. I'm just happy all five are safe," Silas said.

Cassandra sat perfectly still as the faint memory at the back of her mind stirred. *All five... safe...* She tilted her head at the collection of precious gems. Why did that sound wrong?

"All good?" Silas murmured, seeing her drift off in thought.

She flashed him a quick smile. Everything was great, right?

Silas stood and took her hand, murmuring to the others. "If you'll excuse us..."

His eyes glowed, and she smiled, for real, knowing exactly what he had in mind.

"Have fun, kids," Kai called.

Boone whistled, and Nina thumped his arm.

"Hey!" he protested.

"That was once us," Nina admonished him.

"That's still us." Boone laughed, tugging her out of the chair. "If you'll excuse us, everyone..."

Silas chuckled, keeping Cassandra close as they walked toward the path to his house. Behind them, footsteps, giggles, and lusty growls indicated that the other couples were also heading to their own private corners of Koa Point with their jewels.

Cassandra wound her arm around Silas's and breathed deeply, looking around. "Such great people. Such a peaceful place. And it's yours."

"It's ours," he corrected as they walked up the path. "Every part of it."

She laughed. "All I really care about right now is the bed. And not for sleeping."

Silas's arm slid up and down her back, making her hungry for him all over again. But that uneasy *something* still tapped at her brain, and she couldn't quite let go of it.

"What's mine is yours. The bed. The house." Silas lifted one finger after another as he spoke. "The car. The estate. Oh, and the library, of course."

She stared at his hand. Five fingers. Five Spirit Stones...

A blurry image raced through her mind as quickly as the ruffled pages of a book.

"The library," she murmured, taking off for the stairs.

Silas jogged after her. "The library?"

"Yes. No. I mean, sorry," she mumbled, trying to catch a stray thought that refused to be caught.

She was panting by the time she reached the top level of the house, and when she burst into the library, she crouched by the box next to the door and pulled out one book after another.

"Filimore's books?" Silas asked, giving her space.

She nodded, not sure which one she sought. She'd only skimmed through a few briefly. She pushed one book aside to check the one under it, then backed up to a green, leather-bound volume.

"This one..."

A moment later, she had it open on the table and under the lamp. Silas leaned over it with her, and she started flipping through the pages. The worn leather cover carried the scent of centuries, and the detailed illustrations on each page were from an era when tasks were measured in years, not hours.

"What are you looking for?" Silas asked in a hushed voice.

"There was something in here about the Spirit Stones..."

"I think I've read everything that exists on Spirit Stones," Silas said in a weary tone.

He sounded as though he'd be happy never to read a book again, but she pressed on.

"Have you ever read these?"

"No. I haven't had time."

She flipped through the hand-decorated pages, searching for something that might trigger a memory. Then she stopped at a lushly illustrated scene with a field of dense script along one side.

She peered closer, holding her breath.

"What is it?" Silas asked.

She looked, stunned, fighting the instinct to hide the page. Shouldn't she allow Silas to enjoy peace for a few more days? Surely, this new complication could wait.

On the other hand, she couldn't keep a secret from her mate, especially one as critical as this.

She tapped the page, telling herself whatever trouble this new discovery created, they would face — and conquer — it together.

"There. Look."

She pointed. In the center of the image was a woman holding out both hands, one higher than the other. In the background, a burgundy dragon circled a volcano that shot lava high in the air.

"Have you ever seen this?" she asked.

Silas leaned closer, studying the details. "No. Filimore had so many books..." He ran a finger under the script caption. *"The Queen of the witch clan creates the Spirit Stones..."*

"You can read that?"

He nodded. "It's an ancient script, but yes, I can read it. My parents were sticklers for a classical education." He sighed. "Lucky Kai. He got off easy."

"Look at her hands."

The woman in the center — the witch queen — held both palms up with her fingers curled tightly, displaying a full set of rings. One on each finger, with the gemstones showing.

"A diamond...a ruby..." Cassandra pointed at each one. "A sapphire..."

"An amethyst, and an emerald," Silas finished. "The Spirit Stones."

He seemed content to leave it there, and she bit her lip, wondering what to say.

Say the truth, the voice inside her urged.

She pointed at the book. "There aren't five Stones. There are six. Look at her other hand."

When Silas leaned in for a closer look, his body tensed along her side.

"There's one more ring with one more gem," she said. "Something multicolored..."

Silas's eyes darted from the image to the text and back again.

"What does it say?" she begged.

He ran a finger under the script and read aloud. *"Five Spirit Stones, born of fire..."*

She waited impatiently.

"Commissioned by the great dragon lord..."

If there were a fast-forward switch to Silas's commentary, she would have hit it.

His voice dropped. *"And the Keystone shall unite the others..."*

Silas trailed off, and they stared at each other.

"The Keystone?" She gulped. "Have you ever heard of it?"

He shook his head immediately. "Never. But it says here, *First, the queen created the Keystone, and with it, she breathed life into the diamond, the ruby..."*

Cassandra had felt so happy a short time ago. Now all the anxiety pressed back in.

"So it isn't over. There's one more Spirit Stone out there."

Silas nodded slowly. "Sounds like there could be."

She tilted her head at the image. "What kind of gem looks like that?"

"Like a rainbow? I have no idea."

Cassandra looked at the box by the door. "You brought those from New York, right?"

He nodded. "They're the oldest books from Filimore's collection — the ones he kept in a separate vault. I took them in case Drax came along, but I haven't been able to read them yet."

Cassandra's blood ran cold. "Do you think Moira knows about this?"

His chin dipped, and for a moment, he looked older. Wearier. "I doubt she knows. I doubt anyone knows."

"Maybe this book is wrong," she tried.

He shook his head immediately and showed her the title page. "By Marius Baird. He's a legend among dragon scholars. I doubt he would be wrong."

She wrung her hands. "Damn it. Just when I thought we had everything figured out..." Then she sighed. "If nothing else, I think I just found myself a new job."

He tilted his head in a question, so she went on.

"Learning to read that script and going through all these books. We're going to have to if we want to find out more about that sixth stone."

Silas rubbed his chin. "That means another trip to New York."

"To clear out my apartment?" She'd already pictured the process, and frankly, she couldn't wait.

He smiled. "That, and to go through Filimore's penthouse."

"The penthouse. Of course." She waved a hand like it was nothing.

Silas nodded toward the box of books. "There are a lot more books there. You think you're ready to give up bartending?"

She laughed. "If I get to explore these books, yes. Maybe I'll finally learn a spell or two. I love the idea of helping Tessa too." Her face fell into a frown. "After we figure out what to do about this Keystone, that is."

Silas tipped her chin up and flashed her a bittersweet smile. "That could take years. But you know what?"

"What?"

He hugged her fiercely. "First, we have a long time. Your life span will be as long as a dragon's, thanks to the mating bite. And second, I am putting problems aside for tonight. Exploring the fine art of procrastination, as Boone might say. In fact, I am putting problems aside for several nights. Because I have my mate, and nothing is going to stop us from enjoying our time together."

She burst into a smile and slowly shut the book as lust reared up in her again. They couldn't procrastinate forever, but yeah — a week or so would be nice.

"Well, then," she said, inching around until she was sitting on the desk. She pulled Silas into the V between her knees and wrapped her legs around him. "I've always had a fantasy about this table, you know."

She ran her arms over his chest then lay back slowly. Silas pushed the books aside and nestled close enough to make every hard ridge of his body felt.

"And what exactly did you have in mind?" he asked, leaning over her.

"A kiss."

One pencil-thin eyebrow arched. "Just a kiss?"

She tried — and failed — to hide her smile. "Maybe more than just a kiss. But you'd better act fast."

"Oh, yes?"

"Yep. This offer is going once..." she said, wondering if her eyes were shining as brightly as his.

He placed his elbows on either side of her and settled in close.

"Going twice..."

His lips twitched, and his eyes glowed.

"Gone," he whispered, kissing her lips.

Books by Anna Lowe

Aloha Shifters - Jewels of the Heart

Lure of the Dragon (Book 1)

Lure of the Wolf (Book 2)

Lure of the Bear (Book 3)

Lure of the Tiger (Book 4)

Love of the Dragon (Book 5)

Lure of the Fox (Book 6)

The Wolves of Twin Moon Ranch

Blue Moon Saloon

Perfection (a short story prequel)

Damnation (Book 1)

Temptation (Book 2)

Redemption (Book 3)

Salvation (Book 4)

Deception (Book 5)

Celebration (a holiday treat)

Shifters in Vegas

Paranormal romance with a zany twist

Gambling on Trouble

Gambling on Her Dragon

Gambling on Her Bear

Serendipity Adventure Romance

Off the Charts

Uncharted

Entangled

Windswept

Adrift

Travel Romance

Veiled Fantasies

Island Fantasies

visit www.annalowebooks.com

About the Author

USA Today and Amazon bestselling author Anna Lowe loves putting the "hero" back into heroine and letting location ignite a passionate romance. She likes a heroine who is independent, intelligent, and imperfect – a woman who is doing just fine on her own. But give the heroine a good man – not to mention a chance to overcome her own inhibitions – and she'll never turn down the chance for adventure, nor shy away from danger.

Anna loves dogs, sports, and travel – and letting those inspire her fiction. On any given weekend, you might find her hiking in the mountains or hunched over her laptop, working on her latest story. Either way, the day will end with a chunk of dark chocolate and a good read.

Visit AnnaLoweBooks.com

Made in the USA
Coppell, TX
29 November 2020

42428660R00152